THE
BOOK
OF
WONDERS

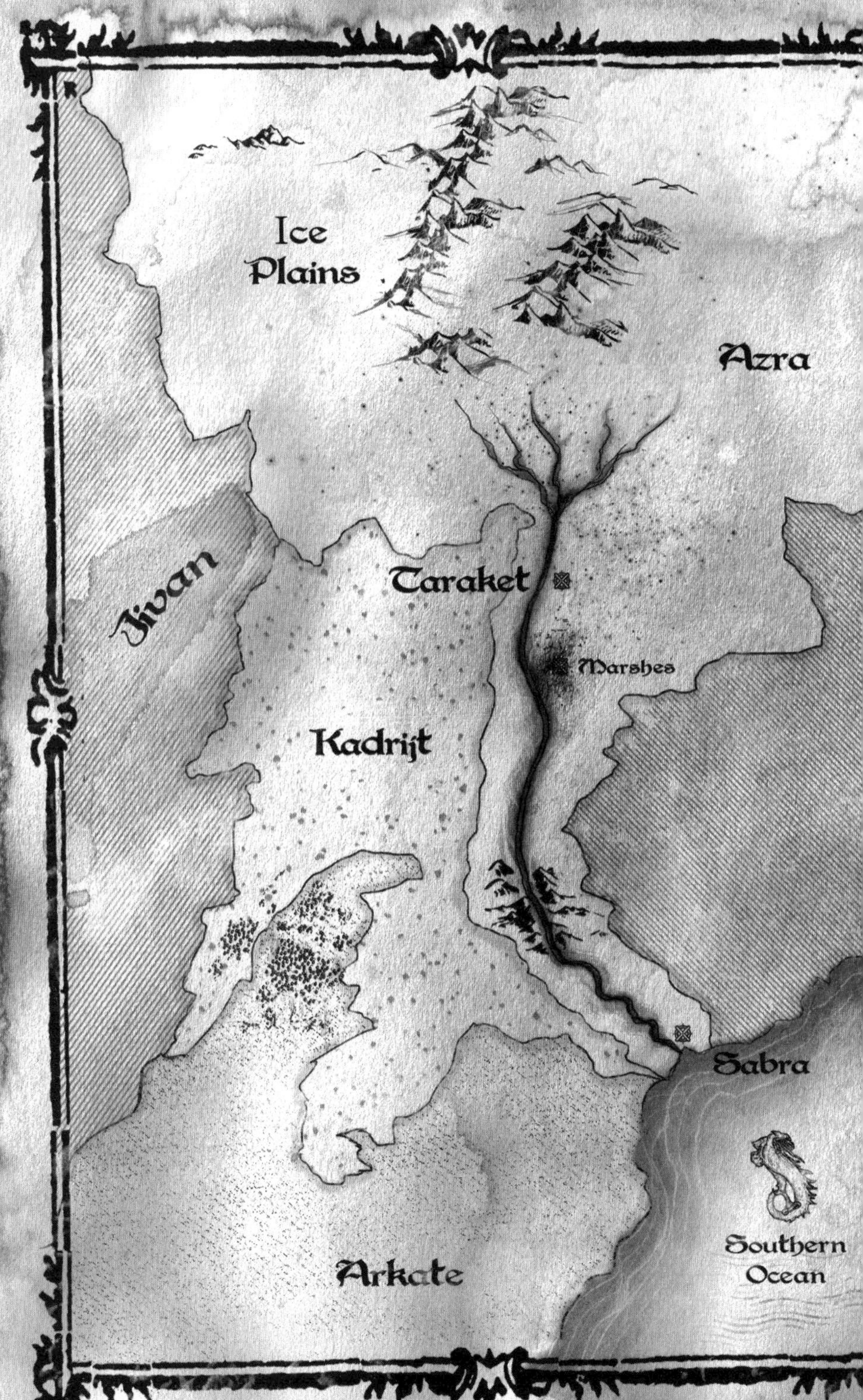
Ice Plains
Azra
Jivan
Taraket
Marshes
Kadrijt
Sabra
Southern Ocean
Arkate

For David Nasralla,
slayer of beasts,
traverser of battlements,
corrector of commas,
and bona fide hero

The Book of Wonders

For information address HarperCollins Children's Books, a division of HarperCollins Publishers, 10 East 53rd Street, New York, NY 10022.
www.harpercollinschildrens.com

Library of Congress Cataloging-in-Publication Data
Richards, Jasmine.
The book of wonders / Jasmine Richards. — 1st ed.
p. cm.
Summary: In a tale loosely based on the Arabian nights, thirteen-year-old Zardi and her best friend, Rhidan, join forces with Captain Sinbad to defeat an evil sultan and restore magic to the world of Arribitha.
ISBN 978-0-06-201007-0
[1. Fantasy. 2. Adventure and adventurers—Fiction. 3. Best friends—Fiction. 4. Friendship—Fiction. 5. Sinbad the sailor (Legendary character)—Fiction.] I. Title.
PZ7.R3846Boo 2012 2011009153
[Fic]—dc22

Typography and title type by Erin Fitzsimmons
Title type set in Jasmine
12 13 14 15 CG/RRDH 10 9 8 7 6 5 4 3 2
❖
First Edition

HARPER
An Imprint of HarperCollins*Publishers*

Sea
of
Sands
Andalus
Issyria
Desolation
Island
Valley
of
Diamonds
Falcon
Camp
High Peak
N
E
S
W
Arribitha

VARDAR
BOREAS
ZEPHYOS
SHAMAL

Contents

PART 1 Home

ONE
The Storyteller
1

TWO
Widow Reaper
13

THREE
The Impatient Seed
22

FOUR
The Praisemaker
36

FIVE
Zardi's Choice
47

SIX
Our Very Own Quest
59

PART 2 Voyages

SEVEN
The Marsh
67

EIGHT
Captured
82

NINE
The Pirate Ship
94

TEN
Through the Eye of the Needle
108

ELEVEN
The Medicine Woman
119

TWELVE
Visions of Home
129

THIRTEEN
The Captain's Revenge
142

FOURTEEN
Flight of the *Falcon*
157

FIFTEEN
Worm on a Splinter of Wood
167

SIXTEEN
Answers
175

SEVENTEEN
The Brass Rider
182

EIGHTEEN
A Truth Revealed
194

NINETEEN
The Roc
202

PART 3 Prisons

TWENTY
The Emerald's Secret
213

TWENTY-ONE
The Valley of Diamonds
224

TWENTY-TWO
Slither
234

TWENTY-THREE
What Lies Beneath
243

TWENTY-FOUR
Cyclops This Way
253

TWENTY-FIVE
The Djinni's Price
264

TWENTY-SIX
The Riddle
271

TWENTY-SEVEN
The Windrose
286

TWENTY-EIGHT
To the Future
293

TWENTY-NINE
Spelltrap
302

PART 4 Reckonings

THIRTY
The Flying Machine
317

THIRTY-ONE
The Sorcerer's Creation
328

THIRTY-TWO
The Sleeping Sailor
340

THIRTY-THREE
The *Falcon*'s Cry
349

THIRTY-FOUR
Plan B
358

THIRTY-FIVE
The Graveyard
369

THIRTY-SIX
The Hunt
379

THIRTY-SEVEN
The Farewell
392

PART ONE
Home

1

The Storyteller

"I heard the noise first. A howl, which sounded like all the djinnis in the world were crying out as one." The sailor stared out at his audience, green eyes sparkling. "I looked up to see the scaled underbelly of a beast—the width of a leathery wing—and knew at once that it was—"

"A dragon!" Zardi shouted.

The sailor frowned. "Yes, a dragon. The great dragon,

Thuban, in fact and—"

"Was it big?" Zardi asked eagerly.

The sailor's chiseled face darkened with annoyance. "Well, yes, as big as the sultan's grandest ship. Thuban's tail alone was as long as—"

"But could he breathe fire?" Zardi queried.

"Will you be quiet?" someone behind her snapped. "Stop interrupting the story."

Zardi turned round to see the exasperated faces among the crowd that stood with her on the docks. "Sorry," she mumbled, her cheeks warming with embarrassment. But she needn't have worried; she was already forgotten. Everyone was looking past her at the ship's captain, who was telling the story.

"Thuban was here to do battle," the seafarer declared, leaping up onto his moored vessel, "and I would not disappoint him." He strode over to the boat's falcon-shaped figurehead, his jewel-bright clothing a rippling flag in the breeze. He turned to face the crowd. "I wrapped my hand in a roughly woven cloth, took a red-hot spit from the cook's fire, and climbed the mast." The sailor looked up to the sky and bared his teeth as if he could see the dragon circling above his head. "Thuban lunged at me with a roar and I swung out, thrusting the glowing spit into the beast's eyeball." He smiled grimly. "It exploded with a sizzle and a pop, and then with a shriek, the dragon crashed into the sea." The captain's eyes gleamed with satisfaction. "My dear listeners, Thuban was dead, but my adventure was not over yet."

Zardi found herself leaning in closer as the seafarer's voice became low and smoky, and for a moment imagined that she too was a member of the captain's crew, ready to start the next part of the quest. "A map drawn by the ancient wizard Eria guided me to the caves of Kadrijt. Even the knowledge that a beast far worse than the dragon I'd just faced guarded the magical treasures hidden there could not stop me." He thrust his shoulders back and tilted his head proudly. "I am Sinbad the sailor. When someone joins my crew I promise them adventure and, by my soul, adventure I will give them!"

A few in the audience whooped at this, while others clapped in approval. Several of the female onlookers smoothed down the pretty silk scarves pinned in their hair and shot admiring glances at Sinbad.

A grin split the captain's sun-kissed face. He bowed gallantly in the ladies' direction and continued his tale, but Zardi found it impossible to hear him over the clapping and whistling. She scowled. It wasn't fair that she got told off for interrupting the story when everyone else was now making such a racket. Listening was made even more difficult by the loud huffing noises that Rhidan was making at her side. She knew her father's ward would rather remove his toenails than listen to tales like this. He was only here because she had begged him to stop and listen to the captain's story for a while before they went on to the market.

She turned to him. "Stop that, will you?"

Rhidan's violet eyes were mutinous. "We need to get the ingredients for tonight's feast. Don't you want to celebrate your birthday?"

Zardi glared at her friend, noticing for a moment how silver his spiky hair looked amid the sea of ebony tresses that surrounded him—like a star exploding in the night. "We'll go in a minute. I just want to see how the story ends."

"Fine, let's stay." Rhidan's lips became a thin line. "I mean, it's not as if mentioning wizards or magic is forbidden in Arribitha or we could get arrested by the sultan's guard for even listening to this nonsense." He snorted and pulled anxiously on the silver amulet that hung around his neck. "Oh, wait, all those things are true."

Zardi's gaze caught on the two engraved snakes that bordered Rhidan's silver talisman. Their sinewy length twisted around a plum-colored stone, their mouths open as if ready to bite. She shuddered. The snakes made her flesh creep, but she would never dare tell Rhidan that. The amulet was his only connection to his past, the only clue to the origins of the violet-eyed baby boy left on the shores of the Tigress River twelve years ago. According to her father, Rhidan's tiny hand could not be pried from the amulet when he was found. He only released it once he was brought to live with Zardi's family as decreed by Sultan Shahryār.

"A mightier monster had never been seen," Sinbad's voice suddenly boomed, and Zardi found herself sucked back into the captain's story.

"It had three heads, teeth as sharp as sabers, and claws made to slice and dice." With a flourish, Sinbad released his sword from its leather scabbard and made to parry and thrust, right there on the deck of his ship. "We battled the beast from dawn until dusk and finally it began to tire." Sinbad stabbed his weapon forward with a cry. "My blade found its belly, and the rest, as they say, is history." He sheathed his sword nonchalantly. "The beast was slain, my men and I entered the cave, and our fortunes were made."

Applause built like a wave and Zardi couldn't help herself—she began to clap wildly along with everyone else. She knew she'd never get to meet a wizard like Eria or duel a vicious beast. Still, she loved hearing stories about them.

"It is, my dear friends of Taraket, an embarrassment of riches." The captain waved his hand toward the wooden chests that his crewmen were stacking on the riverbank. "We have so many magical talismans and trinkets that it weighs down our ship and we cannot continue on our adventures." He looked out at the crowd earnestly. "We need your help. We need you to take some of these charms off our hands. I have everything: amulets that will protect you from the evil eye, tablets that will capture curses, even pendants that will bring you luck and love."

Sinbad flashed a smile at his listeners, but Zardi noticed that it didn't quite reach his eyes—they remained watchful. "It has been too long. Let magic come into your lives again." The captain's voice was soft and melodic. "Remember its taste and brightness. Here is your one chance to possess some bona fide magical treasure—any charm for thirty dirhams."

As the words left his mouth the crowd surged forward, trapping Zardi and Rhidan in their midst. She exchanged a resigned look with her friend and they allowed themselves to be swept along by the eager buyers. Better to go with them than be trampled to death.

Sinbad raised a hand. "Form a line, please. My crew will pass down the queue with the charms—I ask that you have your money ready, please." There was some shuffling but no line actually appeared. Sinbad didn't bother to press the point. "And for those of you waiting to purchase something, I am happy to sign autographs."

"But we have no ink," a voice piped up from the crowd.

Sinbad flashed his teeth again. "Do not fear." He took a slender golden tube from the folds of his loose-fitting trousers. "This is an invention I picked up on my travels. It's called a *pen*. There is no need for a reed and inkpot. The ink is already in the cylinder."

One of Sinbad's crewmen produced a piece of parchment and Sinbad signed his name with a flourish. The crowd gave a collective gasp as they saw the pen form the curving characters.

"Now *that* is pretty impressive." Rhidan stood on tiptoe. "I wonder how it works."

Zardi shook her head. "I can't believe you're more excited about a writing instrument than a tale about a quest, a monster, and a wizard. You're so weird sometimes."

Rhidan ignored her.

"So, which lucky soul should get this autograph?" Sinbad called out. Forty hands went up at once. "Ha! It is impossible to decide," he cried, and threw the parchment into the crowd.

The audience watched, mesmerized, as the paper floated down toward them. A woman well past her sixtieth year broke ranks first and leaped upward, snatching the autograph out of the air. Zardi winced as another woman dived at the old lady's legs, taking her to the ground. Within seconds several other people had piled on top of them. The old lady was not down for long, though. A few well-placed blows with her elbows, and she was free, scarpering off down the riverbank with her prize.

Zardi winked at Rhidan. "That lady's as determined as my grandmother."

"True," Rhidan agreed, as the crowd finally started to form a line, "but Nonna would never be pulled in by this charlatan."

Zardi grimaced. *Why does he always have to use such big words?* she wondered with annoyance. *And why must he always ruin things with logic?* "How do you know he's a *charlatan*?" she challenged. "Maybe he *has* defeated a vicious beast with three heads and been in a cave full of magical treasures."

"Now, that's extremely doubtful." Rhidan dismissed the idea with a wave of his milk-white hand. "He has no knowledge of real magic. He's just a smart sailor who can spin a superior yarn. I guarantee the only thing he is selling today is junk and dreams." Rhidan looked round at the jostling crowd. "He's a good salesman, though, I'll give him that. Somehow, he's convinced everyone here to forget that it's a crime to think about magic in Arribitha, let alone try to buy a piece of it."

She was just about to reply when Sinbad sidled up to them.

"Greetings, my young friends. Can I interest you in an autograph?"

Zardi disguised her laugh at the look on Rhidan's face with a cough. Suddenly, she was struck with a rather brilliant way to get back at her friend for being so grumpy. "I have no paper, I'm afraid," she told Sinbad. "But I'd *love* to hear more about your adventures."

Rhidan narrowed his eyes at her, not impressed with the game she was playing.

"Ah, a young lady with a taste for thrilling quests and breathtaking escapades," Sinbad said. "Let me see if I can think of a new story." He rubbed his chin. "You know, it's a shame you're of the fairer sex, otherwise you could join us on the *Falcon*. We're always looking for new recruits."

A dull ache pooled in Zardi's chest. Sinbad could not know it, but she'd spent countless hours at the docks, watching the ships sail down the mighty Tigress River, envy making her throat close up until it was reed-thin. Her future was already written. She'd stay here in the city of Taraket, as certainly as the river rolled across the land and out toward the ocean that lapped Arribitha's south coast.

Yet despite this, the world beyond the riverbank called to her, making it impossible to be at peace with her fate. More than anything, she wanted to be a part of a ship's crew, to sail on the open sea. But such a thing was unheard of for a girl, much less for the daughter of the sultan's vizier.

"Don't look so sad, my lady." Sinbad rummaged in his pocket and took out a small wooden carving of a proud-looking bird. He folded it into Zardi's hand. "If you can't come to the *Falcon*, then let it come to you. You know, a falcon is the most loyal of birds. Her cry fills grown men with fear, for they understand that she'll fight for her master until her last breath." He winked at her. "The falcon will look after you."

Zardi smiled up sadly at the tall captain as she thanked him. For the first time, she noticed a tiny, crescent-shaped scar near his left eye. She wondered what had made the mark. A sword? The claw of a beast . . . ?

Sinbad turned to Rhidan. "Pale one, maybe you would you like to join me? After all, you are far from home. Strange, I didn't think your people left the Black Isle."

Rhidan made a sound as though he'd been punched in the stomach. "Y-you've seen people who look like me before?"

Zardi met her friend's surprised look with one of her own. No one had ever been able to identify Rhidan's origins. He didn't mention it often, but his need to know why his parents had abandoned him—where he came from—was as much a part of him as the dimples in his cheeks.

Sinbad chuckled. "With hair and eyes like yours, how could I mistake you? You have classic Ilian features. It's just a shame that—"

A member of the *Falcon*'s crew suddenly dashed up to them. "Capt'n, we've got to move. *Now!*" The sailor's mouselike face was ashen. "Sultan Shahryār's guards are coming this way and—" He faltered and then swallowed hard. "It'll be our heads if they find out we've been selling these fake charms and telling stories about wizards."

"No, don't go!" Rhidan's plea was hoarse. "The Black Isle. Please, tell me about the Black Isle."

"Mirzani, you imbecile, keep your voice down!" Sinbad glowered at the crewman, oblivious to Rhidan and Zardi. "Must all of Arribitha know our business? Start to pack away the goods and lift the anchors. I'll tell Musty we're moving out."

"But—" Zardi began.

The captain interrupted her. "I'm sorry, young ones. Our time is up. And if you have any sense, you'll get out of here before the sultan's guards arrive." With a final nod, Sinbad and his companion threw themselves into the crowd and were instantly swallowed up.

2

Widow Reaper

"Sinbad!" Rhidan dived after the sailor. "Wait! Please!" Rhidan turned to Zardi, his eyes wild. "I've got to speak to him."

Pain and want was scored into her friend's face, and in that split second Zardi remembered all the times Rhidan had walked up and down the riverside docks, showing sailors and merchants his amulet—asking if they recognized it, or whether they could tell him where he was from. There was no way she was going to leave him without answers, not when they were so close. "Don't worry," she said. "We're not finished with Sinbad yet. Come on."

They tried to follow the captain, but the swarm of people in front of them was impossible to penetrate. Word of the sultan's guards had reached the crowd, and fear spread like a sickness, making the citizens of Taraket whimper and shake. Many tried to flee the approaching menace, but the crush of bodies made it difficult to move. All around her, Zardi could hear the whispered predictions of what would happen to those caught by the sultan's men, of the blood that would be spilled on the executioner's block.

Rhidan gave a low growl and tried to shove his way through.

"Rhidan, stop!" She grabbed his arm. "The guards are coming. We've got to get out of here."

"No, I can't. You heard what Sinbad said." Rhidan's voice rose with each word. "On the Black Isle there are people who look like me . . . just like me."

"I know, I know," Zardi soothed, even as fear pinched at her skin. In the distance, she could see the steady advance of the sultan's guards marching along the riverbank. Curved sabers hung from their waists, and Zardi knew that they needed little reason to use them. Crimson tattoos of staring eyes covered their faces, necks, and arms. The ink left their expressions stiff, a red mask of judgment that told every man, woman, and child that the sultan's guards were always watching. They moved in perfect unison, standing shoulder to shoulder like bricks in a wall. *The wall! That was it. That was how they could get to Sinbad!* She dragged on Rhidan's arm. "We need to get to the sultan's arch."

He looked at her in confusion.

"Don't you see?" she said. "All ships have to pass under the arch to leave Taraket. If we get on it, we'll be able to see the *Falcon* go through." She paused, not quite believing she was about to say her next words. "And when it does, we'll jump down onto the deck. We'll be able to ask Sinbad everything he knows about the Black Isle!"

"You're a genius." Rhidan's violet eyes blazed. "Let's go!"

Pushing along with everyone else, they eventually broke free of the frantic throng and sprinted along the riverbank, but the way ahead was heaving with yet more people. Beggars pulled at sleeves and held out hands for a coin, while skinny urchins in rags watched the crowd with calculating eyes. Traders from all over Arribitha had traveled along the Tigress River to Taraket, eager to sell their wares, and Zardi and Rhidan found themselves dodging street sellers proffering mirrored glass from Azra, sidestepping women trading animal skins from the northern Ice Plains, and finally barging past men selling musk, fireworks, and porcelain from the distant kingdom of Mandar.

Over her shoulder, Zardi could see Sinbad's ship. The *Falcon* was striking a course down the middle of the Tigress, doing its best to avoid the other boats. For a moment her breath was stolen as she looked at the majestic vessel. Its sails were jade, ruby, and amber, and the hull was made of a rich ebony wood that proudly reflected the eddies and swirls of the river. Zardi blinked hard. She didn't have time to be mooning over the ship. She and Rhidan had to get on top of the sultan's arch before the *Falcon* passed through it.

They charged on, the soft ground of the riverbank squelching beneath their sandals, and finally arrived at the arch. It reared up in front of them—a huge stone structure stretching over the Tigress. Its curving surface was made of massive, spaced columns that jutted upward. The arch had never been stepped on; it was a whim of the sultan's, a symbol to show that all were beneath his greatness. Under their breaths, some dared to call the arch the widow reaper because of the countless men who had died during its construction, some slain by the guards for not working fast enough, others crushed beneath falling rocks.

Rhidan's and Zardi's fingers instantly began to search for handholds to climb to the top of the first pillar, but they found none. Zardi hunkered down and formed a cradle with her fingers. "Hop up," she said.

Rhidan didn't hesitate and placed a foot in her hand. As Zardi vaulted him up onto the widow reaper's lowest column, she marveled at the transformation of her usually cautious friend. He normally had his nose in a book of riddles or mathematics and certainly never climbed walls. He hadn't even questioned what would happen to them if they were seen on the arch or how they were going to get off the ship once they got the answers he needed, not that she'd quite worked that out either. He seemed so different that, for a heartbeat, she wondered if he might leave her behind. But without pausing, Rhidan offered his hand and pulled her up beside him.

With a glance Zardi saw that Sinbad's ship was coming swiftly to the widow reaper, its multicolored sails swelling with the wind. She surveyed the columns ahead, each one sitting a bit higher than the last, huge rocky steps rising upward.

All we need to do is reach the middle. She looked down at the river and the spiky clusters of rocks that stabbed out of the water within the shadow of the arch. *And not fall off . . .*

Zardi took a deep breath and leaped for the second column. She landed safely, and after a moment Rhidan appeared beside her. Without pausing, she jumped for the next column of stone and then the one after that. The river wind buffeted them fiercely, doing its best to bully them off the edge of the arch, but they gave it no quarter.

They climbed higher, their pace slowing as the columns began to get narrower. Zardi took the lead but found that she had to be even surer of her leaps, her footwork more controlled. Mid-jump, a strong gust tore the silk scarf from her head and pulled some of her hair from its long braid. The strands blinded Zardi for a moment, forcing her to use instinct rather than sight to land safely.

She watched her silk scarf dance away on the breeze. On the same wind, from the tallest watchtower of Taraket, she could hear the sultan's praisemaker reciting the rules of Arribitha in a high, pure voice:

Subjects will think not, know not magic.
Subjects will report any that seek to undermine the sultan's will.
Subjects will not walk the streets after dusk.
Sultan Shahryār shall be respected at all times—for even with his eyes closed he can see.
All will praise him. Praise him all.

There was a sharp blow of a horn and then came the daily call of names of those who had disobeyed the sultan's rules. Names of those who'd been executed that morning.

"Maysa Amari . . . Aida Kalil . . . Jamal Temiz . . . Salam Nas—" The praisemaker's voice faltered on the last name, as if the horror of all these deaths flowing and tumbling over each other had stolen her ability to speak.

Zardi turned to stare at the watchtower. She could see the silhouette of the praisemaker standing on the ledge of the window, the shadow of a guard looming behind her. The wind that came off the river made the girl's dress flap around her like an angry bird, and her shoulders were hunched as if she was trying to fold into herself.

A blade of anger slipped beneath Zardi's ribs, making her gasp. She hated that the praisemaker had no choice but to be in that tower. She hated that the names of the executed had already faded on the air, never to be spoken again. She would honor them by her actions. The sultan could not be defeated, but with every step she took on the widow reaper she was rebelling against his orders. Feeling braver, she tucked her hair back into its braid and leaped faster toward the middle of the arch. As the *Falcon* began to pass under the widow reaper she found herself standing directly above the ship. They'd made it! The thought of jumping aboard a *real* ship made Zardi's heart pound like a stonemason's mallet.

Over her shoulder, she saw that Rhidan was still a few columns behind. "Hurry!" she called. "The *Falcon*'s coming through!"

Zardi felt a surge of pride as she watched her friend grit his teeth and leap for the next stone pillar. He landed awkwardly—arms spinning like windmills.

Springing forward onto the column closest to her friend, Zardi reached out and steadied him.

"Thanks." Rhidan's hands were shaking.

They both looked out at the water. His stumble had cost them dearly. The *Falcon* was now on the other side of the arch and in full flight.

"He's gone." Rhidan's voice was flat, but Zardi felt the ache of his disappointment.

He did not move a muscle as he watched the *Falcon* sail away with the answers he'd been seeking his whole life.

The Impatient Seed

Zardi pushed open the door of the kitchen, her toes curling in pleasure as she breathed in the scent of baking bread.

"Smells good in here," Zardi said, spotting her grandmother over by the hearth.

"I'm glad you approve," Nonna replied, turning away from the two cauldrons that sat over the fire. Wispy gray tendrils stuck to her forehead and her cheeks were flushed. "I'm just about to start the soup. Did you get the sesame seeds for the tahini?"

"I got everything but the pomegranates." Zardi tumbled the contents of her sack onto the kitchen table.

"No matter, my dear," her grandmother said. "Maybe your sister will be able to get them. Where's Rhidan?"

Good question, Zardi thought to herself. "He had some things he needed to do," she said. "He'll be along later."

Rhidan had been strangely calm once they had gotten off the sultan's arch. They had been lucky that no one had seen them from one of the many watchtowers of the city, and they were quick to leave the widow reaper far behind. Rhidan had told her to finish running the errands for Nonna and promised he would catch up with her at home. When she'd asked what he was planning to do, he'd replied that he was going to find Sinbad.

"Someone's bound to know where he's heading next," he had gone on to explain. "Sinbad's not exactly the shy and retiring type. All I need to do is a bit of investigating."

"Well, he had better not be late," Nonna muttered, interrupting Zardi's thoughts. "I'm making chorba soup tonight, and I don't want its flavor to dull from overcooking."

"You know that's Rhidan's favorite," Zardi replied. "His nose will lead him home."

Nonna chuckled, walked over to the table, and started to sort through the ingredients. Zardi watched her grandmother fondly. She was a round woman with a face well worn from smiling and laughing. In other wealthy families, it was unheard of to have a member of the family doing the cooking, but her grandmother didn't give two hoots about status or what other people thought.

Zardi grinned to herself, remembering all the cooks her father had tried to employ in the past. Somehow, Nonna always managed to drive them away. Putting dead mice in their stews or adding too much salt to dishes while they weren't looking were her favorite methods, but she had a whole range of pranks in her armory. Unsurprisingly, Nonna's views on nannies were very similar to her opinions on cooks, and her methods of expulsion equally ingenious.

The door swung open, and Zardi turned to see Zubeyda skip into the kitchen. Her sister's name meant "little butter ball" and she was exactly that—soft and round with skin as smooth as buttermilk. Zubeyda's heart-shaped face was glowing, and she brought the smell of lavender and excitement.

"Nonna, isn't it a glorious day?" Zubeyda greeted her grandmother with three kisses on alternate cheeks. She turned to face Zardi with a grin. "Hello, birthday girl. Thirteen years old today—you're practically ancient."

Nonna laughed at this and bustled over to the hearth at the far end of the kitchen to begin adding ingredients to the soup.

"You're four years older than me, Zub," Zardi pointed out to her sister.

"But never too old to enjoy sherbet. I'm going to make some. Watermelon and mint flavor suit you?"

Zardi's mouth watered. She loved the fruity iciness of sherbet. "That sounds perfect."

"Wonderful. Maybe O—" Zubeyda stopped, her long lashes becoming a fan on her suddenly blushing cheeks.

"Zub, why have you gone pink?" Zardi asked suspiciously. "What's going on?"

Her sister smiled shyly. "Well, I've got some good news," she whispered, glancing over at Nonna. "But I want to save it for later so we can celebrate properly."

Zardi looked at Zubeyda closely. Her sister's green eyes, with their flecks of gold, sparkled like dew on riverbank reeds. "It's something to do with Omar, right?" she asked.

Zubeyda's mouth opened in surprise. "How'd you know?"

Zardi snorted. "He's the only one who can make you look this sappy."

Zubeyda put a hand to her chest, right over her heart, and sighed dramatically. "He's going to ask Baba for my hand in marriage. Omar is going to be my husband!"

"Oh, Zub, he finally asked." Zardi hugged her sister, the sweet scent of lavender water surrounding her. "I knew he would."

"You know how shy Omar can be," Zubeyda said. "He just needed a bit of time to work up to it. He's only lived next door to us our whole lives!" She rolled her eyes. "I'll give you all the details, I promise, but don't tell Nonna yet. I want it to be a surprise." She picked up Zardi's empty sack from the table. "Nonna, I'm off to get the ingredients for the sherbet," Zubeyda said loudly. "Do you need anything else from the market?"

"Your sister couldn't find any pomegranates—get me two if you can," Nonna called back.

"Will do." Zubeyda turned to leave the kitchen, but Zardi caught her hand.

"Be careful, the sultan's guards are out today," she said. "Stay out of their way."

"Those tattooed bullies don't frighten me." Zubeyda raised a perfectly shaped eyebrow. "Besides, our father would have something to say if they bothered me, and they wouldn't want to annoy him now, would they?"

Distaste made Zardi's lip curl as she thought of Shahryār and how her father was his most trusted advisor. "Just be careful, Zub. Those guards are as mean and as mad as the sultan."

Zubeyda tapped Zardi on the nose. "I'm the older sister, and I'll do the worrying, all right?" And with a swift triple-kiss farewell, she was gone.

Zardi gazed round the room at the steaming cooking pots and the delicate pastries that were all ready to go into the clay oven. She let out a sigh. It felt like everyone else in the world liked cooking except her. It was Zubeyda or Rhidan who normally helped Nonna out with the meals.

Rhidan, Zardi thought with a jolt, and with half a mind to head to the docks to find him, she began to creep out of the room.

"Where do you think you're going, young lady?" Nonna asked, not looking away from the soup she was stirring. "I need you to chop up a few onions."

"I hate chopping onions!" Zardi exclaimed. "They make me cry."

"Scheherazade, you have plenty of tears to spare. Now get dicing."

Still grumbling under her breath, Zardi peeled the skin from the onions. Her grandmother was the only person to ever call her by her full name. Baba never did. But why would he? It was the name of his dead wife. His beautiful Scheherazade, who had died to give Zardi life thirteen years ago today . . .

When she thought about it, Baba didn't say much at all, really. According to Nonna he used to be full of words and fire, determined to change the regime and depose the sultan. But then his wife had died, and something had died inside him too. He was now one of the sultan's key advisors and spent every day trying to discourage Sultan Shahryār from his never-ending impulse to destroy and devastate. It kept him busy. Too busy to be a father . . .

She felt the sting of tears. *Stupid onions,* she thought as she began to slice through their crunchy whiteness.

Zardi blinked away the wetness and concentrated on the task, her fingers becoming deft and quick.

"Good knife control," Nonna commented, walking toward her.

Zardi liked the praise but felt the sting of guilt at the same time. She was pretty good at anything that involved hand-eye coordination; it had nothing to do with burgeoning culinary skills. "Can I go now?" she asked as she finished chopping her third onion.

Her grandmother sighed. "I've never met a girl who hates the kitchen as much as you." She picked up a handful of sesame seeds from the table and let them run through her fingers. "Did you know that sesame pods burst open when they're ripe, almost as if they can't wait to be eaten? You're just as impatient, Zardi, but you must learn caution. We all must."

Nonna stared into the distance. She did this sometimes when she was deep in thought. Rhidan called it going to Nonnaland. Zardi swiftly put her knife down—a chance to escape! She hurried toward the kitchen door.

"Always outside practicing with that bow and arrow or getting me to tell you about magic, ogres, and djinnis," Zardi heard her grandmother murmur to herself.

"My impatient girl, I failed you."

Zardi stopped and turned. "What do you mean, 'failed me'?"

Nonna blinked hard before looking at her directly. "It's your thirteenth birthday today, Scheherazade. You're on the brink of adulthood, but I have failed to prepare you for it." Her eyes were serious. "Not very long from now, your father will have to start thinking about a husband for you and—"

"Nonna, stop right there! I don't want to talk about this." Panic crested in Zardi's chest, threatening to swamp her. Her sister might be ready to get married, but she certainly wasn't.

"My darling girl, I am old but not deaf." Nonna spoke softly. "Omar will ask for Zubeyda's hand in marriage, and it is well past time. Your sister will be safe now, but what of you?" Nonna's face creased with worry. "You understand why you need to get wed sooner rather than later, don't you? It is the only way you will be kept safe from the sultan. Safe from the Hunt."

Nonna's words pummeled Zardi like waves, but she couldn't swim away from them. The truth was simple. The sultan of Arribitha was a killer. Every season, Shahryār took a young woman, still unwed, and turned her into a praisemaker. He held his praisemaker prisoner in the tallest watchtower of the city and forced her to sing his praises in public each morning. Then, after the season was finished, he released the girl into the grounds of his vast palace before hunting her down like an animal. It was his favorite sport. A praisemaker for each season—four praisemakers a year—four Hunts a year. It had been like this ever since Shahryār came to the throne after murdering the last sultan, his wife, and their newborn child, Aladdin, fifteen years ago.

Silence lay heavily between Zardi and her grandmother.

"I am sorry that it has to be this way, my darling, habibti." Nonna stepped forward and cupped Zardi's face in her weathered, olive-colored hands. "I've always wanted you to have a normal life, without fear or dread, but we do not live in a normal time. The sultan holds Arribitha in a deadly grip. We all suffer, but it is women who pay the highest price." Nonna began to tremble. "He hunts us because he is afraid of us. Before he came to power it was women who were the most skilled in magic. Now you are thirteen, now you are a woman; a shadow looms over you and it will only deepen."

Zardi balled her hands into fists but couldn't bring

herself to say any more. What was there to say?

Nonna clucked her tongue sympathetically. "Come, Scheherazade. I want to show you something that will make you feel better. I will prove to you that your future isn't as terrible as you imagine."

Nonna picked up a small case full of saffron from the table and led Zardi over to the second cauldron of water on the fire. It was bubbling in earnest now, spitting and hissing fiercely.

Nonna glanced at Zardi. "You must promise me that you will never tell a soul what I am about to do."

Zardi tensed. "No, Nonna, please. It's too dangerous to do magic."

"It is just a bit of soothsaying," replied Nonna. "I am not as talented as some I have known and lost to the sultan's cutting block." She picked three saffron strands from the case and threw them into the water. The burnished-orange strands instantly began to twist and turn in the bubbling liquid.

"Look!" Nonna exclaimed. "All three of your strands have floated. You are blessed. It is good luck to have even two strands float and you have three!"

Zardi looked at the threads uncertainly. They were all floating, but was this explanation just something that Nonna had concocted to make her feel better? Suddenly, each strand began to twist and turn more violently and curled inward, forming three circles that were interlinked.

"What does it mean?" Zardi asked, her skin prickling with unease.

Nonna's face had gone pale. "I don't know," she replied. "But I don't like it. I don't like it one bit."

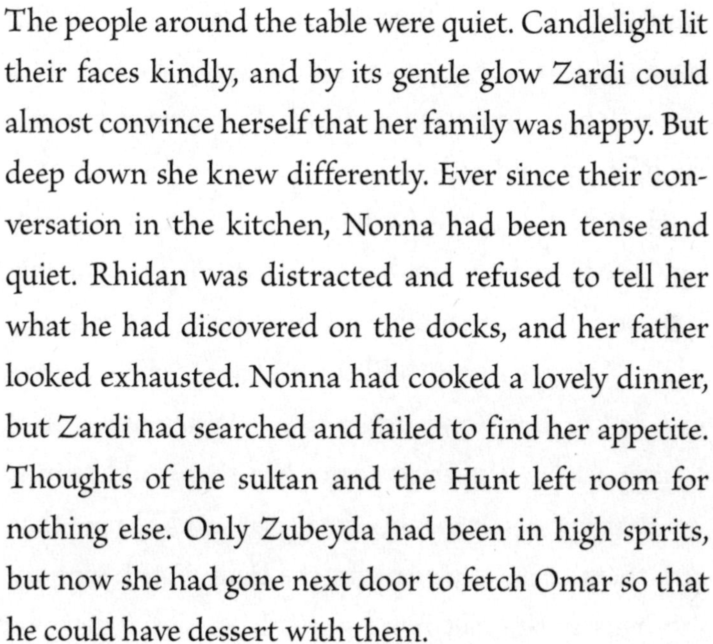

The people around the table were quiet. Candlelight lit their faces kindly, and by its gentle glow Zardi could almost convince herself that her family was happy. But deep down she knew differently. Ever since their conversation in the kitchen, Nonna had been tense and quiet. Rhidan was distracted and refused to tell her what he had discovered on the docks, and her father looked exhausted. Nonna had cooked a lovely dinner, but Zardi had searched and failed to find her appetite. Thoughts of the sultan and the Hunt left room for nothing else. Only Zubeyda had been in high spirits, but now she had gone next door to fetch Omar so that he could have dessert with them.

From the end of the table came a small, polite cough. Looking almost embarrassed, Zardi's father produced a wrapped gift from under the table and handed it to her. "I hope you like it," he murmured.

Zardi stared at Baba in shock. From the crescent shape of the package, she had a good idea of what it contained. She ripped the paper off to reveal a wooden bow. It was short and tightly strung and covered with varnished leather that made the weapon waterproof. Lying beside it was an archer's belt with a quiver that flowered with thin arrows topped by delicate white feathers. Looking closer, she could see that the quiver had a clip for her bow and was embossed with an image of a golden lion. "Baba, I don't understand," she finally managed to say. "I thought you said archery wasn't *suitable* for a girl."

Her father laughed, his handsome, tired face lighting up. "Zardi, you may not have noticed, but I gave up telling you what was suitable a long time ago." He smiled sadly. "You are so much like my darling Scheherazade, just as stubborn and determined. Whenever I tried to argue a point with your mother, she would remind me that her name meant 'lion-born,' and I knew then and there that I'd never win the fight. You have your mother's spirit, that lion's spirit. It is so sad that you never met her. She would have been proud of you." He stood and kissed Zardi's forehead. "Enjoy the bow and the arrows, my daughter. You're a talented archer and you might as well have equipment that is the right size for you."

Zardi was speechless as she watched him sit down in his chair. Not only had he given her a gift that until now had been *totally* taboo, he'd also mentioned her mother! What in all of Arribitha was going on?

"Baba, thank y—"

A high-pitched scream interrupted her. Zardi froze, her skin alive with goose bumps. "What was that?"

"I think it came from next door," Rhidan said.

"Stay here," Zardi's father ordered. He and Nonna erupted from their chairs and ran toward the front door.

Zardi's eyes met Rhidan's, which were almost indigo with worry. "You coming?" She pushed her chair back, slung the bow over her shoulder, and fastened the archer's belt around her waist.

"I'll be right by your side," Rhidan replied.

They raced after Baba and Nonna, and Zardi tried to ignore the watery dread that filled her stomach.

Zubeyda was next door.

Another cry tore the night apart, and Zardi ran faster, fear pounding in her skull. She heaved the front door open and spilled out into the darkness.

4

The Praisemaker

There was nothing unusual in the street in front of her. It was as quiet as a graveyard, except for Baba and Nonna banging on the door of Omar's family's villa. Zardi and Rhidan skidded along the tiled path and joined in with their efforts. But there was no answer.

"Let's go to our balcony," Rhidan suggested. "We'll be able to see into their courtyard from there."

Baba nodded, his face a portrait of fear in the moonlight.

Zardi led the way, racing back inside the house, up the wide marble staircase and out onto the balcony at the side of the villa. She looked over into the courtyard next door. Scudding clouds covered the moon, and it took a second for her eyes to adjust to the darkness. When they did, ice scraped her spine. A ghostly figure in white was being held by two of the sultan's guards, their red tattooed faces smudges of blood in the night.

The figure twisted in their arms, and Zardi caught a glimpse of a heart-shaped face, wet with tears.

"Zubeyda!" The name was torn from Zardi's throat, a cry of a wounded animal.

Her sister wore the white dress of a praisemaker, and it might as well have been a noose around her neck. The edges of Zardi's vision darkened and pushed inward until all she could see was her sister's terrified eyes. She gripped the wrought metal of the balcony railing, its coldness beating back the darkness.

Sitting astride a powerful, flame-colored horse, surrounded by guards, was a man, his face in shadows. A gust of wind chased the clouds away from the moon's surface, and in the eerie light the man's features were suddenly revealed: high cheekbones, an aquiline nose, a handsome face ruined only by the cruel twist of its mouth. The sultan. He was smiling widely as he took in the scene unfolding before him.

Every fiber of Zardi's being screamed in protest as she saw Zubeyda writhe like bait on a line, trying to get away. But the guards held her sister tight, one of them covering her mouth. More guards stood to the side, swords drawn, keeping back Omar and his brothers.

Another scream pierced the night air, and Zardi realized that it came from her grandmother. Nonna had collapsed to the floor in a heap and was making a low keening sound. Baba stood completely still, tears streaming down his face as he stared down at his daughter in white.

Rage filled Zardi, clogging her throat, making it hard to breathe. Swinging her new bow from her shoulder, she withdrew an arrow from the quiver on her belt. The sharpness of the arrowhead cut against her fingertip as she traced its edge, and she suddenly felt powerful.

All noise fell away. The screams, the shouts. They became muted, drowned out by the thumping of her heartbeat. *I can do something about this,* she thought. *I can save my sister.* She nocked the arrow to the string and pulled back, the cord making a creaking noise as it flexed for the first time.

The sultan raised his head at the sound. His mouth twisted into a mocking sneer as he stared straight at her.

Rhidan grabbed her wrist. "What are you doing?"

"I'm taking care of the situation." Zardi aimed her weapon straight at Shahryār, and still the sultan stared at her. He leaned back in his saddle as if daring her to shoot.

"Those guards will kill you," Rhidan rasped. "An injury to one of the sultan's guards is an injury to the sultan himself."

"I'm not going after the guards." Zardi's eyes never left the sultan's.

Rhidan stepped in front of her, the tip of the arrow pressing into his chest.

"This is suicide. He's too far away—you won't get him."

"We'll see about that."

"I won't let you do it." Rhidan's voice sounded as though it was shaking with the effort to remain calm. "If you want to shoot an arrow it'll have to go through me first."

Why is he stopping me? Her hands trembled on the bow. *Doesn't he see that we have to do something?*

"Daughter, listen to him," Baba's voice said softly from behind her.

Zardi swung round to see her father helping Nonna to her feet. Suddenly, the anger that she felt toward the sultan changed direction and flew like an arrow toward her father. "Why aren't you doing something, Baba?" Tears stung her eyes. "He's going to take her, my sister—your daughter—and you just stand here."

"Please, Zardi, I will make this right." Her father looked wretched as he took a step toward her. "But violence will not help us here. I will go to the sultan. I'll make him give Zubeyda back. He will listen to me."

"He's never listened to you before," Zardi snarled. "My whole life, I've heard you say that you work for Shahryār to protect the citizens of Taraket, to keep the sultan's madness in check." She shook her head. "Too many have died at Shahryār's hands. My sister won't be one of them."

Turning from him, she roughly pushed Rhidan aside so she could see into the courtyard below, but Zubeyda was gone. Omar was being picked up off the ground by one of his brothers. Blood streamed from a wound above his eye, but he did nothing to stop it. He stared through the open gate of the courtyard and into the distance. Zardi followed his gaze. She could just make out the shape of the sultan's horses galloping against the night sky, billows of dust being kicked up by their hooves.

I'm too late.

I failed her.

Failed.

Her grandmother had used that same word earlier in the kitchen. Zubeyda would now be imprisoned in the city's tallest watchtower, forced to call out the sultan's decrees day after day until the time of the Hunt. Then Shahryār would begin his sport, and release Zubeyda into the grounds of his palace only to pursue and kill her.

A wave of dizziness hit Zardi, her knees crumpling. She placed her forehead against the balcony's railing and drew in a painful, ragged breath.

There was a loud, rapping knock on the door downstairs, and Zardi stood straight once more, although all she wanted was to curl into a ball of forgetfulness.

Her father wiped his tear-stained face with trembling hands, his wedding ring glinting in the moonlight.

"That will be the sultan's general to give me formal notice that my daughter has been taken as a praise-maker."

Baba laid his shaking hands on Zardi's shoulders. "I will talk to him in the library. Whatever you hear, you must not interfere. Promise me. Your sister's life depends on it."

Zardi nodded.

Baba turned to Nonna. "The same goes for you, Mother. Wait in your room and rest. I will let you know what happens."

Zardi watched her father step through the balcony doors. He walked like a man being led to his execution.

"Habibti, will you come inside?" Nonna asked beseechingly.

"Not yet," murmured Zardi.

Nonna took Zardi's face in her hands. "I love you, Scheherazade. My lion-born. You fought for life even when you were just a few hours old. The doctors said that you would lose the battle, but I knew you would not." Nonna kissed her forehead. "I think I understand what I saw now, what the saffron strands were trying to show me. You will fight for life again—your own, your family's, and Arribitha's—and you must win." Looking old and frail, her grandmother turned and stepped into the dimly lit house.

Zardi and Rhidan stood alone on the balcony, but she couldn't bring herself to look at her friend. By stopping her from shooting that arrow, he'd almost certainly saved her life. But she could not forgive him or herself for allowing Zubeyda to be condemned to death, and Nonna's words weighed heavily on her.

They stood in awkward silence.

"Your father will make this right—I know he will," Rhidan finally said.

Zardi felt cold although the night was balmy. Her whole body began to tremble. "She'll be so scared," she whispered.

Rhidan reached out a hand to comfort her, but Zardi pulled back.

"Please, I just need to be alone." The words came out sharper than she'd intended, but she couldn't take them back.

"All right," Rhidan said softly. "But I'm coming to find you later."

She stared at Rhidan's retreating back as he left the balcony and then looked down at her bow. She was as tightly strung as the weapon in her hand. Somewhere in her house, the sultan's general spoke to her father about Zubeyda's future. The urge to find the general, to make him pay with his life for her sister's kidnap exploded in her like a firework from Mandar. She needed to do something before she broke her promise to Baba not to interfere.

She flew through the balcony doors, down the stairs, and out into the garden. The orchard was always lit with flaming torches at this time of night, as her father liked to come home and walk through the sifsaaf trees. Nonna said it was the one time in the day when he got to be alone with his own thoughts.

Tonight though, the garden was empty. The air smelled of jasmine and night queen, and the sweet scent filled her head and made her feel calmer. She padded across the grass, past the citrus trees, and toward the date palm at the bottom of the garden. The tree was something solid, with five concentric rings carved into its enormous trunk, a target that she, Zubeyda, and Rhidan had made one long summer years ago.

Zardi took up her shooting stance, one foot set slightly back. She nocked an arrow in the center of her bowstring and let the shaft of the arrow rest on the bow, just above where her hand gripped. Holding the bowstring with her first three fingers, she felt it settle into familiar creases. She drew the string back until her thumb was against her jawbone and her index finger almost touched the corner of her mouth. Facing her target, she aimed and fired.

The arrow sprang forward, as if relieved to finally be in flight, and the sound of it thunking into the tree was reassuringly solid. Zardi let another arrow fly. It swiftly found refuge in the innermost ring of the target. She strained every sinew to keep herself still and steady; she got ready to shoot again, allowing her frustration to flow through her and down the length of the arrow. As she let each arrow fly, the frustration, too, flew from her. She felt lighter but realized that her grief over Zubeyda's fate would not leave. Her sister was a praisemaker. She would be hunted and killed and Zardi didn't know how to stop it from happening. She continued to fire arrows until her arm felt sore before yanking the arrows from the tree and putting them back in the quiver on her belt. She then clipped her bow onto the side of the arrow case.

Zardi made her way into the house. She needed to speak to her father and find out what the sultan's general had said. Arriving at the door to his library, she stopped as she heard Baba's voice rise in anger.

Zardi put her ear to the hard wood.

"Why my daughter?" she heard her father say in a cracked voice. "Shahryār, I have served you loyally. I have done all that you have asked."

Zardi flinched. The sultan was here, in her house.

"Really, Faisal, did you think that just because you were my vizier that your daughter could not become my praisemaker?" There was a low hiss of breath. "You should be thanking me for the honor. Fate smiles on you, Faisal, for only this very evening my former praisemaker accidentally fell from the watchtower. Such a shame, she was only two days into her season." The sultan tutted. "Oh well. Zubeyda has now taken her place in the watchtower, and in ninety days' time, as the sun reaches its zenith, it will be her turn to be hunted."

5

Zardi's Choice

Ninety days. Blood flowed over Zardi's teeth as she bit down on her tongue to stop herself from crying out. *Ninety days until the Hunt.*

"You want thanks?" Baba snarled. "You tell me with a smile that you plan to kill my daughter and you think I should be pleased. You're deranged, Shahryār, rotten inside."

The sultan growled with anger. "You forget yourself.

You have no idea of what I am, or what I am still capable of."

"Forgive me for raising my voice." Zardi's father gave a shuddering sob. "Please, I beg you, release Zubeyda."

The sultan laughed. "Oh, you are a worm of a man to beg. I saw your younger daughter tonight. Zardi, I believe?" The sultan said her name as if he enjoyed the shape of it in his mouth, and Zardi sunk her nails deep into the hardness of the door, wishing it was his face.

"She was ready to take action, her eyes full of fire. Shame on you that your child has more bravery in her little finger than you do in your whole body." Shahryār laughed again. "I look forward to hunting her. But I must not be impatient, one daughter at a time."

Her father screamed in rage. There was the thud of one body slamming into another. The sound of wood breaking.

"Baba!" Zardi pushed against the door but it was bolted shut.

"Move again, Faisal, and my guards will break your neck." The sultan's voice from behind the door was as cold and flat as a blade.

"Why do you seek to destroy me?" Baba asked brokenly. "My entire family."

"Because you would seek to destroy me," the sultan snapped back. "You were told to discover whether the stories about Aladdin being alive were true. You reported that he was not, but my spies tell me differently. They say that as a baby, the prince of Arribitha was secretly smuggled from these shores. Now my enemies search for him, hoping he will lead a rebellion. Whispers of a revolution grow, and somewhere in the city of Sabra, a secret order of warriors has risen: the Varish. They train in the arts of assassination, fueled only by their desire to slay me. You let your ruler down, Faisal. My taking your elder daughter is your punishment, not a crude impulse. I have been planning it for many weeks, watching Zubeyda's every move. She was always going to be the next praisemaker."

"Let her go, Sultan Shahryār." Baba's voice was a whisper. "None of what you have heard is true. It is just rumor."

"Rumor is dangerous!" The sound of a fist coming down on a table punched into Zardi's ears. "As my vizier you should have snuffed it out. For all I know you might be involved in this planned rebellion." There was a sharp, brisk clap. "Guards, bind and gag him."

Zardi jumped back as the library door flew open.

She found herself looking up into the sultan's sharply carved face. Three guards stood at his back.

"Tsk, tsk, little one. Has no one told you not to listen at doors?" The sultan brought his face right up to hers. "You might not like what you hear." He blinked, and Zardi could see a pair of red eyes tattooed onto his eyelids.

Even with his eyes closed he can see, she thought, remembering the praisemaker's mournful voice from the watchtower.

Two guards dragged Baba forward. Zardi's fingers crept to the bow at her waist, but another of the sultan's guards was on her immediately, a saber at her throat.

"Why, you are like an angry kitten," the sultan said approvingly. "All ferocity but no strength. Maybe I should just imprison you now so that you can join your sister for the Hunt?"

Baba gave a muffled cry through his gag and tried to break away from the guards who held him.

"Leave her alone," a voice said from behind them. Despite the blade at her throat, Zardi turned to see Rhidan on the marble stairs. His normally spiky silver hair was even messier than usual, as if he had been raking his fingers through it again and again.

"What will you do if I do not?" the sultan asked, looking at Rhidan with a strange intensity.

"I'll fight you." Rhidan's voice was unsteady, but he took more steps down the stairs. "I'll fight you a-and you'll be sorry."

The sultan snorted. "Is that all you will do?" He looked disappointed. "Not yet fully hatched, I see, young Rhidan. But surely it can't be long." The sultan clicked his fingers at the tattooed guard towering over Zardi and the soldier withdrew his saber. "I will leave your precious Zardi alone, but remember this kindness when the time comes. You and I will stand together one day."

The sultan's eyes slid to Zardi. "We will see each other again, angry kitten. I promise to keep your father safe—under lock and key, in fact." He gave a bark of laughter. "He can keep your sister company until the day of the Hunt. And when I return with my slain prey, he will truly be sorry for failing me. And that sorrow will be the last thing he thinks of before I kill him."

The sultan stalked toward the door, his guards dragging Baba behind him.

Zardi's eyes met her father's. She expected to see fear in their depths, but she found something else entirely.

She saw love for her, regret, and a plea. Her whole life she had struggled to understand her father, but in that instant, before he was dragged out of the door and into the night, she did.

There's only one thing left to do, Zardi realized. She began to climb the stairs to her bedroom.

Rhidan grabbed her hand as she passed. "We have to talk," he urged. "What are we going to do about your father, about Zubeyda?"

Zardi couldn't look at him. Rhidan was as good at reading her face as he was at reading a book of epigrams. She couldn't risk him guessing her plan. "I need you to tell Nonna what has happened," she said, refusing to meet his gaze. "We'll talk in the morning." Impulsively, Zardi hugged him. He smelled fresh and cool like rainwater. "Thank you for standing up for me."

She ran up the rest of the steps before Rhidan could respond. Once inside her room, she lit the lanterns and bolted the door shut before walking over to the mirror on the dressing-table at the end of her chamber.

Staring at her reflection, Zardi unpinned her scarf and pulled the long rope of her braid over her shoulder. She unraveled it, feeling its unruly thickness beneath her fingertips. A memory of her sister teaching her how to braid hair when she was just four years old caught and held her fast. Zubeyda had been so patient, sitting with her as she practiced intertwining the three strands again and again. She could almost hear Zubeyda's squeal of delight, feel her sister's hugs and kisses when she had finally got the braid right.

In the sheet of glass, Zardi gazed at the oval face, long nose, strong jaw, and the black eyebrows that swept upward like two cormorant wings above hazel eyes. She willed herself to remember this image of herself, for it was time to remove it from the world. She would not let the sultan come for her.

Reaching into the dressing-table drawer, she picked up a dagger with an ivory hilt. The blade glinted fiercely in the candlelight. *This was it.*

Taking a deep breath, Zardi grabbed a handful of hair and cut through the locks with one clean slice. She opened her hand and let the strands fall to the ground but refused to look at herself in the mirror. She couldn't stop now. Not until her transformation was complete.

She took another handful of her thick ebony locks and cut again, and then again. The blade took on a life of its own, hacking away until most of her waist-length hair was on the floor. At last, she faced her reflection.

Zardi, reinvented.

She put the dagger down and ran her fingers through her new choppy haircut. With the weight of her long tresses gone, her hair curled tightly and she looked just like a boy. A boy who could convince a boat's captain to take her on as a member of his crew. A boy who could get to Sabra and find the secret order of warriors who sought to destroy the sultan. It was what her father would want her to do—she was sure of it.

Crossing over to the chest in the corner of the room, she took out the plain leather bag her grandmother had given her as a birthday present that morning and packed a bar of soap and a muslin facecloth. She then took the carved falcon that Sinbad had given her from her pocket and placed that into her bag as well. Her lucky charm.

Zardi stared around her room, realizing she didn't have much else to take. She couldn't take any of her knee-length tunics or trousers because their swirls of embroidery would instantly give her away as a girl. Where was she going to get boys' clothing?

Rhidan, a voice whispered inside her. Zardi shook her head. She couldn't involve him in her plan. He'd insist on going with her and she wouldn't take him into danger. Her stomach twisted in protest at her decision to leave him. They had grown up together, done everything together. Rhidan was not her brother, he was her twin heartbeat. Zardi kneaded the thin skin around her eyes, forcing herself to collect her thoughts. She'd go to the laundry room and grab a pile of Rhidan's dirty clothes. They might be a bit smelly but she had little choice.

Kneeling down, she pulled a carved sandalwood moneybox from under the bed. She flipped the lid and tipped the box upside down. Silver coins became rain, landing softly on the richly carpeted floor. She trembled as she saw the imprinted face of the sultan on the metal discs, but she forced herself to touch the coins and count them. Sixty dirhams. Not much. *But enough to get me to Sabra if I offer to help on deck as well.*

The idea of finally fulfilling her dream, leaving Taraket and sailing on a boat, made her breath catch. *Wait, Zardi,* she told herself firmly. If her plan was to work she needed to get hold of the clothes, but she couldn't leave her room until everyone was asleep.

She sat at the dressing table with a piece of parchment and her reed and inkpot, wondering how to say good-bye. She couldn't give away too much of her plan in case the sultan's guards ever found it.

In the end, a few lines said it all.

> *To Nonna and Rhidan,*
>
> *I must leave. Try not to worry about me, just believe that I'll come back to you, and when I do, I'll have found a way to save Zubeyda and Baba. The hunter will become the hunted.*
>
> *I love you both.*
>
> *Z*

She looked at the words she'd scratched on the paper, nervousness making her hand shake. Now that she'd written the words, her quest felt frighteningly real. She'd devote her every living breath to finding a way to destroy the sultan and stop his tyranny. Give her life, if need be, to rescue Zubeyda and Baba. Zardi watched the black ink dry on the page, and in her mind's eye the ebony lines and curves blurred and became the cruel planes of Shahryār's face. "I'll find a way to stop you," she whispered into the quiet room. "I'll search the whole world if I have to."

Zardi waited until the house had finally settled into sleep and, with her bag over one shoulder and her archer's belt with its quiver around her waist, she quietly unbolted her door. She crept into the laundry room, a squat outhouse to the side of the villa. By the moon's chalky light she took a sheet from the drying stone and tore it into strips before binding her chest. For the first time in her life she was grateful for her boyish form and that she didn't have the curves of her sister. She then changed into one of Rhidan's outfits, a white tunic over loose pants, and stuffed more of his clothing into her bag.

Zardi took one last look at her home, thinking of Nonna and Rhidan sleeping inside. The stone building looked peaceful, its tiled walls of azure and gold warm and welcoming. But the desolate streets of the city waited for her. She knew that the sultan's guards watched from the towers of the city, even after dark, or lurked around corners, eager to catch someone out after curfew. Her throat began to burn. She desperately wanted to walk back into the house and crawl into bed. She wanted to wake up in the morning and shake her head as Zubeyda managed to convince Baba to let her buy a new dress for the thousandth time, or sit in the kitchen and hear Nonna singing to herself as she made breakfast. "If I stay I'll never find a way to stop the sultan," she reminded herself out loud. "I'll never find a way to save Zubeyda and Baba." *Or myself.* Zardi trapped the last thought and pushed it down deep.

Squeezing her eyes shut against the tears that wanted to fall, she walked away, leaving the villa behind. Wending her way through the streets that led out to the port, she ran through her plan. First she needed to reach the docks without being detected by the guards. Then she'd hide beneath the pier for the rest of the night. At sunrise she would find a boat getting ready to depart for Sabra and offer its captain her services as a temporary deckhand.

She kept to the edges of the path where the shadows were thick as molasses. Soon the grandeur of the villas gave way to squat buildings with flat, woven roofs and collapsing walls. Ragged tents filled the spaces between the buildings. There was evidence everywhere of how little the sultan cared for his subjects, how he was breaking the poor with his greed for high taxes.

Up ahead, the docks came into sight, and Zardi quickened her step. At the same moment, she heard footsteps behind her. She bolted forward, fear cutting at her insides, but she was not quick enough.

A heavy hand grabbed her shoulder and held her fast.

6

Our Very Own Quest

Zardi swung round, ready to fight, but froze as she found herself staring into a familiar pair of violet eyes. "Rhidan, what are *you* doing here?"

"I could ask you the same question." He reached out and touched one of her roughly hewn locks. "I almost didn't recognize you. Luckily I spotted your birthday present." He pointed to her archer's belt. "Where are you going, Zardi? There's a curfew, you know."

"I am well aware of the curfew." Zardi grabbed Rhidan and pulled him down behind two barrels so that they were out of sight. "Answer my question first."

Rhidan's pale face looked guilty and defiant at the same time. "I was going to the docks." He dipped his head. "This afternoon I arranged to sail to Sabra," he said. "Sinbad's heading there next and I need to find him. He's the only one who can tell me where the Black Isle is."

"You're running away?" Anger scorched her insides. "And you didn't even bother to tell me. How could you?"

"Hang on a second!" Rhidan whispered furiously. "You're not exactly tucked up safely in bed." He paused for a moment and looked her up and down. "Hey, are those *my* trousers?"

Zardi looked away, embarrassment warring with anger.

"Come on, tell me what you're planning," Rhidan begged, his voice gentle. "I was going to the docks to tell the captain that I wouldn't be leaving with him at first light. That I needed to stay in Taraket with you."

Zardi felt a swell of warmth go through her. She exhaled deeply, and words began to flow on the same breath. She told Rhidan about the overheard conversation between Baba and the sultan, about Aladdin, the true prince of Arribitha, and how he might still be alive, and why running away to Sabra and finding the secret order of warriors called the Varish was the only way to stop the sultan once and for all.

"I didn't tell you I was going," she finished, "because I knew you'd insist on coming with me. I couldn't take you into danger."

Rhidan shook his head. "Zardi, you are my best friend. I go where you go, all right?"

"All right," Zardi repeated.

Rhidan frowned. "Do you think Aladdin is really alive? And if he is, why hasn't he come back to take the throne from the sultan?"

"I don't know," Zardi replied. "But if we can find the Varish we can ask them."

Rhidan chewed on his lip thoughtfully. "After your father was taken, I spoke to Nonna. She told me that she read your future today—that you have a destiny to fulfill and that I had to help you even if it meant leaving her behind." His violet gaze pinned her to the spot. "Maybe finding the Varish and helping Aladdin to reclaim his throne is your destiny. Let me go with you to Sabra, then we can find Sinbad. I'm sure he'll know about the Varish and the rebellion. We'll save Zubeyda and your father together!"

Hope sparked inside Zardi. She didn't know if she believed in destiny, but Sinbad was well traveled, a man who had really lived. He must know all kinds of people . . . *people who might even kill for money.* The thought stole through Zardi, as quiet and light-footed as an assassin. *Such knowledge would be more of a weapon than even my bow and arrows.*

"It's a good plan," was all she actually managed to say.

"I've already found a riverboat that was willing to take me," Rhidan went on. "The captain said it will take eight days or so to sail down the Tigress and get to Sabra. I'll tell him that you're a friend of mine." Rhidan got to his feet, quickly scanning the area for the sultan's guards. "You'll get to sail on a boat, and I'm sure he'll let you try cutting the sail or whatever it is you want to do."

"It's trim the sail, camel brain." Zardi smiled to herself.

"Come on, then," he said, and they crept toward the docks. "We're looking for the *Triumph.* The captain's called Assam, and he's setting sail as soon as the sun rises." Rhidan glanced at the sky, which was turning from black to indigo, and picked up the pace. "Given the fact that he made me pay up front, I don't think tardiness is an option."

"How much did he charge you?" Zardi asked in alarm, remembering she only had sixty dirhams in her purse.

"Fifty," Rhidan replied. "But I had to promise to help out on deck as well for that price. It was the cheapest I could find, and he seems like a fair man." He glanced at her. "I've got some money if you need it."

Zardi shook her head. "I've got enough, but our dirhams aren't going to last forever once we get to Sabra."

Rhidan flashed a smile at her. "With my brains and your brawn we'll be fine." He assessed her for a moment. "What should I call you now that you're a boy?"

"Good question." Up ahead, she could see the outlines of the moored ships, and she felt a splutter of panic. Very soon she would be leaving "Zardi" behind.

Rhidan thought for a moment. "How about Zee?" he asked. "Short, sweet, and simple."

"Zee," Zardi repeated, rolling the new name around in her mouth like a date seed. "I like it."

"Good, because having a new name is just the beginning, Zee," her friend replied. "The beginning of our very own quest. The Black Isle is out there somewhere, and so is a way to stop Shahryār."

PART TWO
Voyages

7

The Marsh

As the inkiness of night had surrendered to the orange of dawn, the *Triumph* had unfurled its triangular sail, raised its anchor, and set off downriver. Zardi remembered what it had felt like two days ago standing at the prow of the boat and breathing in the sharp, ironlike smell of the Tigress as they left Taraket. The breeze off the water had lifted up the blunt tendrils of her hair and the sensation of the wind brushing her nape had been an unfamiliar but welcome distraction from the ache in her heart.

Images of Baba, Nonna, and Zubeyda had filled her head, urging her to look back at the city and its winding streets that smelled of charcoal and baking bread. Instead, she'd fixed her gaze downriver, where the water was wide and straight. She couldn't push thoughts of those she loved out of her mind, but her quest to save her sister and Baba would not be solved by looking over her shoulder—the answers were ahead.

The sound of retching and the sight of a silver head bowed over the side of the boat dragged Zardi from her memories. *Poor Rhidan.* For a second she considered leaving her perch on the boat's railing and going over to him, but she stopped herself. Rhidan had made it clear, *several times,* that if he was going to be sick, it would be on his own. She really didn't feel like getting her head bitten off again.

They had been sailing for well over two days now, and Captain Assam said that they'd be in Sabra in six more.

Zardi hugged herself. Just thinking the word *Sabra* made her light-headed. Sabra, the harbor town, marked the juncture where the Tigress River met the ocean—the sea she'd imagined but never seen. She frowned as she suddenly recalled how Rhidan refused to even entertain the possibility that Sinbad might have already left Sabra, let alone discuss how they'd find the captain in a port ten times busier than Taraket. *But find him we must,* she thought. *Because once we've docked there will be only eighty-one days until the Hunt.* Zardi just hoped that Rhidan was right and that Sinbad would have some idea of how to find the Varish warriors and that they would be strong enough to defeat a man who was constantly guarded and had the command of a whole army.

"All right there, Zee?" Captain Assam asked, waddling up to her, his significant girth undulating in harmony with the movement of the small boat.

"Good, thanks." Zardi smiled into the captain's wrinkled face. Her new name had quickly become familiar, but a part of her still couldn't believe she was actually managing to pass herself off as a boy.

"You're doing a lot better than your friend." Assam chuckled as he looked over at Rhidan, who was still hanging over the railing making rather hideous gagging noises. "You know, once he gets on a bigger ship the seasickness will go. He won't feel the movement of the water as much."

"I hope so," said Zardi. "Otherwise, our careers as deckhands might be over before they even begin." Her cheeks burned as she told the lie. She and Rhidan had not told Captain Assam or his two crewmen, Rakin and Hakeem, who they really were. To them, Zee and Rhidan were just two friends heading to Sabra, looking for a permanent job on a ship.

Assam looked out at the river, his graying hair ruffled by the breeze. "Not everyone is cut out for a life on water, Zee. Some say it is no better than being a worm on a splinter of wood, but for me there's nothing I love more." He patted the rail of the boat affectionately. "She's called the *Triumph* because owning her, all twelve arm spans of her, is the biggest triumph of my life."

Zardi nodded. Over the last couple of days she'd really become quite fond of the captain. He could talk for hours about sailing and the sea. She loved listening to his amazing tales of enormous ocean-dwelling beasts and mysterious islands.

She smiled to herself. Two days ago, when she'd first stepped onto the boat with Rhidan, the captain hadn't been quite so friendly, but once Zardi had willingly offered to scrub the deck he had become more friendly. Now, Assam readily showed her how to steer with the tiller.

"We'll be approaching the marsh soon." Assam pointed up ahead. "If you like, I'll let you steer all by yourself."

"Really—" The pitch of her voice made her break off. It was *way* too high. Over the last three days she'd mastered her boy's voice well enough but somehow always forgot to use it when she was excited. She gave a little cough to cover the awkwardness. "Will it be difficult?" she finally managed to ask in a much lower octave.

"It can be tricky," the captain replied. "You don't want to get too near to the bank or the rudder will get caught up in reeds, but at the same time you need to keep a lookout for pirates. The marshes are their favorite hunting ground. They know boats aren't going anywhere fast."

They walked down the deck and Zardi took up the tiller. The captain's last words niggled at her. More than once Assam had mentioned that pirates operated on the Tigress River, but she wondered if he might be exaggerating just a *tiny* bit. The river could be eerily quiet at points, but whenever they did come into contact with other sailors, they'd been friendly and as keen to exchange stories as goods.

Up ahead, Zardi could see that the river was becoming murky. As the boat plunged into the brackish marsh water, it instantly slowed, almost as if they were sailing through rice pudding.

"I feel abysmal," Rhidan groaned as he staggered over to join Zardi and the captain at the tiller.

"At least you're not throwing up anymore," she replied, swatting a fly from her face.

"That's because there is nothing left to throw up," her friend grumbled. "Besides, people on the riverbank kept on waving at me. I felt like a real idiot."

"Those are the marsh people," the captain explained. "They know these waters like the backs of their hands. They're an extremely private race—you should be honored that they waved at you."

Rhidan dropped his shoulders wearily. "Right now, I'd be honored if I could stand upright for longer than ten seconds without feeling nauseous."

"Why don't you sit down and watch some of my expert steering," Zardi suggested teasingly. "You might learn something."

Captain Assam chuckled. "That's the spirit, my boy.

Show your friend what you can do."

Rhidan's dimples appeared. "Yes, my *boy*." Zardi noticed that he dragged out the last word mischievously. "Let's see what you're capable of."

She took Rhidan at his word and began navigating the *Triumph* through the marsh. Her hands trembled on the tiller, but she made sure that her face remained composed and her voice steady as she instructed Assam's crew to let the sail out a little.

"Sure thing, Zee," the crewman named Rakin hollered, loosening the rigging, while Hakeem scaled the main mast and dealt with the sail at the top. It was a good call, and the wind caught the triangular sail perfectly and propelled them swiftly downstream, cutting through the soupy water.

Captain Assam's face was filled with admiration. "You've the makings of a fine sailor, Zee. Well done."

Zardi grinned and ran her hands over the hard wood of the tiller. She couldn't believe she was really steering a boat. Her life had changed so much in just three days.

"Captain," Hakeem shouted, still atop the mast. "There's a boat in trouble." He pointed upriver. "They're flagging us down."

Zardi looked along the length of their vessel and

saw the outline of a small boat, no more than six arm spans, by the riverbank. As they got closer it became clear that the boat had been caught by the reeds. A distraught-looking young man stood on the deck, gesturing frantically at them.

"Oh dear," Rhidan commented. "Somehow, I don't think that this guy is as good at sailing as you, Zee."

"What should I do, Captain?" Zardi asked, looking at Assam. She was surprised to see deep worry lines scoring the old man's brow.

"We're not stopping," the captain replied. "I will not become an easy target for pirates."

Zardi bit down on the words of disagreement that rapidly formed in her mouth. If she was serious about passing herself off as a sailor she'd better get used to not arguing with the captain.

She continued on course. However, as they drew level with the stranded boat and she saw the desperation on the young man's face, Zubeyda's frightened eyes, glittering with tears, floated in Zardi's mind. They couldn't just sail past.

"Please, Captain," she implored, turning to Assam. "Can't we help him?"

The captain scowled at her, but after a moment's

more thought, nodded tersely. "Hakeem," he barked, looking up at the crewman on the mast. "Trim back the sail and get down here. Zee, take us in toward the boat, not too close, we don't want to get trapped by the reeds as well. Rakin, drop the anchor on my count, and Rhidan, go and fetch some rope from the cargo hatch. We're going to pull that boat onto the river."

Rhidan, who still looked a bit green, agreed readily, and the rest of the crew set about their tasks. Zardi steered the *Triumph* in toward the bank, carefully skirting the olive-colored reeds that reached upward from the riverbed. Once she'd brought them as close to the bank as she dared, Assam went to the port side of the boat and instructed Rakin to drop anchor.

Zardi peered over at the banked boat and its passenger. The stranded boatman's face was deeply tanned and was all sharp angles, but he was much younger than she'd thought initially, maybe thirteen or fourteen.

"What do you suppose he's doing on that boat alone?" Rhidan asked, padding over to Zardi with the heavy rope slung over his shoulder. "Even I can see it's too big for him to handle by himself."

Zardi frowned. It was almost as if Rhidan had plucked the words straight out of her brain. "Perhaps the rest of his crew have gone to get help," she reasoned, even as a feeling of unease began to creep through her. *What if this is some kind of trap?*

"Rhidan, the rope," Captain Assam bellowed, making her jump.

"All right, I'm coming," Rhidan called back. "Would a 'please' hurt?" he muttered under his breath.

"You too, Zee," Assam beckoned. "The tiller will be fine unmanned for a moment."

Zardi and Rhidan joined Assam and his crew at the boat's railing and looked out at the smaller boat that was now only a few arm spans away.

"Thank you so much for stopping," the boy shouted. "I can't tell you how many boats didn't."

"Are you alone?" Assam asked.

The boy shook his head. "My brother's gone off to ask the marsh people to help get us out of these reeds. He hasn't come back—" He broke off, a worried look on his face.

At once, Zardi knew this was not a trap. The note of fear in the boy's voice was too real. He needed their help.

Assam must have felt the same because he took the rope from Rhidan and tossed one end of it over to the boy. "What's your name?" the captain asked.

"Nadeem," the boy replied.

"Nadeem, listen to me closely. Tie that rope tightly around your figurehead," Assam instructed. "We're going to pull you out."

Zardi watched as the boy tied the rope around the bird-shaped figurehead of his boat. There was something about the carved bird of prey that nudged some recent memory, but she couldn't quite grasp it.

Assam grabbed the other end of the rope and Zardi and the rest of the crew followed the captain's lead and fell in line behind him.

"All right, on my count," Assam shouted. "ONE, TWO, THREE!" The five of them heaved as one. Zardi braced herself for the point of tension, the point where they'd surely meet resistance as the boat freed itself from the reeds that imprisoned it, but there was none. Instead, the smaller boat shot forward, its figurehead smashing into the hull of the *Triumph* and wedging there. Assam's boat rapidly began to take on water; the fractured boards that surrounded the carved wings of the figurehead became teeth in a gaping mouth.

The captain said a word that Zardi had never heard before and then dropped to his knees and desperately began bailing water out of the bottom of the boat with his hands. Rhidan, Hakeem, and Rakin joined the captain, but Zardi was frozen. *The little boat was not stuck,* she realized. *It was never stuck.*

Her gaze met Nadeem's. There was no regret in his dark eyes. Instead, they burned ember-bright with excitement. His mouth curled into a satisfied smile, and Zardi knew that the worst was still to come.

Looking past him, she saw several figures in black drop from the trees that lined the bank. They wore daggers at their waists, and their faces were covered by thick strips of black material so only their eyes were visible. The men dove into the river and slithered like black eels through the water toward Nadeem's boat.

"Captain!" Zardi yelled, not caring this time that the pitch of her voice was all wrong. "We're under attack!"

Assam's head shot up, and his eyes narrowed as he spotted the first of the figures in black to climb up onto Nadeem's boat and stalk toward the boy.

The man was tall and powerfully built, and Zardi wondered if she'd been wrong about Nadeem and whether this man would harm him. She was about to cry out a warning when she saw the two of them shake hands. Nadeem then pointed at the boat and bowed with a flourish. The tall man ruffled the boy's hair and murmured something, while Nadeem beamed with pride. There could be no doubt now—this had been a planned ambush.

"PIRATES!" Assam threw the rope over the side. "We have to push ourselves off this figurehead. NOW!"

Zardi launched herself at the carved wooden bird that had taken roost in the *Triumph*'s hull, barging it with her shoulder. The figurehead's cruel face mocked her attempts, and she was relieved when Rakin and the captain joined her and rammed the full weight of their bodies against it. To her side, she could hear Rhidan and Hakeem continuing to bail water from the bottom of the boat.

Her shoulder ached fiercely as she continued to push at the figurehead, but it refused to budge. The wooden wings of the bird of prey had hooked onto the inside of the *Triumph* and would not release their grip. Looking over, Zardi saw the rest of the pirates climb up onto Nadeem's boat, and then, as one unit, stride across the deck toward them, using the smaller boat as a bridge to Assam's vessel. With the bird of prey still holding them hostage, there was nowhere the riverboat could go.

Zardi whirled from the wooden figurehead toward

the cargo hatch to grab her bow and arrows. She was too late. The attackers swarmed the boat like locusts, and two men blocked her way, daggers drawn. Yet more pirates had swum around the back of the *Triumph* and now climbed onboard. The two men advanced on Zardi, pushing her into the center of the boat where Assam, Rhidan, Hakeem, and Rakin also now stood. They were surrounded.

"Who is the captain of this boat?" The tall man who had ruffled Nadeem's hair asked commandingly.

"I am," Captain Assam spat out, eyeballing the other man defiantly. "And I demand that you get off it."

The man in black wagged a finger. "That's the wrong answer, my friend. I am the captain of this boat until I deem otherwise."

"You? A captain?" Assam's voice dripped with disdain. "A captain holds his head high and leads his men. You hide your face and steal from those who work for a living. You are no better than a hyena stealing from a mighty lion."

The pirate narrowed his eyes and then nodded his head once. Two of his men grabbed Assam and dragged him over to their leader. The tall man then put his hand to his dagger and with deliberate slowness drew it from his belt.

"Don't!" Zardi cried, trying to break through the ring of pirates. "Please, don't hurt him."

"Be quiet," the pirate leader roared, turning to her with a glare that could cleave iron. "Say another word and I will remove your tongue. Is that clear?" The viciousness of his words snatched the breath from Zardi's throat.

"The same goes for the rest of you." The pirate's gaze raked over Hakeem, Rakin, and finally Rhidan. Zardi frowned when she saw the pirate flinch as he looked at her friend. He turned his head swiftly, but not before Zardi saw an angry kind of fear in his eyes. The crescent-shaped scar just by the pirate's left eye was jerking crazily. She gasped. She'd seen that crescent scar before. She'd heard this man's voice before.

It was Sinbad the sailor.

8

Captured

"Zee, stay back, boy," Assam called out. "I don't need you to fight my battles. This man is nothing but a jumped-up thief."

Sinbad turned back to Assam and held the blade under the captain's nose. "You're mistaking me for a man who will tolerate argument." He spoke softly. "I *will not*. There are fifteen men on this boat, and I will call for more if need be. I want to know what you have on this ship, and I want to know *now.*"

Captain Assam looked sullenly at Sinbad and pursed his lips together firmly. With a growl, Sinbad lowered the blade toward the captain's neck.

"The cargo hatch," Hakeem yelled. "All we carry is in the cargo hatch. Some bolts of silk and some sacks of grain, that's all we've got."

Assam scowled at Hakeem but still didn't say a word.

"I wouldn't look so annoyed if I were you," Sinbad told the captain while his men headed for the hatch. "Your crewman just saved your life." The pirate nodded, and the two men holding the captain dragged him over to where Zardi stood with Rhidan and the rest of the *Triumph*'s crew.

Zardi was pleased that the captain had escaped the taste of the pirate leader's steel, but her mind could not stay still. Sinbad was *here,* on the *Triumph*! That was why the figurehead of Nadeem's boat had seemed so familiar. It was a falcon, the namesake of Sinbad's ship. She knew that every ship carried at least one spare lifeboat—Nadeem's boat must be one of the *Falcon*'s. She glanced over at Rhidan. His face was strained, but no trace of hope or excitement shaded his expression. Sinbad clearly recognized Rhidan, but her friend didn't have a clue that the man they were searching for was standing right in front of them.

The pirates were busily throwing the bolts of silk up on the deck and soon emptied the hold of all its contents, including Zardi's bow and arrows.

"It hardly seems worth it," she heard Rhidan mutter under his breath. "All this effort for some scraps of silk and a few sacks of grain."

Sinbad stiffened. "Your boat was the only one foolhardy enough to stop," he snapped, still refusing to look at Rhidan directly. "Those annoying marsh people kept on warning boats that we were waiting for them."

Rhidan's eyes widened. "So *that's* what all the waving was about." He looked over at Assam guiltily. "I'm sorry, Captain, I didn't pay them any attention"—his voice became small—"on account of all the throwing up. . . ."

Zardi shook her head in disbelief. Rhidan had ignored the warnings, and she'd persuaded Captain Assam to stop. Together, they'd caused his boat to be captured. Her eyes fell on the quiver full of arrows and her bow.

Perhaps . . .

Sinbad must have seen where her gaze lingered

because he picked up the archer's belt and unclipped the bow from the quiver, examining it with interest. "Impressive workmanship," he mused, turning to face her. "Is this yours?"

"My father gave it to me," Zardi managed to say through gritted teeth. "It was a birthday present."

"Touching," Sinbad replied. "But you must be far from home, young man, if you have a father who can afford a bow of this craftsmanship." He clipped the bow to the quiver and slung the belt over his shoulder. "It is far too nice for you, young one."

A red-hot surge of anger lanced through her. How dare Sinbad take things that didn't belong to him? How dare he enjoy it so much? He was just as bad as the sultan. Her disappointment in the man she thought might be able to help her defeat Shahryār turned her anger to rage. She couldn't see Sinbad's smug smile through his disguise, but she was determined to wipe it right off his face.

"Actually, I have something else that might interest you." She reached into her pocket and pulled out the wooden carving of the falcon that Sinbad had given her a mere four days ago—it felt like a lifetime had passed since then.

"Zee, what are you doing?" Rhidan asked in a baffled voice.

She ignored him and held the falcon out to the pirate leader. "This was given to me by a sailor in Taraket four days ago. He told me he'd just come back from Kadrijt, where he'd battled a ferocious beast." A deathly quiet descended on the boat. Sinbad's men became as still as scared rabbits as they stared at her. The apprehension in their eyes gave Zardi a thrill of power. "Oh, what was the sailor's name again?" She rubbed her chin. "It seems to have escaped me."

"Sinbad." Rhidan's voice was a croaky rasp.

Zardi turned and saw sudden understanding dawning on her friend's face as he looked at the pirate leader.

Sinbad took a step forward, and Zardi lifted her arm in defense, expecting a blow. Instead, he snatched the wooden carving out of her hand.

"I've heard of this Sinbad," the pirate leader said, fixing her with a piercing gaze. "He is a great sailor, admired by many, and foolishly kind to children who turn up in the strangest of places."

"Why are you talking about this Sinbad?" Assam growled. "I want you off my boat. You've got what you wanted."

Sinbad looked over at his men. "He's right, we're finished here. Pick up all that you can carry and move out." He turned to Zardi and Rhidan. "You two will join me."

Zardi's mouth went dry. The steel in Sinbad's voice told her he would not leave them on the *Triumph*. Not when they could identify him to the authorities in Sabra.

"Show us the way, Captain," Rhidan said. His voice sounded squeaky, whether from fear or excitement she could not tell.

Sinbad turned on his heel and strode off the *Triumph* and onto the smaller boat.

Rhidan rushed after him, but Zardi felt as if her feet had taken root in the wooden deck.

Assam's head snapped round in her direction. "Surely you will not join this man and his band of crooks?"

She swallowed hard. Assam was asking her the question as if she really had a choice. Out of the corner of her eye she could see one of Sinbad's men waiting for her to move off the boat. His hand rested on his crescent dagger. One way or another she was going to be taken from the *Triumph*, and if she didn't leave now someone could get hurt.

"I'm sorry, Captain," she whispered. Ripping her feet from the deck, she followed Rhidan.

"Traitors!" Assam shouted, his voice full of hurt.

Traitor. The word clawed viciously at her insides as she crossed the small boat that had been the *Triumph*'s undoing. Assam had got it *so* wrong. Zardi joined Rhidan, who was standing at the prow of the smaller boat, and they watched as the last of the pirates left Assam's vessel. In the marsh she could see Nadeem and two other pirates guiding a raft loaded with the stolen bolts of silk and sacks of grain over to the bank. Soon the water was alive with even more pirates as Sinbad and his men jumped into the river and struck out for the shore.

She turned to Rhidan. "Stay close to me," she said quietly enough so that Sinbad's men couldn't hear her. "We need to find a way to esc—"

There was a firm nudge at her shoulder. "Swim," the pirate behind commanded.

Zardi did as she was told and dove into the water, closely followed by Rhidan. She was a strong swimmer, years of living by the Tigress had ensured that, but the marsh water was thick with sediment and reeds reached upward, grasping at her legs and arms. As she fought through the muck, dread curled around her and drew in tight. She remembered Nonna's warning about the impatient sesame seed that burst from its pod, almost as if it wanted to get eaten. Zardi cursed herself. Her fate and Rhidan's were joined with Sinbad's just because she wanted to needle the pirate leader. Who knew what lengths he would go to keep his identity a secret? And how was she going to save Zubeyda and Baba when she was a prisoner herself?

Sopping wet, she climbed onto the bank and flicked the riverweed from her hair. Straightaway Nadeem was at her side, guarding her.

"I suppose you think you're really clever," Nadeem said through clenched teeth. "Mocking Sinbad the way you did."

Zardi snorted. "No, not really clever, just smarter than you." She gave him her most withering look, ignoring the voice in her head that said she probably shouldn't be aggravating her captors. "Captain Assam thought you were in need of help and you tricked him. How can you stand to look at yourself in the mirror?"

"You don't know anything about me," Nadeem snapped.

"I've seen all I need to." She narrowed her eyes.

"You're a liar and a coward."

Nadeem opened his mouth to say something but stopped as Zardi's original guard climbed out of the water and came to stand beside them. Nadeem glared at her instead and strode off.

Zardi looked across the marsh at the *Triumph*. Only Assam, Hakeem, and Rakin were on the boat now, and they were desperately bailing water. The *Falcon*'s lifeboat was still lodged in the *Triumph*'s hull, and Zardi hoped Assam had enough wits about him to keep it. Selling the lifeboat would go some way toward covering his losses. Assam must have felt her eyes on him, because at that moment he looked up and stared at her, his face deformed with rage and blame. She quickly looked down at her feet.

Rhidan pulled himself up onto the riverbank. His violet eyes were bright with anticipation, and Zardi found herself clenching her hands. *Does he really think Sinbad is going to tell him anything about the Black Isle? He's supposed to be the smart one. Can't he see that we're probably being led to our deaths?*

Two pirates marched Zardi and Rhidan inland, through a cluster of date palms and along the path set by Sinbad and his men.

"Zardi," Rhidan whispered.

She ignored him. She didn't want to deal with his misguided excitement right now.

"Are you angry with me?" he asked. "Come on—I had to say we'd go with Sinbad. It wasn't exactly a request."

She grudgingly conceded that point in her head but still didn't say anything.

"What happened to the *Triumph* is awful," Rhidan went on, "but I'm sure Assam will be able to fix it."

He fell silent, but she could tell he had more to say. It took all of twenty seconds for Rhidan to crack.

"We found him. Can you believe it?"

Zardi's anger boiled over. "Ah yes, your precious Sinbad." She glared at him. "He's a pirate. For all you know he's taking us somewhere to be killed."

Rhidan flinched.

"We guessed Sinbad's true identity." She emphasized each of the words, enjoying the look of horror that now painted her friend's face. "We're a threat."

"Well, perhaps he can be reasoned with?" Rhidan babbled. "Maybe he'll still tell us where the Varish warriors are or where we can find the Black Isle. Perhaps . . ." He trailed off, his face suddenly crumpling. "Oh, Zee, when did I become such a numbskull? What are we going to do?"

Zardi shook her head, suddenly feeling mean. Now her friend was just as scared as she was. "You're not the numbskull, Rhidan. I should have never let on I recognized him or revealed my identity." She rubbed at her eyes. "He was just being so arrogant—"

Rhidan reached for her hand. "It's all right. We'll think of a way to get out of this."

"Less talking, more walking," a pirate said, pushing them forward. Zardi's gaze was pulled to their guard's curved dagger. There was no arguing with it.

They continued to walk inland. Away from the river the air was oppressively humid and birds screamed from the treetops as if protesting at the heat. At an ancient-looking olive tree with a gnarled and twisted trunk they turned sharply to the right and headed for the banks of the Tigress again. Looking ahead at the river, Zardi could see that the stretch of marsh had ended, and she spotted the *Falcon,* with its distinctive multicolored sails, moored by the riverbank.

Zardi had forgotten how big the *Falcon* was. It was at least six times the size of the *Triumph* and had a high cabin in the back with five windows and a poop deck. The ship was manned by several crewmen dressed in simple white sailor garb, busy preparing the *Falcon* to sail.

As they got closer the ship's landing planks went down and the pirates bounded onboard, throwing the bundles of loot they had seized to their friends. Nadeem was hoisted onto the shoulders of a sailor with nutmeg-colored hair, and the crew began to cheer and congratulate him on a good job. Zardi's eyes met Nadeem's and he smirked.

Following Assam's cargo onboard, Rhidan and Zardi watched miserably as it was safely stowed belowdecks. A new guard, one who must have been left out of the raid, as he was dressed in white, came to stand by their side. He stood stiff and silent, chewing on the end of his long braid. Zardi got the distinct impression that he was just as nervous as she and Rhidan were.

A water buffalo was sitting on the muddy river-bank, its tail slowly swaying back and forth, its broad face peaceful. The beast didn't have a care in the world, not one single worry. Zardi sighed with envy. If a djinni appeared right now she'd wish to swap places with the buffalo in a heartbeat. Then there would be no pain, no fear—just mud.

9

The Pirate Ship

In no time at all the ship's anchors had been raised and the *Falcon* was sailing downstream.

"That didn't take them long," Rhidan said, looking over at the pirates who had changed out of their wet black clothing and were now dressed in white linen tunics and softly flaring trousers. "They're not half as scary now," he continued, sounding bolstered. "They reminded me of giant bats before."

The young guard beside them snorted with laughter, but quickly tried to disguise it with a coughing fit.

Zardi frowned. She didn't expect laughter from these criminals—it didn't fit. She irritably picked at the wet clothes that clung to her skin, then berated herself for even caring. Wet clothes were the least of her problems.

Up ahead, she could see Sinbad talking to an older man with a shock of thick white hair and skin the color of polished mahogany. Sinbad's companion looked over at her and Rhidan before nodding his head at something the captain said.

Zardi's body stiffened as the man started walking toward them. At her side, she could feel Rhidan thrumming with tension.

The old man stopped in front of them. "My name is Mustupha, but everyone calls me Musty." He held out a calloused hand. "I'm the shipmaster, Sinbad's second-in-command."

Zardi looked down at the hand with bemusement. A polite handshake? Musty laughed, his dark brown eyes crinkling at the corners. "Is it not customary to shake hands when you meet someone for the first time?"

"Not when you've been kidnapped," Rhidan pointed out coldly.

Musty dropped his hand. "Ah, yes, that is unfortunate." He looked at their guard with the long braid. "Zain, you can go. I'll look after these two."

Zain bowed his head and left.

Musty turned to face Rhidan and Zardi. "I'm sorry events have unfolded in this way. We're not a bad lot. Hopefully, after spending some time with us you'll see that. Sinbad is busy at the moment but hopes to talk with you later." The shipmaster looked uncomfortable. "You have a choice. You can sit here under guard or you can help me out onboard. Which is it to be?"

Zardi looked around at the sailors who were busy sluicing water off the deck and hanging their wet black clothes on the rigging to dry. The *Falcon* might be a pirate ship but it was a ship, and a big one; she couldn't help but be intrigued by how it operated.

Rhidan sighed. "From the look on my friend's face, I think you'd better put us to work."

The rest of the day swept by like the river. Zardi found herself helping the crew to darn holes in the spare sails, while Rhidan discovered his seasickness had abandoned him altogether now that he was on a bigger ship. Finding his sea legs gave him new reserves of confidence, and he even had a go at climbing the mast, albeit rather slowly. At points Zardi almost forgot she was a captive. The twins who manned the tiller, Mo and Ali, were always making jokes, their smiles identical right down to a chipped front tooth. Only the turban that Mo wore made it possible to tell them apart. And Musty had even showed her how to use a navigational instrument called a kamal. He explained that the rectangular board with its trailing cord was used to keep records of the latitudes of different ports. His soft voice immediately put her at ease, although his eyes missed nothing and he was quick to correct those around him if he thought they had made an error.

It only occurred to Zardi later, as she sat by herself twining rope from strands of salted coconut fibers, that Sinbad's crew was a clever lot. With their smiles and laughter, they almost made her feel like they were good people. Maybe the crew hoped she and Rhidan wouldn't put up a fight when the time came to dispose of them.

Zardi balled her hands into fists. They were wrong. She and Rhidan would get off this ship—she just didn't know how yet.

Night fell, and lanterns were used to light their way down the river. Zardi was finishing her last length of rope when she spotted Rhidan heading toward her from the other end of the ship. Earlier that afternoon he'd been instructed by Musty to help the ship's cook, a man as round as one of Nonna's cooking pots, with the preparation of tonight's dinner.

"Dinner's up." Rhidan crouched down next to her. "It's fish stew." His words were nearly drowned out by a ringing bell. Sailors everywhere dropped what they were doing and stampeded toward the cook, who was standing next to a steaming cauldron. Rhidan wrinkled up his nose in annoyance. "I was hoping we'd get there first."

"Don't worry about it." Zardi set the completed rope beside her. "How'd you find the cooking?"

"Not too taxing." He sat down next to her. "It makes a lot more sense than ship's knots, and the cook is really nice. I even showed him one of Nonna's tricks to clean fish."

"Nonna would be proud. At least one of us has some skill in the kitchen." Zardi smiled sadly as she thought of her grandmother but tensed as she saw a tall figure walking toward them.

Sinbad.

Light and shadow played across his face as he strode

past the lanterns on deck.

Zardi and Rhidan scrambled to their feet.

"He's coming for us," Rhidan hissed.

"We'll jump overboard if we have to," Zardi said. "Be ready."

"That's the great plan?" Her friend sounded distinctly unimpressed. "They'll only fish us out again."

"Just be ready." Zardi's palms were sweaty. Sinbad and his crew had overrun the *Triumph* and threatened Assam in the morning, and then laughed and joked with each other in the afternoon. They were a paradox. Who knew what they were really capable of?

"At ease, young ones," Sinbad said softly as he reached them. "I don't plan on hurting you—it's not my way."

"Captain Assam would say differently." The words escaped from Zardi's lips before good sense could stop them. *Why can't I keep my mouth shut?*

"Would he?" Sinbad looked at her keenly. "Tell me, did I touch a hair on his head?"

She paused, remembering the events on the boat.

"Well, did I?" Sinbad asked again.

"No, I suppose you didn't actually harm him, but you held a knife to his throat."

"But I would never have used it." Sinbad held his head

proudly. "My men and I are simply actors; our boat is our stage. We may pretend to be pirates but never, ever, have we shed a drop of blood."

Zardi felt some of the tension ooze from her body. It was like getting the last bit of puzzle, an answer to a riddle. She realized that she'd already seen Sinbad's crew play many different parts: rich merchants, adventurers, pirates, and today just plain old sailors. She wondered which role was the true one; she wondered if they even knew.

"But you steal. That's not acting," Rhidan said.

Sinbad inclined his head. "I lived on the streets of Sabra until I was twelve years old. Stealing was the key to my survival—it's a hard habit to break."

For an instant, Zardi was reminded of the pickpockets who roamed the streets of Taraket. She remembered the hungry look in their eyes. Had Sinbad once been a boy like that? She stared into the captain's face, but his gaze still held that mocking gleam that had so infuriated her on Assam's boat—it refused sympathy. "So what do you plan to do with us, if you're far too nice to kill us?" she asked.

Sinbad grinned wolfishly. "All in good time, *my lady.* Have you eaten yet?"

Rhidan shook his head.

"Well, that's no good," Sinbad replied. "The cook should most certainly eat, as should his friend. Nadeem!" The boy, who was at the other end of the boat, eating, turned round. "Bring two bowls of stew for our guests."

Nadeem did the captain's bidding but he wasn't happy about it. "I don't see why we have to feed them," Nadeem said with a scowl as he arrived with the bowls. "They look like they have had plenty of good meals in their lives." He thrust the food into Zardi's and Rhidan's hands and then stomped off.

He really doesn't like us, Zardi thought to herself. *That's fine with me because I don't like him either.* The smell of the fish stew hit her nostrils and chased away all thoughts of Nadeem as she and Rhidan sat down and eagerly began to devour their food. Sinbad sat down beside them, patiently waiting for them to finish.

As they took their last spoonfuls, the captain cracked his knuckles. "Right, and now to it. I don't know what wind of misfortune or cruel coincidence has blown you into my life, but I want some answers."

"Itisn'tacoincidence," Rhidan said in a rush. "We've-beenlookingforyou. Wefollowedyoufrom Taraketand—"

"Hold it." Sinbad interrupted Rhidan's tide of words. "I'm still talking." His face remained relaxed, but Zardi noticed that a strained note had entered his voice.

"Let's start from the top." Sinbad pointed to Zardi. "Back in Taraket you had significantly more hair. Why are you dressed as a boy?"

"I wanted to go to sea, so I ran away," Zardi replied simply. This was only a small part of the truth, but she wasn't about to tell him that she was a daughter of a vizier looking for a way to destroy the sultan of Arribitha, or for that matter that the sultan had imprisoned her sister and father. Sinbad would probably ransom her to Shahryār before the words even left her mouth. "My name's Zee now."

Sinbad nodded. "I suggest we keep the truth about your gender to ourselves. My crew can be a superstitious lot. They'll see it as bad luck to have a woman onboard." He turned to Rhidan. "And you, pale one, what do you mean you came looking for me?"

"Twelve years ago I was left on the banks of the river Tigress." Rhidan spoke more slowly this time. "The only thing I had with me was a piece of parchment with my name on it and this amulet around my neck." He stroked the intertwined snakes. "Zardi's family, or should I say Zee's, took me in." His eyes met Zardi's for a moment, and she silently thanked him for failing to mention that his adoption was under the sultan's orders and that her father was in Shahryār's employ. "Four days ago," he continued, "we met you and you mentioned a place called the Black Isle. You said that the inhabitants of this place look just like me." He fixed Sinbad with a stare shiny and hard with hope. "I need to know where the Black Isle is."

Sinbad rubbed at his temples, and Zardi thought that he looked like a man who'd just been given some *really* bad news.

"Sinbad, please, you need to tell me," Rhidan repeated more urgently.

"I can't." The words were wrung out of the captain. "I can't tell you where the Black Isle is, because it doesn't exist."

Rhidan's eyes widened. "What?"

"I mean that the Black Isle is a myth, a story. A tale my adoptive mother, Sula, used to tell to keep me entertained when I was younger." Sinbad winced. "Who knows, it might be a real place. But if it exists I don't know where it is."

"This can't be." Rhidan recoiled from the captain's

words, pushing backward until he was up against the ship's edge. "Y-you said that I had classic Ilian features."

"You do," Sinbad insisted. "Sula said that the Black Isle is populated by a race of sorcerers with violet eyes and silver hair. . . ." The captain trailed off.

Rhidan sprang to his feet. "Sorcerers," he snarled, his hands clenching into fists. "Do I look like a sorcerer? If I was a sorcerer would I still be a prisoner on this stupid ship? You lied to me, you made me think—" He didn't finish his sentence, launching himself at Sinbad instead.

Zardi leaped after him. Rhidan was upset, but he wasn't going to win in a fight against Sinbad. She grabbed the sleeve of her friend's tunic, but rage had made him strong and he threw her off. Before he could take another step, she jumped onto Rhidan's back and pinned his arms. He bucked like an unbroken horse but she held on.

Sinbad was on his feet, watchful and wary. Alerted by Rhidan's angry shouts, Nadeem and four of his friends, Zain, Dabis, Syed, and Tariq, raced down the deck. The captain held up a hand, stopping the sailors in their tracks. "Everything is fine here," he yelled over to them. "Just a minor disagreement. Go back to your meals."

"Captain, are you sure?" Nadeem asked. "These two can't be trusted. Can't you see it? Something doesn't add up about them."

Nadeem's four friends eyed Rhidan and Zardi suspiciously.

"Nadeem, I am old enough and wise enough to look after myself," Sinbad said gently. "But I do appreciate your concern, my young friend. Go back to your meal. It is fine, really."

Nadeem opened his mouth to object, but his friend Dabis took him by one arm and Zain took him by the other, and all five sailors went back up deck.

Sinbad turned to Rhidan. "Listen, I am sorry I gave you false hope." The captain sounded genuinely regretful. "It was never my intention. Zee here wanted a story and I wanted a sale."

The fight went out of Rhidan and he sank to his knees. Zardi gratefully slid off his back.

"We dock in Sabra in just over five days," the captain went on. "I'd ask that you remain on board as my guests."

"Your guests or your prisoners?" Zardi questioned.

Sinbad ducked his head, his cheeks red. "Both, I suppose. I cannot let you go. You know too much about me and my men." He shrugged. "You're a liability. I don't know what I'm going to do with you."

Zardi almost felt sorry for the captain. Deep inside, she knew he wouldn't hurt them, but whichever way she looked at it, he was her captor. She glanced at Rhidan, expecting a reaction to Sinbad's words, but he was staring down at the silver amulet, his shoulders hunched over.

She stood a bit straighter. "Circumstances as they are, Captain, we accept your gracious invitation." The words were sticky with sarcasm.

The captain bowed deeply and, with one more regretful look at Rhidan, returned to his men.

She watched Sinbad go. For a moment, she wondered if she should tell him about her quest to stop the sultan and ask if he knew anything of the secret order of the Varish warriors. *Don't be stupid, Zardi,* she told herself firmly. Sinbad might not be a killer, but he and his men were driven by their greed for wealth; it would be far too easy for them to betray her to Shahryār.

A claw of sadness raked across Zardi's chest as she remembered one of her sister's favorite sayings. *Trust is the friend of trust.* Zubeyda was always telling Rhidan that he was too quick to judge and he should try to see the good in people. Not that believing in Sinbad had done Rhidan any good. *No, now is not the time to start trusting people, Zub,* Zardi's thoughts whispered. *You and Baba are still the sultan's prisoners, and now Rhidan and I are prisoners of Sinbad.*

Zardi pressed a hand to her temple, reassured by the steady throb she found there. Any hope of answers for Rhidan had been blown away like grains of sand in a storm. But her hopes to save her sister and Baba would not be scattered so easily. Once they reached Sabra, she would escape the *Falcon* with Rhidan and find the Varish.

10

Through the Eye of the Needle

Heat from the midday sun was prickly on her neck, but Zardi didn't care. After five days they had finally reached their destination and were swiftly approaching the southernmost tip of Arribitha. As the Tigress River raced to join the ocean that lapped her kingdom's south coast, she swiftly climbed the rope ladder to the poop deck.

She stepped onto the raised platform, and the *Falcon*

burst from the river into the sea. Her breath became a whistle through her lips. The ocean was so much vaster and darker than she'd imagined—an inky blue swath that went on forever. She wondered how men had ever found the courage to build ships to explore this dark expanse. How had they resisted the urge to run screaming from its hugeness?

She hoped she'd get the chance to find out one day. But saving Zubeyda came first, and the Varish were not to be found at sea. They were hiding somewhere in Sabra. For the past five days the secret order of warriors had been the only thing that Zardi could think about. Questions and doubts plagued her. *Can I find them? What does a secret order of warriors look like? Will they help me?*

"It's going to be tight," she heard Sinbad say to Musty. The two men stood below her and were looking out at Sabra's busy port, which jutted out into the sea.

Following their gaze, she could see hulking ships and stout fishing boats arranged like dates on a stem. Even more vessels jostled for position on the coast's waterfront.

"Tight!" the shipmaster exclaimed. "It'll be like threading a camel through the eye of a needle." Musty headed for the tiller and shooed Mo and Ali out of the way, much to the twins' annoyance.

Zardi looked inland. The quay was teeming with activity: men building boats, boys wheeling crates full of salt to trade, and women selling oranges to thirsty sailors. The harbor curved, almost as if it were smiling in welcome—welcoming her to Sabra and the Tigress to the sea.

"If you grin any wider, your face is going to crack." Rhidan's voice from below made her jump.

"Oh, sorry, I didn't realize . . ." She trailed off. It seemed wrong to be smiling when Zubeyda and Baba were still in danger and all hope of Rhidan finding out the truth about his origins had been destroyed. She clambered down from the poop deck to stand next to him.

"What are you apologizing for?" Her friend sounded annoyed. "I was only teasing. I know how much seeing the ocean means to you. You dreamed of this."

"You dreamed of a few things too, but you didn't get them," she replied softly.

"No, I didn't. But that doesn't mean I can't be happy for you." He smiled, although it looked a bit wobbly. "How many times have you told me that you wanted to sail on the open sea? That you wanted to know what lay beyond Taraket?"

"A few times," she replied, knowing what an understatement that was. She could talk about sailing all day.

"A few times plus a thousand, perhaps!" All teasing left Rhidan's face. "Zee, somewhere in this vast world there must be a power greater than the sultan's. We'll find it and stop Shahryār before time runs out. We've still got eighty-one days until the Hunt." He paused as Sinbad's sailors started to cheer and stamp their feet in approval as they watched the *Falcon* slip into the tightest of moorings. "Of course, we'll need to escape first."

"I'd like to see you try." Zardi turned to see Nadeem, his tanned face as sour-looking as the earliest plums. Over the last five days, she'd come to rather like the *Falcon*'s crew. The men were quick to help and quick to laugh, but the youngest member of Sinbad's crew was different. He would just sit and watch them, his eyes narrowed as if trying to work something out. "Leave us be, will you?" Zardi asked.

"Just letting you know the facts," Nadeem snapped back. "You're not going anywhere until Sinbad says so." The boy curled his lip. "More's the pity. We don't need your kind round here."

"What d'you mean, 'your kind'?" Rhidan demanded.

"Annoying, stuck-up people like you," Nadeem

replied. "You might try to dress like us, but you're not one of us. You come from money, I can tell from your accents, the way you stand, even. The only question is why you're here and not in your fancy home." He crossed his arms. "Where do you really come from?"

"Enough, Nadeem." Sinbad's voice cut through the boy's sharp words as he walked up to them. "These two are our guests. You will show them some respect."

"But, Captain," Nadeem protested, "these two stink of trouble."

"I said, enough," Sinbad responded. "Go and help Syed and Tariq take the cargo off the ship."

Nadeem's face flushed red but he obeyed without further comment.

"Sorry about that." Sinbad watched Nadeem's retreating back. "He doesn't trust strangers and gets very protective of the *Falcon*. This crew's the only family he's got." The captain rocked on his heels. "I've been thinking," he said finally. "I believe I have a solution to our little problem."

"You mean the little problem of us being your prisoners?" Rhidan asked flatly.

"Yes, exactly that." Sinbad clasped his hands together. "Come and work for me. Not as my prisoners but as full-fledged crewmembers of the *Falcon*." His face was solemn. "I'm not ordering you to do this, I'm giving you a choice." He glanced at Rhidan. "I think I owe you that much at least."

Zardi blinked hard. Sinbad's request was a surprise, but so was the realization that if this were another time or place, if she lived in a world where her sister was safe and her father was free from the sultan's clutches, she could have made a home on the *Falcon*. An image of Assam's face suddenly filled her head. Zardi saw his hurt and anger again and she realized that this was not true. She could never live a life like Sinbad's, taking what wasn't hers. That would make her no better than Shahryār.

Zardi met Rhidan's gaze and saw her own feelings reflected in his eyes. "Thanks, but no thanks," she told Sinbad firmly.

"Rhidan?" the captain asked.

He shook his head, his silver hair dazzling in the sunlight.

Sinbad sighed. "That's a shame, but I can't say I'm surprised." He tilted his head to one side. "Luckily, I have another proposition." The captain quickly explained that he had a friend in Sabra, a fellow captain, who owed him a favor. "He trades wool and silver between here and Mandar," Sinbad went on. "I'm sure he'll find space for two extra crew hands, if I ask nicely." He winked. "It's good money."

"Mandar!" Rhidan exclaimed. "That's a bit far away, isn't it?"

"I think that's the point," Zardi said wryly. "If we're on a ship to Mandar, we won't be able to tell anyone in Sabra that you are a scoundrel, correct?"

Sinbad shrugged. "People know me as a seller of trinkets, an occasional charm perhaps, but not a pirate, and I want it to stay that way. How about it then?"

Zardi paused for all of a second to examine their options. Sinbad's good humor could only last for so long. Besides, they didn't have to go to Mandar, they just needed to make Sinbad believe that they would and then they could escape. She looked at Rhidan and his eyes told her that he'd go wherever she wanted. "Deal." She held out her hand and Sinbad shook it.

"Until I speak to my friend, I'd like to invite you to stay with my mother, Sula." Sinbad sounded every inch the gracious host. "She lives here in Sabra. She's the local medicine woman."

"I'm guessing that's Sinbad for 'I want to keep you out

of sight until I can get rid of you,'" Zardi commented.

The captain let out a roar of laughter. "Am I that obvious?"

"It was pretty obvious," Rhidan replied, not missing a beat.

Sinbad shook his head. "You may be able to see through me, but you will not find Sula so easy to read." He absently rubbed at the scar by his eye. "She saved my life, took me off the streets, and raised me as her own, yet she's still a mystery to me." He looked over toward his cabin. "Let me get a few things and I'll meet you back here." He strode off.

"Shame we don't have your bow and arrows," Rhidan said once Sinbad was out of earshot. "What if this is some kind of trap?"

"Sinbad doesn't need to set a trap. If he wanted to hurt us he would have done it already." Zardi looked over at the captain's cabin. Her bow and arrows were in there somewhere, and she felt a wave of sadness as she thought about the gift from her father. She straightened her shoulders. "If we're going to escape, we need to make him think that we're going to Mandar. If that means going to his mother's, we'll go to his mother's."

The door opened, and Sinbad walked out with a

large sack slung over his shoulder. "Let's go."

Zardi and Rhidan said farewell to the crew of the *Falcon* and then followed Sinbad across the landing planks and onto the docks. The port was peppered with tea and coffee houses, and outside them salt-encrusted sailors puffed on water pipes that made the air thick with apple-scented smoke. Men with small boat-shaped fiddles played happy tunes and serenaded anyone who would give them a coin. Traders and fishermen rubbed shoulders with scribes and storytellers. The busy port was like a bulging sack of grain about to split at the seams, and Zardi wondered how she would ever find the Varish in such a busy town. Where would she even start?

Crossing the port, they headed in toward the heart of the city. Zardi noticed straightaway that there were hardly any watchtowers here. Also the streets in Sabra weren't as narrow as the ones in Taraket, and all the houses were painted white, reflecting light into the narrowest of alleys. Sabra smelled different as well, the sea making the air briny and pungent. As they walked farther on, she could see young men weaving rugs, their fingers a blur as they manipulated the threads of color. A wizened old man, claiming to be a sage, gripped Rhidan's arm with a clawlike hand

and offered up a bejeweled spyglass.

"Don't you want to see the future?" the man asked, waving the spyglass at Rhidan and Zardi. "This will show you."

Zardi reached out to touch it, but Sinbad stopped her with a hand on her arm.

"They don't need that spyglass. I can see the future already," Sinbad interjected. "And I don't see a sale for you, old man."

The sage gave a cackling laugh. "I think you may be right. My humble little spyglass is not right for these two. More powerful magic will come their way, I think."

"More powerful magic?" Zardi repeated.

"Don't get pulled in, Zee," Rhidan cautioned.

The sage looked at Rhidan in amazement. "You don't believe in magic? But you have the look of a sorcerer."

Rhidan rolled his eyes. "Yes, I know, I have classic Ilian features." He lifted a shoulder. "I believe in magic. I just don't believe that there is anyone left in Arribitha who can do it." He looked grim. "The sultan saw to that, and you should really be more careful about what stories you sell."

The sage cackled again. "You're in Sabra now. Things that are hidden in other places will be revealed here.

You just have to know where to look."

Zardi stared at the sage. His words seemed loaded with meaning. Maybe he knew where the Varish were? But how could she ask him with Sinbad right beside her?

"Come on," the captain urged. "Let's keep moving."

As they continued to walk, Zardi kept careful track of their route. Once she and Rhidan had escaped Sinbad, she wanted to find the old sage and ask him some questions.

They passed herbalists promising potions that would bring wealth and health and snake charmers who made their serpents dance for eager audiences. It took a moment, but Zardi finally put her finger on the real difference between Sabra and her home. Sabra was a city that breathed, whereas Taraket held its breath. Magic did not hide its face so much here. But then this city didn't have Sultan Shahryār squatting at its center like a large, poisonous toad.

"This way." Sinbad turned down a narrow alleyway and toward a small stone-white villa. The doorway was covered with gauzy slips of brightly colored material, which the captain easily swept aside. Sinbad smiled. "In we go!" And the three of them crossed the threshold and entered the house.

11

The Medicine Woman

The house was much larger than it looked on the outside. Cavernous chambers led off from one another and hundreds of candles lit the way. They walked deeper into the house, leaving the outside world far behind. The smell of incense hung heavily in the air, and Zardi's eyelids drooped as she breathed it in deeply. The edges of everything became softer.

"Hey, which way did he go?" Rhidan asked.

Zardi opened her eyes to see Rhidan squinting in the low light. "No idea." She pointed over to the first chamber. "I guess we should look in there."

They walked into the room calling Sinbad's name, but there was no reply. Sitting by one wall of the chamber was a tall dresser, and above it were wooden shelves lined with glass jars. Many were filled with familiar spices like saffron, sumac, and star anise. But inside some were much more unusual things: pear-shaped blue stones that glowed with icy brightness, preserved butterflies that hung motionless in their containers, and something she could only compare to lightning that flashed, fizzled, and flashed again.

"What in all of Arribitha is this stuff?" Rhidan murmured as they stepped right up to the shelves.

Zardi felt her stomach knot in excitement. "Magic," she whispered. "Maybe Sinbad's mother can do magic!"

"But how did she escape Shahryār?" Rhidan asked. "He executed so many with magic when he came to power." He reached out to touch a jar full of burnished bird feathers. "Ow!" He snatched his hand away. "It's hot!" He sucked his fingers, staring at the jar indignantly.

"Don't touch anything else." Zardi's gaze wandered

over again to the jar filled with the blue jewels. She could feel herself being drawn toward them. As she leaned in even closer, her world shifted like a sand dune during a storm. The jar next to the jewels contained a miniature girl, no bigger than a little finger. She floated in water, suspended, her hair drifting all about her face. Zardi swallowed hard.

"Come away from there," came a woman's lilting voice from behind her. "That Snolot will suck the life right out of you if she wakes up and catches you staring."

Zardi whipped round to face a tall woman with floor-length white hair.

"I am Sula." The woman bowed her head in greeting. "Sinbad will be along shortly; he is just freshening up. Scheherazade and Rhidan, you are both welcome. I have been waiting for a long time."

"How do you know my full name?" Zardi asked in amazement. "I never told Sinbad."

"Neither did I," Rhidan said, looking at Sula hard.

"All in good time, my children." The white-haired woman stepped forward and took Zardi's hands into her own. Any questions vanished from Zardi's mind as a thick mantle of peace settled over her.

Sula's hands were as smooth as marble, just like her

face, which was without blemish or wrinkle. Only the wisdom and experience that shone from her eyes and her long white hair told Zardi that this lady had lived a long time.

The medicine woman let go of her hands and turned to Rhidan, taking his burned fingers into her grasp and examining them closely. "You are lucky that these burns have not blistered. That can happen with phoenix feathers. Don't worry, I have something that will heal them."

"Phoenix feathers," Rhidan repeated dumbly as Sula dropped his hand and reached into the folds of her dress to produce a small vial filled with an amber liquid. "There are no phoenixes in Arribitha. Shahryār killed them all."

The ageless lady gave a trill of laughter. "Oh, he tried, but he did not succeed. Phoenixes are still with us. They're just a little bit disguised with magic. We would be quite lost without them." She pulled the stopper out of the vial and poured a drop of the liquid into her hand. "Of course, it does not surprise me that you went straight for the feathers. After all, power always attracts power." She reached for his fingers.

Rhidan's mouth hung open.

He's speechless, Zardi thought, smiling in spite of herself. *That has to be a first.* "What is that stuff?" she asked, pointing to the amber liquid in Sula's palm.

"It is many things." The medicine woman rubbed the liquid onto Rhidan's scalded skin. "A salve for burns, a cough medicine, drops for earache." She examined Rhidan's fingers. "Give it a moment or two to work."

He sniffed his fingers. "It smells of sesame."

"The medicine's main ingredient is sesame oil." Sula smiled. "Sesame seeds are one of nature's dearest gifts to us. They cure many ailments." The medicine woman put the vial in her pocket. "Speaking of gifts, Zardi, I have a present for you."

Sula walked over to the wooden shelves, reached for the jar of blue stones, and plucked one out.

Zardi's heart began to pound. She didn't know why, but she wanted this stone desperately.

The medicine woman opened the top drawer of the dresser and took out a gossamer-thin length of thread that glinted in the low light. Hanging from the center of it was a tiny spiderweb. Sula placed the pear-shaped blue jewel into the web's center, and Zardi gasped as the thin strands started to twine around the stone, seemingly of their own accord. In no time at all the blue gem was securely enclosed in the web's grasp.

Zardi could only watch as Sula walked over to her and placed the newly made necklace around her neck. Looking down at it, she could see that the stone shone more brightly as it touched her skin.

Sula looked happy. "See that light? It means the stone is pleased. It has accepted you as its owner."

Zardi reached to untie the necklace. "I can't take this. It's far too valuable."

"You are a guest in my house, Scheherazade Lion-born. I'll be offended if you do not accept it. Just promise to take good care of it."

"I will," Zardi said as the gem settled in the groove at the base of her neck. Somehow, it felt as if it had always been there, and Zardi knew she would not be without it.

The medicine woman smiled. "Good. These stones are incredibly rare. A gift of the stone's own choosing will be given to its wearer—at a time of its own choosing."

"Is it magic?" Zardi asked. Saying these forbidden words, she could almost feel the executioner's blade on her neck.

"Yes. I think you may require the stone's power one day."

"So, what power will it give me?" Zardi asked,

stroking the stone.

Sula laughed. "So impatient, just as I always imagined you to be. The stone does not have the kind of magic that moves mountains, but it can grant a helpful magic."

Sinbad appeared in the doorway. "Ah, there you are, and I see you've met my mother." The captain grinned. "By the looks on your faces, she has made quite an impression. Come on, I think you need to sit down."

"Yes, do come through. I've cooked us all some lunch." Sula bustled past Sinbad and led them through to the next room.

A familiar smell filled the room.

The captain shook his head. "Mother always knows when guests are coming. It is really rather extraordinary."

"I suppose extraordinary is one way of putting it," Zardi heard Rhidan mutter under his breath.

A roughly hewn table stood in the center of the room, and a large pot was bubbling away on a grate over the fire.

Sula gave the air a sniff. "Mmm, I think it's ready." She glided over to the bubbling pot and tasted its contents.

"You're cooking chorba soup, aren't you?" Rhidan asked.

Sula turned around to look at Rhidan. "Well, it's your favorite, is it not?"

Rhidan's eyes were wide and he gripped his amulet nervously. "Um, yes it is."

Sinbad grinned. "Don't worry, young ones. You'll get used to it. Mother has a way of knowing things. That's what makes her the greatest medicine woman in all of Arribitha." He walked over and kissed his mother on the forehead.

Sula smiled up at him, and Zardi wondered if, for all of the medicine woman's knowingness, she had any idea what her son truly did for a living.

"Enjoy your lunch," Sinbad said. "I've got to get to the docks and look for the captain who will take you to Mandar." He opened the roughly woven sack and looked over at Zardi. "Before I go, I want to give you something."

"This hardly seems fair," Rhidan said jokingly. "Why is she getting all the gifts today?"

Sula placed two bowls of steaming soup on the table. "Don't worry, Rhidan, your turn will come. Gifts come in all shapes and sizes, and knowledge is the greatest gift of all."

Zardi watched as Sinbad reached into the sack and pulled out her archer's belt. The sight of it made her catch her breath.

"This is yours, I believe?" He grimaced slightly as he handed it over to her, and she smiled to herself. This act of selflessness clearly pained the captain.

"Thank you," she said, fastening the belt around her waist. Welcoming the weight of the quiver against her hip, her fingers lovingly traced the lion embossed onto the leather.

Sinbad flushed with embarrassment and pleasure. "I'll see you later then. Who knows? By the end of the day you may be off to a land afar!" He lowered his voice so that Sula couldn't overhear. "I'll have you out of town before Assam arrives."

Zardi felt her stomach twist. She couldn't bear the idea of seeing Assam again. What must he think of them? She felt eyes upon her and looked over to see Sula gazing at her sympathetically. She shuddered—it was like this woman could see straight into her soul.

Sinbad bade them farewell, and Zardi and Rhidan sat down to eat their soup. Zardi took her first mouthful and was instantly transported home. Once again she was in the kitchen with Nonna, chopping onions. There was no arguing with her taste buds—the soup was a perfect match with Nonna's. Rhidan obviously agreed; he finished his soup even more quickly than she did.

"Any more?" Sula inquired.

"Not for me," Zardi replied, feeling pleasantly full. "But thank you. It was lovely."

"As good as Nonna's?" Sula asked with a secret smile.

Rhidan slammed his spoon down on the wooden table. "Enough! You have magic, that is clear, but what do you want with us?"

"What do you mean?" Sula leaned back in her chair casually.

Zardi frowned. The medicine woman was enjoying this. "You said you have been waiting for us for a long time. Why?"

"And what did you mean when you said that I'd be attracted to the phoenix feathers—that power attracts power?" Rhidan demanded.

"So many questions." The mischievous glint left Sula's eyes. "But are you truly ready for the answers?"

12

Visions of Home

Zardi met Sula's gaze full-on. "Try us."

Sula cleared the bowls from the table before sitting down. "Let us start at the beginning," she said. "My mother spun flax into thread and my father is a djinni. Do you know what a djinni is?"

"My grandmother told me that a djinni is a rare being that can grant any wish except the command to kill another person." Zardi fell silent for a moment, remembering how she, Rhidan, and Zubeyda would sit by the fire and listen to Nonna's stories about Arribitha before Shahryār came to power and how you could find magic around every corner. Zubeyda and Rhidan were always nervous when Nonna spoke about things that were forbidden, but Zardi had always urged Nonna onward. "Nonna said that years ago some of the richer families in Taraket even had their own djinnis. They were found in lamps, bottles, or rings that you had to rub to summon them."

Sula smiled. "Zardi, your description is a good one. You are right, once upon a time djinnis could be seen in Taraket. Even the sultan that Shahryār deposed had one. She'd served the royal family for many generations." Sula made an arch with her fingers. "You are also correct that djinnis bound to an object like a lamp or ring cannot kill human beings, but you should understand that not all djinnis are tethered like this. Those that sided with Eria, the great wizard, during the Battle of Akkad many eons ago are free beings, while those that did not were cursed to become the servants of mortals and were each shackled to a physical object. I am half djinni, but that is only of interest insofar as my djinni blood has given me certain skills."

Zardi braced herself, almost as if she was on the *Falcon* and it was skirting the edge of a whirlpool. Her whole life, magic was something forbidden. Now here it was right in front of her.

"If you have magical abilities, why didn't Shahryār have you killed, like he killed everyone else?" Rhidan asked shortly. "How do we know you're telling the truth?"

Sula's eyes flashed angrily. "I live because I hid. Because for years, I denied who I was. I still hide. Not even my son knows the whole truth about me. It is safer for everyone that way."

"So why are you telling us?" Zardi asked.

"Because I have been waiting for you. An important destiny awaits you both, though it is still shadowy in my mind." Sula looked resolute. "My dreams have told me that I am the only one who can set you on your path, and so that is what I will do. You must follow your destinies, even if it means that the two of you will have to be parted."

"Zardi, let's get out of here." Rhidan was on his feet. "*We* have our destiny already. Zardi's father and sister are in trouble and we're going to save them *together*."

Sula stood slowly, and Zardi was struck by just how

tall she was. Her presence filled the whole room, almost as if the very sense of her was expanding right in front of them. The medicine woman stared straight at Rhidan. "You have been looking for answers your whole life," she said. "Are you really going to walk away when you are so close to finding what you seek?"

Zardi touched Rhidan's arm. It was quivering with rage and something else—fear, maybe. "Sit down. We have to let her finish."

"Fine." Rhidan threw himself into the chair. "Pray tell, Sula, what answers can you give me?"

"I think it will be easier to show you," Sula replied. She walked over to one of the chamber's walls and plucked a glass bottle off a shelf. Arriving at the table, she pulled out the bottle's stopper and tipped the vessel upside down. Three thick silver drops fell onto the tabletop. The globules instantly gathered together and then spread until the entire surface of the table was a shiny sheet.

"Show him," Sula said, waving her palm over the reflective surface.

Zardi gasped as an image of a barren strip of land edged with high cliffs of black onyx appeared on the silver tabletop. An imposing fortress made out of the same shiny black stone rose out of the center of the isle and slashed the stormy sky like a blade. The fortress was all angles and sharp edges and had no apparent entrance. Surrounded by dark and torrid water the color of steel, this strange island was awesomely cold and dismal.

"What is this place?" Rhidan questioned.

"Your home," Sula replied. "The Black Isle."

Rhidan's violet eyes seemed to fill his whole face. "B-but . . . Sinbad said that this place didn't exist," he stammered.

"My son thinks of my stories as fables and fairy tales." Sula leaned in close, her face soft with kindness. "His instincts were right when he identified you as an Ilian. He just didn't know it."

"How do we get there?" Rhidan asked, not taking his eyes from the table's surface.

The medicine woman shook her head. "The Black Isle is far away and has a powerful dissembling spell," she said. "That means it can disguise itself, become invisible, or move at will. You'll be driven crazy trying to chase it."

Zardi's stomach churned. A moving island, a dissembling spell? "Why is it disguised?" she asked. "Are the people on it hiding?"

Sula gave an elegant shrug. "The sorcerers of the Black Isle are extremely powerful, but they have not been seen here in Arribitha since Shahryār came to the throne. They have many enemies who have long tried to steal their magic. Perhaps they are just trying to protect themselves."

Rhidan was making little puffing sounds as though he was short of breath. "If I come from the Black Isle, does that mean I'm a sorcerer? That I can do magic?"

"There is no doubt you are of sorcering stock." Sula studied him. "Whether you can do magic is an entirely different matter." She sat down at the table and stared at the two keenly, as if challenging them to keep up. "There are different types of magic in this world. Sorcerers have Kanate magic. They absorb the natural magic that exists all around us, from every object, from every drop of water. But it is no easy feat; it takes much stamina. You'll need to discover for yourself whether this is something that you can do and, what's more, whether this is something you can control."

Rhidan looked down again at the image on the surface of the table. His gaze became intense. "We have to find the sorcerers of the Black Isle." His voice sounded rougher and lower than usual. "They can help us. Help us defeat Shahryār."

There was a humming sound, and the air suddenly felt charged like the sky before a thunderstorm. Zardi bolted out of her chair as everything in the room started to radiate a faint purple light. She spread her fingers and saw purple threads fill the gaps. Her breath lodged in her throat as the strands of light began to peel away from her and all the other surfaces in the room. The light swirled upward and twisted itself into a rope of violet that wrapped around Rhidan, making him iridescent. His skin sparkled. She wanted to ask what was happening, to ask if Rhidan was going to be all right, but her tongue was thick with shock.

Just as quickly as it had materialized, the purple rope fell away from Rhidan and the light disintegrated on the air. Her friend looked completely normal and was staring down at the table, tugging on his amulet the way he always did when he was anxious.

"What in all of Arribitha just happened?" Zardi exclaimed.

Sula put a finger to her lips and pointed at the table.

Zardi followed the medicine woman's gaze and saw the fortress and the Black Isle fade. A new glowing image began to form. It was a thick golden disc. At its center was an etching of a towering tree. Its roots trailed down and turned into rivulets of water that appeared to swirl across the surface of the metal. The inner ring of the disc was studded with red stones that flickered like firelight, and around the bejeweled circumference elaborately scripted words were engraved. She only recognized one of them: *Shamal,* the name of the wind that buffeted Taraket every summer.

"What *is* it?" Zardi asked, squinting down at the object. It looked so real, it was almost as if she could reach out and pick it up.

"It is the Hunter's Elemental," Sula replied. "But most call it the Windrose, for it is the four winds that bend most easily to its power, although it has also been known to call on the elements of earth, fire, and water." The medicine woman gazed at the Windrose, the image of the golden disc reflected in the dark brown of her irises. "Rhidan, you wanted to know whether you had some aptitude for the magical arts. Well, this is a promising start. If you can find the sorcerers of the Black Isle, they will be able to teach you how to wield your magic properly."

"But I didn't do anything," he protested.

Zardi thought back to the amethyst light that had just filled the room and how it had wrapped itself around Rhidan. He had definitely done *something*, even if he hadn't realized it.

"Nonsense," the medicine woman replied. "Now that you know of your heritage, your magical abilities have awoken, even if just for a moment. You requested a way to find the Black Isle and one has been shown to you."

Rhidan looked pleased with himself, but bewilderment also shaded his expression. He stared at the strange object on the table, and asked, "What does it do?"

"The Windrose can use its powers to guide a person to anyone or anything in the world, even things that are hidden or disguised," Sula explained softly. "Many have died trying to obtain the Windrose. A djinni known simply as the guardian protects it. He is powerful and undefeated, but you, at least the part of you that just revealed that little bit of magic, want to find it."

"Where do we find this guardian?" Zardi asked, ignoring the worm of jealousy trying to burrow into her head. *So, let me get this right,* she could hear the worm saying. *Rhidan is now a sorcerer with magical powers, while you're just . . . you?*

Zardi looked at her friend. He was so excited, so happy—she realized that envy had no place here. Zardi stamped on the worm and, almost hearing it squish, gave a satisfied sigh. She knew she faced a decision. *I either try to find the Varish and ask for their help to save Baba and Zubeyda or I get Rhidan to the Black Isle.* Even as Zardi voiced the options in her head she knew there was only one choice. The Varish were just men; they might not even exist. But the sorcerers of the Black Isle had magic—magic that could defeat the sultan and save her family. *With magic on my side, the sultan won't stand a chance.*

"The guardian's location is secret," Zardi heard Sula say. "But all djinnis are linked. Any djinni would be able to tell you where the guardian resides. A djinni powerful enough could even take you there."

Rhidan looked at Sula hopefully. "You're half djinni. Can't you send me to the Windrose?"

Sula gave an almost indistinct shake of her head. "The djinnis are a proud, haughty race. Half is not good enough." Sula looked thoughtful. "I do know a djinni shackled to a golden lamp who owes me a favor." The medicine woman smiled to herself. "If there is one thing a djinni hates, it is being in debt to anyone. I will ask for his help, and you will wait for me aboard the *Falcon*."

Rhidan opened his mouth to say something, but Sula held up a hand. "If this djinni aids you by taking you to the Windrose's guardian, it will be at great personal cost to himself. A djinni can only serve one master at a time. If he chooses to grant a wish to someone who is not his master he will have to use some of his own life essence to do so. This is true of all djinnis. They are immortal, but if they lose too much of their life essence they will become the walking dead."

Zardi's thoughts were a whirl with everything she had learned, but one thing was absolutely clear: finding the Windrose was the key to saving Baba and Zubeyda. "Are we finished here?" she asked.

"Such impatience, Scheherazade. Have you no interest in learning about your own destiny?" Sula looked at her quizzically. "I dreamed of you both. I am here to set you both on your paths."

Zardi rested a hand on her hip. "Rhidan's path is my path. I'm going to get him to the Black Isle."

The medicine woman shook her head. "Your path is your own, Zardi. No doubt the Windrose has a part to play, but tell me what it is that you want more than anything else."

"To rid the world of Shahryār." The words jumped out of Zardi's mouth, uttered before they were even thought.

"Then let me show you your destiny, lion-born." The medicine woman once again swept her palm over the silver surface of the table. A cluster of trees, their branches heavy with oranges, came into view. A flash of white appeared, darting through the trunks—a girl, wearing the dress of the praisemaker. Something gold was clasped in her hand. At her heels were hunting jackals and, behind them, a man on a powerful flame-colored steed. The sultan. The fleeing girl tripped and went sprawling into the dirt, the white scarf coming away from her hair. Shahryār dismounted and stalked forward. A shudder racked Zardi's body as the girl turned toward the hunter and she found herself looking at her own face. A red light flooded over the moving images on the table and they vanished.

"How can this be?" Rhidan's face was waxen. "Zardi isn't a praisemaker."

"This is part of her destiny," Sula replied. The medicine woman looked at Zardi, her eyes sad. "Your path will take you to this point. There is nothing you can do about it."

"You are wrong." Zardi looked away from the table. "I will never let Shahryār catch me. If that's the future, I'll change it." She walked toward the door. "I think it is time you went and found this djinni. The sooner Rhidan and I can find the Windrose, the sooner we can get to the Black Isle and its sorcerers."

13

The Captain's Revenge

"Can you see her yet?" Rhidan yelled.

Zardi shaded her eyes from the low-hanging sun as she scanned the crowds on the dock. From her vantage point, up the tallest mast of the *Falcon,* she had a pretty good view of the port. "No. Nothing."

She looked down and saw Rhidan shake his head and begin pacing the deck. Zardi quickly shimmied down the mast. He really needed to stop looking so jittery or the crew was going to start asking questions. Sinbad hadn't been pleased when they'd come back to the *Falcon,* but at least he hadn't made them stay in his cabin. "It looks like my friend will take you on as crew on his ship," Sinbad had told them eagerly. "You'll be off to Mandar first thing tomorrow morning." The captain had allowed himself to crack a relieved smile. "Now you two stay on board here and stay out of sight. I've got merchants to see."

Zardi jumped down beside her friend.

"I can't wait any longer!" Frustration made Rhidan's voice shrill. "I'm going into town to see if I can spot her. Maybe she needs my help."

"It is highly unlikely that a half-djinni medicine woman is going to need your help," Zardi said, keeping her voice low. "But if it makes you feel better I'll go into town and see if I can spot her. You may be a sorcerer, but your sense of direction stinks."

Rhidan opened his mouth and then closed it again. "Fine, you go and find her."

Zardi grinned. "I'll do one circuit of the docks and then I'll come back. In the meantime keep your eyes peeled."

"Didn't you know?" Rhidan said, dimples appearing in his cheeks. "Peeling one's eyes is a sorcerer's specialty."

"Pleased to hear it," she called, bounding across the landing plank and onto the dock.

As she walked through the crowds, searching for Sula, Zardi was suddenly struck by the ordinariness of the scenes around her: people laughing, talking, and arguing. The world looked the same, but it wasn't. She thought all magic had been driven from Arribitha, but it was still here. Strangest of all, she and Rhidan were part of it.

Thinking of her friend brought a smile to her lips. She was glad that they could laugh about him being a sorcerer, although she knew the idea hadn't quite sunk in for either of them—not yet.

During their walk back to the *Falcon,* Rhidan had confessed that he didn't know how he made the purple light appear. He normally loved figuring out how things worked, but with his magic he didn't even know where to start.

Zardi had told him not to worry about it. With the help of a sorcerer from the Black Isle, all their problems would be solved. Rhidan would learn how to use his magic and Zubeyda and Baba would be saved.

But only if we find the Windrose first, Zardi thought. Unbidden, she saw the image of herself among the trees, the sultan's jackals chasing her down. She wanted to dismiss it, *would* dismiss it. She and Rhidan would get to the Black Isle and make sure that this version of the future never happened.

Suddenly a hand gripped her shoulder from behind. It was so reminiscent of the time that Rhidan stopped her in that dark alley in Taraket that she turned around with his name on her lips. But it wasn't Rhidan.

Captain Assam stared down at her. "Zee, what a pleasure to see you." The words were friendly but his tone was not. "I was hoping to bump into you."

"Captain!" Zardi exclaimed. Her happiness at seeing him fled as the hand clamped on her shoulder tightened. "I'm so glad you're safe. Is the *Triumph* all right?"

"Yes, the *Triumph* is fine." The captain's face was stony. "I'm afraid your little plan to have my boat rammed and leave it to sink didn't work."

"What plan?" Zardi tried to pull back from his grasp but she was held fast. "I didn't mean for anything to happen to your boat."

"Yet you and Rhidan seemed keen enough to leave my boat and affiliate yourself with a band of pirates."

His eyes were like ice. "You have a lot of explaining to do, and I know the sultan and his guards are eager to hear it." He let go of her shoulder and grabbed her arm, holding it in an ironlike grip.

Zardi felt herself go cold. "The sultan's here?"

Assam raised an eyebrow. "Life is full of surprises, Zee—or should I say *Zardi*? After you and your pirate friends left the *Triumph* to its fate, another ship came down the river. It was the sultan's vessel, the *Swift*." The captain leaned in, bringing his face right up to hers. "His guards asked me if I'd seen a boy with silver hair, possibly traveling with a girl. I told them about Rhidan but you see I was confused because his companion was a boy not a girl."

Assam smiled darkly, and Zardi hated to see the meanness on his face.

"Then the sultan himself came out of his cabin and questioned me," Assam continued. "I told him all I knew. In return, he told me a few things, including your true name and the fact that you and Rhidan are wanted in Taraket for several crimes."

Zardi began to protest, but the captain talked over her.

"I've heard many say that the sultan is a cruel man,

but now I see that for the lie that it is. His ship towed the *Triumph* to Sabra, and I vowed there and then that I'd find you and Rhidan for him." Assam tightened his hold a bit more. "It helps, of course, that there is a reward for your capture: a thousand dirhams for you and five thousand for Rhidan." He chuckled unkindly. "Some would say that justice will be served if I turn you in. What would you say . . . Scheherazade?"

Fear choked her. *Shahryār is in Sabra.* The words screeched in her mind, louder and sharper than any seagull, while fragmented images of jackals, orange trees, and the billow of a white dress spun behind her eyes. She'd never dreamed that the sultan would come after her. *And why is he so determined to capture Rhidan? It doesn't make sense.*

Zardi's legs trembled, and she concentrated on the muscles in her limbs, willing them to become strong and stable. She wouldn't give in to her fear. Her mind stilled, and she suddenly remembered that Assam had never seen Sinbad's ship. If she could just lose him and get back to the *Falcon,* she'd be safe.

The captain shook her roughly. "I asked you a question."

She looked calmly at him, knowing that she couldn't allow herself or Rhidan to get caught. "I'd say I'm sorry that things have turned out this way." She swung her arm upward, breaking out of the captain's grip, and then bolted to the left.

"Stop there!" Assam shouted. She could hear the captain's footsteps behind her but she didn't dare look round. Instead she ducked under a nearby archway and raced down the busy street, past the rug weavers, fabric sellers, tailors, and women selling hummingbirds in brass cages, past the camels burdened with provisions to carry across the desert and the men with quills and scrolls listing the flow of goods into Sabra.

Knowing she couldn't head for the *Falcon* straightaway, Zardi veered sharply to her right, throwing herself into the heart of a complex maze of back alleys. The streets were much quieter here, and the sound of her breathing filled the silence. She turned down another road only to find that it ended with a high wall blocking the way. She ran at the partition and with her gained momentum leaped upward, her fingers finding the top of the wall. Pulling herself up, she balanced on the stony ledge. Only now did she dare to look over her shoulder.

Assam had just turned into the street. His round face was red and he was wheezing for breath. He spotted her on the wall and came to an abrupt stop, looking angry and defeated. They both knew that he could not climb the wall. Zardi felt a sharp pang of guilt for making a man of the captain's age and girth chase her and lose. "I'm sorry, Captain," she called and then leaped down, landing deftly on the other side of the wall.

Zardi stood up from her crouched position. She was in the corner of the spice bazaar and, ducking her head, she weaved in between stalls covered with the gold of turmeric and the pink of dried rosebuds. The hot, sweet smell of cinnamon quills draped the air of the market, making it hard to breathe. She raced to the *Falcon,* the conversation with Assam repeating itself in her head like the lapping of water on the shore, her fear of the sultan a crest on every wave.

She pelted onto the landing planks of Sinbad's ship and as she did so she spotted the captain talking to Musty.

"I thought I told you to stay on board," Sinbad said as she stepped onto the *Falcon*'s deck.

"Sorry, Captain."

Sinbad pulled his eyebrows together in annoyance but continued his conversation with the shipmaster.

She paused beside them, trying to work up the courage to tell Sinbad that she'd seen Assam.

"Zee, we need to talk." Rhidan grabbed her shoulder, dragging her to one side.

Zardi winced. Rhidan was holding the same shoulder that Assam had gripped earlier. It felt bruised, like a piece of meat that had been bashed thin to make tender.

"Did you find her?"

Zardi shook her head and watched as his face drooped with disappointment. She felt a stab of anger. "Don't you dare look like that, Rhidan," she said through clenched teeth. "Finding Sula is the least of our worries right now."

Bewilderment and then guilt scuttled across his face. "What happened?"

She pulled away from Rhidan and rubbed her shoulder. "The sultan is in Sabra," she said in a low voice before quickly telling him about Assam and how she'd escaped him.

Rhidan frowned. "The sultan's hunted you all the way to Sabra?"

"Hunted *us*, Rhidan. He's prepared to pay five thousand dirhams to have you captured. Five thousand!"

She bit the edge of her thumb. "Do you remember, on the night he took Baba, he said that you were not fully hatched yet? Do you think he knows you're a sorcerer?"

Rhidan's frown deepened. "Shh, we can't talk about this now. Someone might be listening. Sinbad would sell us down the river for a fraction of what the sultan offers."

Zardi looked around, checking that no one had overheard their conversation. She needn't have worried. Only about half the crew was onboard and none were close by. She froze as she saw Nadeem sprinting toward the ship, his sharp face pinched with fear.

"Captain!" he yelled as he jumped onto the deck. "We've got to go. They're coming."

Sinbad strode forward. "Who's coming?"

"The sultan's guard."

Rhidan and Zardi shared a look of horror.

"Nadeem, there's no sultan's guard in Sabra," Sinbad dismissed.

"There is now," the boy replied, still gasping for breath. "I was in the market, selling the red silk to your favorite merchant. He asked how things were on the *Falcon,* told me he'd seen a strange boy with silver hair on our ship earlier today. Said he was funny-looking and wanted to know where he was from."

Rhidan's cheeks flared with color, and Nadeem managed to smirk despite being out of breath.

"I told him not to be so nosy, and to fix on a price for the silk. That's when I could feel someone watching me. I turned round. It was that old captain, you know, Assam. He'd heard everything—your name, the name of the ship. So I ran for it. But the old bird wasn't alone. All these guards started coming out of nowhere, trying to dive for my legs. The old man was screaming at me the whole time. He said he worked for the sultan now and that Shahryār would see me and the rest of the pirates that robbed the *Triumph* in prison, or worse." Nadeem pointed at Zardi with a lean finger. "He said that the sultan would stop at nothing to hunt the *Falcon* down and capture Rhidan and the girl." He stared round at his crewmates. "See, I told you. I always said something didn't add up about these two." His eyes met Zardi's. "Who's the liar now?"

The gaze of the crew bored holes into her skin. They knew. They knew she was a girl, and that the sultan wanted her and Rhidan. She looked over at Sinbad, and his face was sad.

He's going to hand us over to Shahryār. Zardi's stomach

squirmed as if it had a life of its own. But the captain didn't say a word to her or Rhidan; instead he turned to the crew on his ship.

"If what Nadeem says is true then the sultan's guard and Captain Assam are looking for the *Falcon* at this very moment. We're leaving, right now!"

Nadeem's hands were clenched by his sides. "We should hand them over, Captain. The sultan might look on us kindly then."

Sinbad glared at him. "The sultan is incapable of kindness, and I will sacrifice no one that is in my care. We set sail now,"

At his words Zardi felt a frisson of shocked gladness go through her.

"But, Captain," Musty protested, "half our crew is still on shore."

Sinbad gripped the shipmaster's shoulder roughly. "Unless you want to see the inside of a prison cell or the executioner's blade, I suggest you do as I say."

"Yes, Captain." Musty turned and instructed Zain and Tariq to haul up the anchors while the rest of Sinbad's skeleton crew set about hoisting the sail. Even the cook helped. Zardi and Rhidan assisted, but progress was slow. Normally it took a whole crew of twenty a quarter of an hour to rig up the sails. She did a quick head count: They only had twelve men on board, not including Rhidan, herself, and Sinbad.

Finally the first sail was up and they swiftly started on the second. But halfway up to its fully rigged position, the sail stuck fast. A piece of rope had become twisted.

Zardi ground her teeth as they lowered the sail and began working at the knot. *We're not going to get out of here in time.*

Sinbad must have had the same thought because his next order was an astonishing one. "Get that knot out, then hoist this sail. We'll go out to sea without rigging it up."

"But, Captain," his men chorused.

"You heard me!" Sinbad bellowed. "We'll hold the sail in position with brute strength alone. Our muscles will scream and our bodies will say no, but we will not slacken until we're on the open sea." His words seemed to transform his men, and panicked expressions were chased off their faces by steely determination. Sinbad grabbed the sail's trailing uphaul rope and pulled. "We'll rig the sail properly once we're away from the port."

Zardi turned to Rhidan. "Come on, we need to help."

"No, *we need* to find Sula. We're getting off this ship." Rhidan strode toward the stern of the ship.

She grabbed his wrist. "If I get caught, I'll be made a praisemaker, and who knows what the sultan's plan is for you. Do you really think you'll get to speak to Sula again if Shahryār gets hold of you?"

The ship lurched forward. The two sails were up and had caught some wind, which pulled the *Falcon* out of its mooring. As the gap between the ship and the dock opened up, Rhidan wrenched his wrist away and moved toward the railing. He stood there for a moment and she could see his whole body bunching up, getting ready to jump.

She dived in front of him, standing in his way, as he'd once stood in her way on the balcony at home. "We'll be back, Rhidan, I promise." She grabbed his hand. "Stay . . . please."

Rhidan's throat worked furiously as if he was trying to swallow tears or maybe a scream of frustration, but he dragged himself away from the ship's railing and slumped down onto the deck.

Zardi knelt beside her friend. Disappointment came off him in waves and blended with her own. They had been so close to starting their quest to find the Windrose and the Black Isle. To finding sorcerers to stop Shahryār. She looked toward the port, catching a glimpse of a lady with a mane of white hair whose hand was raised in farewell. Zardi blinked and the woman was gone.

"Sula." Zardi put her hand to the blue jewel around her neck. It pulsed a welcome like a heartbeat, and Zardi knew that magic wasn't quite done with them yet.

14

Flight of the Falcon

"Oi, could you two give us a hand?" Sinbad roared. The strain of holding up the unrigged sail was carved into his face.

Zardi and Rhidan sprang forward and grabbed hold of one of the ropes that normally tied the second sail to the mast, pulling it taut.

Both sails were fully unfurled now and the *Falcon* was picking up pace as it surged into the open sea.

A stiff breeze had also sprung up, and any gust that caught the second sail sent violent vibrations down the ropes and through the arms of the sailors that held them. The friction of the rope gnawed at Zardi's hand, and her arms thrummed from the effort it took to hold onto the cable, but she did not let go.

She gave a tired cheer with the others when Sinbad finally gave the order to begin rigging the sail up properly.

We escaped. Zardi finally allowed herself to think these words as they set about the task of the rigging. She couldn't quite believe that Sinbad had chosen to run instead of handing her and Rhidan over to Shahryār. The *Falcon,* which earlier that day had been their prison, was now their refuge. She worked happily alongside Rhidan and the other sailors, drinking in the blueness all around her.

"Well done, men," Sinbad congratulated them once the rigging was completed. "We were in the jaws of danger and your strength and courage broke its teeth."

His crew stamped their feet in approval, but Nadeem was not smiling. He stared at Zardi for a moment, his eyes sharp flints of anger, before turning and climbing the mast. Sinbad held up his hand for quiet. "As you know, our friend Captain Assam and the sultan's guard are looking for the *Falcon*. We'll have to lie low. Become nomads of the sea for a while. Assam and his new friends will get bored soon enough and go home. Once the coast is clear we'll go back to Sabra and pick up the rest of the crew."

Musty took out a large book full of navigational charts. "Where to next then, Captain?"

Sinbad rubbed his chin. "Andalus, I think. We haven't been there for some time."

Musty began flipping through the pages.

Suddenly, a cry from atop one of the masts interrupted the celebrations. "Captain," yelled Nadeem, "we have company. I think it's the sultan."

His words silenced the crew. Zardi looked behind her, shielding her eyes from the deep glow of the sun. Sure enough, in the distance, she could see a large ship racing toward them. Unlike other ships she'd seen in the harbor, this vessel had three sails instead of one or two. The hull of the boat was also longer and thinner than a normal ship and sat higher in the water, skimming the surface like a flat stone. *The* Swift, Zardi thought, coldness seeping through her. A red flag emblazoned with a golden jackal—the sultan's insignia—flew from the ship's mast, and just like a jackal the sultan's ship was greedily devouring the distance between them.

The crew did not have a chance to panic. Sinbad wouldn't let them. Instead, he ordered them to move for the wind. Nadeem immediately climbed down from the mast and headed quickly with the whole crew to the starboard side of the ship. She and Rhidan followed. As they did so, they felt the ship tilt and saw the sails catch more wind, giving the *Falcon* a surge of speed. The twins, Mo and Ali, took charge of the tiller and expertly began to guide the rudder, so that the ship turned to bring the wind directly onto the starboard side.

They raced on, and while the sun began its steady descent in the sky, Sinbad called on every sailing trick he knew to lose Shahryār's ship . . . but the sultan continued to cut down the distance between the *Swift* and the *Falcon*.

"All food, all boxes, overboard," Sinbad ordered. "We need to make ourselves as light as possible." He turned to the shipmaster. "Musty, cut two of the anchors."

Rhidan, Zardi, and the rest of the crew set to work unloading the ship.

"You imbecile!" she suddenly heard the captain roar.

Zardi turned around to see one of the sailors, the mouselike Mirzani, at the ship's rail about to dump a box of weapons into the water. "Don't you think we might need those, seeing as we're being chased by a ship filled with guards with very, very pointy swords?"

"Sorry, Capt'n." Mirzani dropped the weapons onto the deck. "You said all boxes."

"I know what I said," Sinbad growled. "But we're going to need those daggers."

Zardi suddenly felt incredibly scared. Sinbad's men weren't really fighters. If they were caught they would be no match for the sultan or his guards. Shahryār was a ruthless hunter and the *Falcon* was his prey only because she and Rhidan were on it. Zardi looked at their pursuers, hoping to see space opening up between them as the *Falcon* was unloaded of its provisions, but the other ship continued to gain on them.

She picked up a bag of rice. It was heavier than she expected and she felt a twist of worry as she thought about Nonna all by herself in the house, perhaps having to lift bags just like this. Zardi shook her head. She had to keep moving and help the *Falcon* escape. *Or I might never see Nonna again.*

The *Swift* was close enough now for Zardi to make out the faces of those on board.

She stiffened as she spotted a figure dressed in expensive white robes and a silk turban standing at the prow of the pursuing ship. Even from this distance, she felt the sharp point of Shahryār's gaze. Did he recognize her? Zardi's stomach flipped, but she refused to look away. Instead Shahryār did, and she watched as he left the prow. She felt a surge of elation at the victory, small as it was.

As she turned to grab another bag of rice, something fast and hot whizzed past her ear and embedded itself in the mast at the center of the ship. It was an arrow, its flaming tail dripping clusters of fiery ash onto the deck. She looked at the sultan's ship. Shahryār stood there again, but this time with an archer by his side who was preparing a bow that was as tall as he was.

On deck, the crew of the *Falcon* had been stunned into stillness by the sudden appearance of the flaming arrow. Dabis was the first to leap into action, and he plunged the arrow into the rain barrel before the fire could touch the sail.

"We're doomed," Mirzani wailed as he crouched for cover on the deck.

"And it's her fault." Nadeem's eyes were slits as he watched Zardi duck low and scramble over to them.

"We can fight back," Zardi said, ignoring Nadeem's words.

Mo, Ali, Syed, and Tariq looked at her pityingly.

"Is that for show?" Tariq pointed to the bow and quiver on Zardi's belt. "You're not much of a bowman, if you can't see that fighting back is futile."

"Zardi's the best archer I know," Rhidan said angrily.

"That may be so, but how far can she shoot with that bow?" Tariq's swamp-colored eyes were despondent.

"Two hundred and fifty arm spans," Zardi replied confidently.

"And how far away is the sultan's ship?" Syed asked, wiping at the sweat that beaded on his shaved head.

Rhidan glanced at the *Swift*. "I don't know, about four hundred arm spans?"

"Well, there's your answer." Zain pulled anxiously at his long braid. "We haven't got any weapons that can reach that far."

"The sultan and his guards have the better ship and the better weapons," Musty confirmed. "We're a sitting duck."

Sinbad looked at them all, his normally handsome face a haggard mask of worry. "It's a warning shot. They're showing us that they can hurt us and that there's nothing we can do about it."

"We'll burn on this ship." Mirzani's face crumpled with fear. "They'll fire off arrows until the *Falcon* is cooked."

The captain looked like a man who was being torn apart from the inside. "I do not believe that it is their intention to sink this ship. They could have fired more arrows but they have not. However, I'm not prepared to lose a single life in a fight that we cannot win," he said firmly. "We must surrender and give the sultan what he wants."

His eyes strayed to Zardi and Rhidan, a silent apology in his expression.

Zardi couldn't feel betrayed by the choice. Sinbad's crew was his family and he would do whatever necessary to keep them safe . . . just like she would do anything to protect those she loved.

"No!" Rhidan cried. "He can't catch us. He's not taking Zardi."

"I'm sorry, there is no other way," Sinbad ground out. He turned to Nadeem. "Raise the white flag and do it quickly." The words seemed to choke him, and the captain couldn't look at Nadeem as the boy started his ascent to raise the white flag of surrender.

"I said, *NO*." The words exploded from Rhidan. "We have to get away from here. Anywhere."

Zardi stared at her friend in amazement. His voice had taken on a timbre that she'd never heard before. It was a voice full of darkness and power. All around her, purple light sprang forth from their surroundings: the sailors, the ship, even the sea. Just like before, in Sula's house, the light peeled away from every surface and wrapped itself around Rhidan. But this time the light stream did not shut off. It kept on pulsing into her friend, lifting him off his feet.

"What's happening?" Sinbad asked hoarsely.

Zardi said the only two words that made sense. "It's magic."

The purple light continued to surge into Rhidan, pulse after pulse. His face was transformed, suddenly gaunt, his skin so translucent she could see the veins that lay beneath the surface. His eyes were lighter too, almost silver. His outline began to shimmer with purple light and a fierce wind sprang up all around them. The sea became choppy, battering the sides of the *Falcon,* tossing the ship about like it was in the hands of an angry god.

Zardi heard a cry from above, and looked up to see Nadeem being thrown from the mast. He fell through the air, landing with a sickening crunch.

"Rhidan, stop!" she screamed. "You're going to kill someone." She tried to get close to her friend, but the energy thumping out of him threw her back. The ship was now spinning in a whirlwind and she tumbled down the deck, only just managing to grab hold of a length of trailing rope.

The sailors around her were a blur, Rhidan the only point of clarity—a still figure in the center of the chaos as the purple light engulfed him entirely.

15

Worm on a Splinter of Wood

The sound of howling wind and crashing waves filled Zardi's ears. She knew she was screaming because her throat hurt.

The *Falcon* continued to spin on the water, and sea spray lashed Zardi's face. She turned her head only to be faced with the *Swift*. The sultan's crew was battling hard to avoid being capsized by Rhidan's tornado, but the masts of the royal ship were snapping under the force of the onslaught.

The howling wind became a screech, and Zardi's stomach clenched as the *Falcon* was sucked up by whirlwind and the *Swift* was left far below.

Sea and sky bled into one another. The *Falcon* swirled through the air, and then all became gray as the walls of the whirlwind closed in around them. Gritting her teeth, Zardi wrapped the rope in her hand around her wrist. Wails and prayers surrounded her and Sinbad's men scrambled to find something to cling onto. She saw Dabis grab hold of Nadeem and haul him to his feet. Nadeem put weight on his left foot and gave a scream of pain, but with Dabis's help he managed to stagger over to the boat's rail. Relief smacked into her. Nadeem was hurt but he was alive.

Her eyes sought out Rhidan again. The light around him was fading now, and she saw his feet come to rest once more on the deck. The whirlwind that surrounded them began to slow. The screeching wind became a sigh. Rhidan dropped to his knees, as the ship skimmed across the water, his eyes glazed with exhaustion.

He needs me, Zardi thought. Her fingers began unwrapping the rope from her wrist.

She got to her feet and, for the first time since the

whirlwind had subsided, glanced around her. There was no sign of the *Swift*, just a wide expanse of sea. She felt a swell of pride. Rhidan had saved them.

"Zee, what are you doing?" Sinbad's voice suddenly bellowed from behind her. "Hold on to something. We're going to hit those rocks."

"Rocks? What ro—" But Zardi was interrupted by something near her head splintering apart. She was thrown forward. Her fingers grazed the roughness of rope as she flew down the deck, but she couldn't grab hold of it. Her eyes desperately searched for Rhidan's, and for a second met his horrified gaze before she was flung over the side of the ship. The water rushed up to meet her and Zardi crashed into the waves.

The shouts and screams of the *Falcon's* crew shut off as she plunged downward, her nose, ears, and mouth filling with icy liquid.

She tried to work out which way was up but all she found was blackness. Pressure built up in her chest and she forced herself to relax and then kicked hard.

She broke the surface and thirstily drank in air.

Eyes stinging with salt water and tears, she tried to see. Ahead was a strip of land bordered by jagged silvery-white rocks. They jutted out of the sea like swords, and the *Falcon* was being smashed against their sharp edges, again and again.

Crack.

Something struck her head. Zardi's legs stopped treading water and she was dragged under once more. She fought back. Her head again broke the ocean's skin; she saw that the sea was littered with planks of wood and timber chests from the *Falcon*. She grabbed onto a piece.

The waves hammered at her but she managed to scan the water. There was no sign of the ship. Had it been destroyed? Could it have happened so quickly? Her heart pounded painfully. The *Falcon* and Sinbad's crew might all be underwater. Rhidan was gone. *I've lost him.*

Zardi didn't know how long she held onto that piece of wood, her eyes searching for the *Falcon*, but it never appeared. Her fingers cramped into claws and her teeth chattered so hard she thought they might break. The smiling faces of her family filled her drowsy mind. They held open their arms to her, told her she would be cold no more.

"Zub, I'm coming," she whispered.

Her eyes fought to stay open.

"Baba, I'm coming."

Zardi's fingers slipped off the wood and the waves carried her away.

"I'm coming home."

Darkness washed over her.

When she regained consciousness, her cheek rested against sand, and her mouth was filled with it. Spitting the grains out, Zardi sat up, her archer's belt digging uncomfortably into her side.

She was on a deserted beach. The air smelled of both earth and salt, and the sky was tinged with saffron. Silver sand with a blue sheen stretched off in one direction, and in the other an enormous rock ridge that looked like an upturned cooking pot jutted out into the sea.

Zardi shook her head.

This isn't Taraket.

When she squeezed her eyes shut, memories gradually began to lap over her and she remembered—*everything.* She remembered the look on her sister's face when she was captured by the sultan's guards, the plea in her father's eyes to stop Shahryār while he was dragged away. She could see the Windrose on Sula's table, and heard the sound of Rhidan's whirlwind screeching in her ears.

Zardi staggered to her feet, her legs feeling old and weak—as if they belonged to someone else. She steadied herself against a tall palm tree, heavy with coconuts, and began to cough violently, salt water wetting her lips. The whole length of the silver-blue beach was spread out before her and, farther inland, lush and strange vegetation: trees with maroon-colored bark and cascading leaves the shape of arrowheads. For an instant Zardi felt a spurt of excitement as she wondered what mysteries lay among the trees. But the thought felt like a betrayal. She had to find the *Falcon* first. Find survivors. Find Rhidan.

She walked along the shore, taking off her sandals, which were flabby and sodden with water. The wet sand squelched between her toes, comforting her even though the sight of silver-blue sand was so strange. The ocean was more lavender than azure, reflecting the sky above, a violet bruise, streaked with orange and red.

After some distance she neared a cluster of white boulders. They cut down the middle of the beach like a pyramid of giant marbles. Zardi froze. She'd spotted movement on top of the white pyramid. Squinting, she could see a lone figure lowering himself from the rocks and running toward her. It was a boy with hair like bright moonlight and a silver amulet around his neck.

They met in a jumble of words and hugs. Neither allowed the other to get a word in, excitement and relief making them both selfish and eager.

Zardi felt tears well up as she took in her friend's appearance. He had a long scratch down the left side of his face; it cut into his cheek like a gully. Ridiculously, it occurred to her that Rhidan now looked a lot more like a pirate than a sorcerer. "You're alive!" she managed to gasp out.

"So are you." His voice was hoarse. "I knew I'd find you. I had to believe that."

She gripped his hand. There was so much she needed to ask him but for a moment it was just enough to feel his palm in hers. "How's the *Falcon*?" she said finally.

"The ship survived," Rhidan explained. "We got lucky and one of the waves carried us past the rocks and onto the beach. We're on the other side of that thing." He pointed to the white pyramid. "Sinbad and Musty have everything under control. All those who can stand are pulling the ship farther up on the beach."

"How is everyone?" Zardi asked. There was another

unspoken question in her words and Rhidan heard it.

"There're a few injuries but everyone made it." He looked down at his feet. "No thanks to me. I almost killed us all, Zardi. My magic, I just couldn't control it."

"But you got us away from the sultan," Zardi reminded him. "You saved us from him."

"And shipwrecked us here," Rhidan shot back. "Musty lost his compass and all the navigational charts in the whirlwind. No one has any idea where we are. All we can work out is that we're on some kind of island."

Zardi sighed patiently. "Will you stop worrying? You're a sorcerer. You can use your magic to get us back to Arribitha. No problem."

"Actually, yes problem," Rhidan burst out. "A big problem, in fact. I can't get us home. I can't get us back to Arribitha. My magic is gone."

16

Answers

"Gone?" Zardi repeated. "You made a whirlwind appear out of thin air. How can your magic be gone?"

Rhidan spread his arms wide. "There is this emptiness inside me—it wasn't there before." His eyes glittered. "When I made the whirlwind come, it was like the amulet was telling me where to go and I felt so powerful. My whole life that ability to absorb magic had been inside me and I didn't know it. But now it's gone and I don't know how to make it come back. I've been trying everything."

An image of Zubeyda and Baba imprisoned in Taraket's tallest watchtower stamped itself behind her eyes, and Zardi struggled to keep her frustration from her face. They needed to get back to Sula and find the Windrose if they were ever going to defeat Shahryār.

She sucked in a calming breath. "Your magic will come back, Rhidan. It will come back because it has to."

"I hope so." Rhidan tugged on his amulet anxiously. His brow suddenly creased, his whole face becoming a question as he held the entwined snakes in his hand.

"What is it?" Zardi asked.

"The amulet," Rhidan replied. "It feels different, heavier somehow." He shook his head. "It doesn't matter. Come on. Sinbad and the others will want to see you."

"Really?" Zardi rubbed her arms. "Sinbad told me that his men would think it bad luck to have a woman onboard a ship. I've only proved them right."

Rhidan snorted. "I wouldn't worry about silly superstitions. Out of the two of us it's me that they're really mad at, especially after I told them that my magic is gone."

They climbed over the white boulders and, as they dropped down onto the beach, Zardi was faced with the ruined beauty of the *Falcon*. The ship was being dragged up the beach by the twins, Mo and Ali, and several other sailors. Nadeem looked on, resting heavily on a makeshift crutch.

The *Falcon*'s two masts had snapped and hung uselessly like dislocated arms, the colorful sails crumpled butterfly wings against a sky streaked with red. On the deck, splintered planks stood up on end and water gushed from the battered hull like blood from a gaping wound. The proud *Falcon* figurehead had been shattered as well. A friend lost forever.

"No need for the long face, Zee." Sinbad walked up to them. One of his eyes was bloodied and swollen shut but she could see no other injury. "Those rocks almost destroyed my ship, but we'll restore the *Falcon* to her former glory. It's nothing that a little hard work won't fix."

"It is going to take a bit more than that, Captain," Musty said, bustling up to them. "If we want to get off this island, it is not a matter of fixing the *Falcon* but rather rebuilding her." He turned to Zardi. "Glad to see you made it."

"Me too." She frowned as his earlier words sank in.

Zubeyda had been kidnapped by the sultan nine days ago, which meant that the Hunt was only eighty-one days away. She and Rhidan had to get off this island. "How long will we need to rebuild the ship?" she asked.

"We'll need to make a proper survey of this island and see if we can find the right materials first," Musty replied. "As far as we can tell, the island has no inhabitants, but we must go forward with care."

Zardi turned her head and looked into the depths of the forest that bordered the beach. A spark of excitement flared inside her despite her anxiety. This island was so different from anything she'd seen before. She spotted a cluster of trees with golden, spiral-shaped leaves and bark that looked like bubbles on mud. She couldn't wait to explore further.

"What do you mean by the right materials?" Rhidan asked.

Musty rubbed his chin. "Well, we don't even begin to have enough nails or bolts to repair the ship, so we need rope. Lots of it, so that we can sew the planks of the deck back into position."

"That doesn't sound too bad," Sinbad said cheerfully. "I have no doubt we'll be off this island by the next full moon."

Musty looked at Sinbad with exasperation. "Of course we'll need to make the rope first, which we'll have to make from the green coconut husks that we still need to gather. Then we have to soak the husk fibers in salt water for several weeks to make them strong enough before twining them into rope to bind the boards together. Oh, and let's not forget the husks we'll need to pack into the seams of the hull to make the *Falcon* watertight."

"I'm guessing that's a lot of coconuts," Sinbad said, scratching his head.

"Yes, Captain, it is an awful lot of coconuts. Hundreds in fact."

Sinbad narrowed his eyes. "It's a shame we can't magic up a few nails, eh, Rhidan? Or even a whirlwind to take us back to Arribitha."

"My magic is gone," Rhidan murmured, tugging on his amulet. "I told you."

"Yes, you did," Sinbad said. "You told me that you have no magic, but you haven't told me who you really are or why the sultan is so eager to catch you." He folded his arms and looked at them intently.

Musty coughed politely. "Captain, I think I should go so you three can talk in private."

Zardi shook her head. "No, stay, Musty. I want you to hear this. Your crewmates are shipwrecked on this island and that is due to me and Rhidan."

Musty looked at her with kind brown eyes. "Guilt is such a useless emotion, Zee. You learn that by the time you get to be my age. Besides, if I remember correctly, we were the ones that kidnapped you. Our fates were tied to yours the day we made that choice." The shipmaster looked at Sinbad disapprovingly, and the captain's cheeks became ruddy with color.

Zardi gave Musty a grateful smile and began her story. She started with why she'd left Taraket and explained about the image of the Windrose that Rhidan had conjured up on Sula's table.

At the end of her extraordinary tale, Sinbad let out a low whistle of astonishment. "If you'd told me, even two hours ago, that you were waiting for my mother to introduce you to a djinni who was shackled to a golden lamp I'd have called you a liar." He studied Zardi and Rhidan. "As it is, I saw the purple fire on the boat, and if Sula says you have a destiny then I will help you fulfill it." He slapped a hand on Rhidan's shoulder. "The days to come will not be easy. Some of the sailors will be scared of you—many would have just been children themselves when magic was scoured from our lives. But Shahryār is evil, not magic."

Sinbad turned to face his wrecked vessel. "It will take time and patience, but we can make the *Falcon* fly again. We'll get back to Arribitha."

Zardi gazed at Sinbad's ship. She'd work until her hands bled to get it fixed as quickly as she could. She looked over at Rhidan. He was staring down at the back of his amulet. She felt a flash of annoyance. His focus should be on getting back to Arribitha, not on studying the amulet.

She was about to say so when a high-pitched sound froze them all for an instant. It came from deep in the forest. Metal screeching against metal. Zardi had heard something like it at the blacksmith's forge. The ground beneath her feet shuddered, and there was an awful pounding noise as if the whole of the sultan's battalion was galloping toward them.

"What's that?" Mo cried from farther up the beach.

"Trouble," Sinbad replied. "And it's heading straight for us."

17 The Brass Rider

With a roar, a giant metal man, as tall as Taraket's highest watchtower, came out of the forest. The sun glinted off his highly polished body and he rode on a giant steed made from the same shiny metal. Hexagonal emerald eyes glinted fiercely in his masklike face and he gripped a metal club. Zardi had seen this metal before; her grandmother's favorite tea set was made out of it: brass.

"Strangers are forbidden on Desolation Island," the brass rider said, bringing his massive horse to a thundering halt. "You will be destroyed." His voice reverberated like the clang of a bell.

Sinbad held up his hands and cautiously approached the brass giant. Zardi and the rest of the *Falcon's* crew followed him. "We've been shipwrecked on your island. Let us fix our vessel and we'll leave," the captain said.

"My instructions are clear," the brass rider replied. "Strangers are forbidden on Desolation Island. You will be destroyed."

"Hang on there," Sinbad said calmly. "Who gave you these instructions? Can we speak to your master?"

The brass rider looked confused. "I know not who made me. Strangers are forbidden on Desolation Island. You will be destroyed." The brass rider lifted his club and the horse reared up on its hind legs. Sharp metal hooves glimmered like knives in the sunlight. Fear charged through Zardi. Those hooves could slice flesh, shatter bone.

"Stop right there." Rhidan ran in front of Sinbad. "Take another step and you'll be sorry."

The brass rider roared in rage at the threat and galloped forward. But Rhidan stood his ground.

Zardi dashed to Rhidan's side even as everybody else fell back toward the shore. "What are you doing?" she screamed over the pounding of the horse's metal hooves. But Rhidan didn't reply. Instead his face scrunched up in concentration and she saw the amulet around his neck throb with purple light. The snakes around the amethyst stone began to writhe and twist.

Zardi gasped. She had never seen the amulet do anything like that in the past.

"I think the boy is going to use magic on him!" Zardi heard the cook exclaim from behind her.

Hope filled Zardi up. She didn't understand how it'd happened, but Rhidan was getting power from the amulet! She watched as her friend gripped the writhing snakes for a moment and then held his palms out. A stream of purple light flew from them, hitting the brass rider squarely in his chest. The metal giant flew out of his saddle and fell to earth with a ground-shuddering thud. Spooked, the brass horse reared up on its hind legs, let out a screeching, tinny cry, and then galloped away up the beach and into the forest.

The crew cheered. "That's it, Rhidan!" Zain yelled. "Show him what you're made of."

The brass destroyer staggered to his feet.

"Go on, boy," Sinbad said, and Zardi turned to see the captain dancing on the spot jubilantly. "Give the giant another blast of that purple fire."

Rhidan let rip with another flash of light, and Zardi got ready to cheer but it died in her throat. The purple bolt of magic was much fainter than the last and, although it hit the brass giant directly on his chest again, it only halted him for a moment.

Rhidan's face fell and he desperately gripped the amulet. "It's not working," he wailed. "I think it's run out of power."

The brass giant was only a few strides away now, and behind her Zardi could hear the pounding footsteps of the crew as they scattered like frightened geese to the left and right.

Rhidan was still grasping at the amulet, his face set determinedly.

"We need to get out of here," Zardi bellowed, trying to pull at her friend. Rocks and planks of wood suddenly flew above her head and rained down on the giant. Sinbad's men hadn't deserted them. They were throwing anything they could find at their attacker, but the missiles didn't even leave a dent.

The destroyer was on top of them now and still

Rhidan did not move. The faintest of purple light was gathering around his fingertips.

The giant lifted his club above his head.

Zardi dived at her friend's legs, pushing him out of the way of the descending weapon. Her tackle flung Rhidan's arm high and an almost translucent streak of purple left his fingertips and soared upward, striking out the giant's emerald eye. Zardi and Rhidan watched as the gem flew from its socket and landed in the sand next to them.

The brass rider gave a screeching cry as he dropped to his knees and covered his eye socket with a hand. Black oil ran from the wound, leaving a tear's track.

"We've got to get that other eye out," Zardi said as the giant got to his feet with a howl of rage. "It's the only thing that hurts him."

"There's nothing left in the amulet," Rhidan panted as they both scrambled to stand. "It came alive to help us but it's dead now."

The brass giant, still howling, swung his club wildly above his head.

"Head for the forest!" Zardi heard Mirzani yell from behind her.

"Don't run, fight," Sinbad shouted back. "Can't you

see that the giant is hurt?"

But his men paid him no heed. Mirzani, Dabis, Syed, Zain, and Tariq ran toward the trees.

The destroyer spotted them and, with terrifying speed, turned and chased down the fleeing men. Under the swing of his mighty club, Mirzani fell to the ground. The trees with the golden spiral leaves were knocked down as the giant barreled into the forest, and Zardi yelled out a warning as she saw one of them fall toward Dabis.

The sailor screamed as he tried to dive out of the way but he was not quick enough. The tree smashed on top of him, his shout of terror snuffed out like a flame.

Scalding tears streamed down Zardi's face. There could be no doubt about it: Dabis was dead. As the sound of crunching bone and more screams pierced the air, Zardi unclipped her bow and grabbed an arrow.

"Rhidan." Her voice was hoarse. "I need you to get the giant's attention. I'm going to shoot out that other eye."

Her friend nodded, his face as pale as bone. He reached into his pocket and produced the giant's emerald eye. "I picked it up after you tackled me."

"Perfect. You know what to do."

Rhidan stepped forward. "Hey, you," he yelled over to the giant, waving the emerald in the air. "I've got something that belongs to you. Want it back?"

The brass rider swung round and spotted his eye. He pounded toward them. Rhidan stumbled back to stand next to Zardi. She nocked an arrow.

"What are you doing?" Sinbad asked, arriving at their side with Mo, Ali, Nadeem, and Musty. His eyes were wild. "I will not lose another today."

"Don't worry, you won't," Rhidan said, looking at Zardi.

"Shoot straight and true, Zee," Musty whispered. "Do it for Dabis."

Zardi raised her bow arm, waiting for the destroyer to come closer. She drew the string back until her thumb was against her jawbone and let the arrow fly. It soared in an arc toward the brass giant's face but dipped before it reached his remaining eye.

How did I miss? Zardi felt rising panic. *I never miss.*

Rhidan turned to her. "Your arrows are still wet; they're heavier than usual. Adjust your aim. You can do this."

Zardi nocked another arrow, tilted her bow ever so slightly upward, and then released it. She watched as it hurtled through the air and knew that this time its path was true. The arrow embedded itself between the giant's eye and socket, flicking the emerald out.

Blinded, the brass rider ground to a halt, his club swinging about crazily. "Where are you?" the giant bellowed in his strange metallic voice. "You will be destroyed."

Sinbad put a finger to his lips and silently urged them all to step back toward the sea.

The captain then bent down and picked up a heavy rock. Zardi expected him to throw it at the giant, but instead the captain turned and threw the rock into the sea. It made a loud splash and the destroyer's head flicked toward the water. His eye sockets gaping black chasms, the giant lifted his club above his head and lumbered toward the sound, swinging his weapon.

Still treading quietly, Zardi and Rhidan followed the other sailors out of the way of the thundering giant. They watched as he charged into the sea, still swinging his club. When his massive foot caught on the edge of one of the silver rocks, he toppled into the water like a tree felled by a woodcutter's axe. Before he could recover, his body was dragged onto the rocks by the waves. The waves then pushed him toward the shore only to draw him back and dash him onto the rocks again. The sound of metal on stone rung through the air and soon the destroyer was smashed into pieces.

Zardi sucked in a mouthful of cool air. Her throat hurt from her screamed warning to Dabis.

Turning away from the sea that was littered with fragments of brass, she looked into the forest. Sailors started walking out of the trees, cautiously at first and then in a flood. Zain held Dabis in his arms. Nadeem stared at them, his face a mask of grief. Tariq, with the help of Syed, managed to stagger forward, blood trickling from a gash on his forehead. Everyone else was safe.

No, not everyone.

An unmoving body lay on the ground, just a little distance away from the forest. It was Mirzani.

Zardi ran to his side. The sailor's eyes were closed and his mouselike face was pale. His arm lay at a strange angle.

The rest of the crew joined her and looked down at their fellow crewman.

"I wish we had a doctor," the cook said mournfully.

Sinbad looked down at Mirzani, his eyes dark with worry. "We'll just have to do our best," Sinbad said gently.

Musty set the injured sailor's arm and bound

Mirzani's chest to hold his broken ribs in place. Mo and Ali built a stretcher from two strong sticks and spare sail material, and Sinbad and Zain gently lifted Mirzani onto the makeshift bed and carried him farther up the beach.

Zardi and Rhidan climbed onto what was left of the *Falcon* and found some thick cotton material in one of the surviving chests. Remarkably, it was dry, and they brought it to Mirzani and tucked it around him. The rest of it was used to cover Dabis.

The injured sailor finally rewarded them all for their care by opening his eyes for a moment and looking at them with something like comprehension. "Is the metal monster gone, Capt'n?" he whispered.

Sinbad smiled down at him. "He is fish bait, Mirzani, rusty old fish bait."

As night fell, they built a fire. Each man looked into the flames and seemed to be reliving the day; remembering how they'd put Dabis's body in the ground and said their good-byes. Zardi closed her eyes. Over the last few hours fear, despair, and hope had all churned in her stomach. But more than anything, she was grateful that she and the crew of the *Falcon* would be alive to see another sunrise.

They ate what fruit they could find near the beach, and before saying good night Sinbad chose a few sailors to help him keep watch over the camp. The rest of the crew settled into sleep, but Zardi could not find peace.

She lay still and listened, her eyes aching as she searched the darkness. Beside her she could hear Rhidan's gentle breathing, and she wondered how he could sleep so easily. There were so many questions unanswered. Why had his amulet come alive and why had it stopped again? When she'd asked Rhidan this he had refused to meet her eye and said that he didn't want to talk about it.

And then there was the brass rider.

Someone had made him. What was on Desolation Island that was so precious that it had to be guarded by such a creature?

In the distance, a low roar rumbled through the night and she shuddered. What else was out there? What else might come out of the forest?

Zardi squeezed her eyes shut. When she was little and got scared it was always her sister who comforted her. If Zardi woke screaming from a nightmare, it was Zubeyda who would press her cheek to hers and whisper that all was well and she would never leave. She would say it again and again until Zardi fell asleep.

A sob built up in Zardi's throat and she buried her head in the crook of her arm. Zubeyda was trapped in her own nightmare now, in a watchtower in Taraket, but Zardi would not leave her there. She would find a way to get off this island and back to her sister. Nothing was going to stop her.

18

A Truth Revealed

At sunrise, Sinbad woke the camp. Zardi rubbed at her eyes. They felt as dry and rough as sand.

"Today we go to the forest to forage for food," the captain declared.

There was a collective mew of distress. Zardi wasn't surprised. More than one man had experienced nightmares in the dark hours, and, if she had managed to sleep at all, she was sure the destroyer would have stalked her dreams.

"We need to eat," Sinbad went on, "and find enough coconuts to begin making rope."

The captain sorted them into pairs and Zardi was relieved to find herself with Rhidan.

Mo, Ali, and Nadeem were told to stay behind with the injured Mirzani and act as his protector if need be.

"Captain, I should go with you." Nadeem stood a bit straighter, holding his crutch away from his body as if it had nothing to do with him.

"No," Sinbad replied. "You aren't strong enough to go foraging."

Nadeem's cheeks flushed angrily. "My ankle is much better."

"You'll stay here with Mirzani." Sinbad's voice did not abide argument. "You can start gathering jetsam. We need wood to repair the *Falcon*."

"Yes, Captain." Nadeem's voice was frosty, but Sinbad didn't seem to notice.

The paired-up sailors grabbed sacks from the *Falcon* and then fanned out through the forest.

Zardi and Rhidan soon found themselves alone, deep in the dappled green of the trees. Away from the sea, the air was heavy with humidity. Creepers hung from trees like pythons, brushing the tops of their heads, and wet soil squelched beneath their feet. As they walked on, the warm air filled with the sweet scent of honey. Zardi looked round at the trees. Yellow, waxy fruit with five cut edges dangled off thin branches. They were in a star fruit grove!

"This is incredible," Rhidan said as they started to pick the sunny yellow fruit and fill their sacks. "Can you believe how many are here?"

Zardi felt a smile tug at her lips. In Taraket, you would see the occasional star fruit, but they were rare and expensive. Here on Desolation Island they would be able to have as many as they liked.

Rhidan rubbed the back of his neck. "If I wasn't so scared that something was about to come crashing out of the undergrowth and attack us, I'd be thinking how pretty this forest is." He looked up at the dense canopy.

Zardi frowned. "It might have star fruit, but this place doesn't feel right. It's too quiet. Like a graveyard. I can't hear any animals around here, and I haven't seen any either."

"I think that's a good thing," Rhidan said. "Did you hear that roaring last night from the other side of the island? Who knows what type of creatures live here?"

"I heard it." Zardi chewed the inside of her cheek.

"The sooner we get off this island and back to Sula the better. It's the only way we are going to find the Windrose and its guardian."

"But if the sorcerers of the Black Isle don't help us, then the Windrose isn't the key to saving Zubeyda." Rhidan's face was pulled inward with worry. "Maybe we should look for the Varish instead."

Zardi stared at him questioningly. Her friend looked vulnerable, wounded somehow.

Taking a deep breath, Rhidan lifted the amulet and flipped it round. Zardi's eyes widened as she saw words in tiny script etched onto the amulet's surface. The words spun round on the disc, only slowing as Zardi began to read.

Know me. I am Iridial—your father. If you are reading this, then you have come searching for me. Stop looking. I do not want to be found. Take what magic is in this amulet and go home.

"This message never used to be here," she gasped.

"I think it must have appeared as soon as I landed on the island," Rhidan replied softly. "But I only noticed it just before the brass rider attacked." He raked a hand through his silver hair. "The amulet has felt heavier ever since we landed here, but it was only when I read the inscription that I realized the amulet had magic inside it."

"And that's what you used against the brass rider?"

Rhidan nodded miserably. "I've still got no magic of my own, and there wasn't much power in the amulet and now that's gone too."

Zardi scowled at him. "Why didn't you tell me about this yesterday?"

"Because my father sounds vile." Rhidan plucked the amulet from her grasp. "If we find him, is he really going to help us save Zubeyda or teach me how to get my magic back? I mean, even if we get the Windrose and it guides us to the Black Isle, it could all be for nothing." He looked down at his feet. "I don't want to let you down. I want to save Zubeyda and your father."

"You could never let me down." Zardi's annoyance fled as she thought about how Rhidan must have felt when he read the message. "Our plan is a good one, I promise. Once we get back to Arribitha, we'll find Sula and get that djinni to help us find the Windrose." She put her hands on his shoulders and held his gaze. "It will guide us to the Black Isle, and when we get there your father will have a lot of explaining to do."

Rhidan touched the amulet again. "What if he doesn't want to explain?"

"You're his son, Rhidan. He owes you that at the very least."

"You're right, he does owe me." Rhidan's eyes glittered with tears and determination. "I'll make him tell me why he got rid of me, and then he can help us get rid of the sultan."

Zardi smiled, imagining an Arribitha without Shahryār. Unbidden, the image of herself dressed in white came to mind. Her destiny . . . or so Sula had said.

"Hey, look." Rhidan pointed to a tree. "There're some more star fruit up there, right at the top. Give me a leg up and I'll knock a few down."

Their sacks bulging with fruit, Zardi and Rhidan headed toward camp.

"This fruit weighs a ton," Rhidan complained.

Zardi blew a lock of hair out of her eye. "I know, but think how excited everyone will be when they see these star fruit."

"True. And it would be nice to make them smile,"

Rhidan said. "Especially after what happened to Dabis."

Zardi felt a knot of sadness pull tightly in her chest and she walked a bit faster.

As they neared the edge of the trees and smelled the salt on the air, they heard the flap of many massive wings overhead and high, screeching noises. They both looked up but couldn't see anything through the canopy.

"Listen to that," Rhidan said. "There *is* wildlife on this island." He gave a low whistle. "And they sound big. Actually, they sound big and annoyed."

Zardi strained to make out the sounds.

"I'd love to know what they are screeching about. I bet—" She stopped as the blue stone around her neck began to vibrate and give out an azure light. As the gleam grew, the squawks became words she could understand. They filled her head.

Kill them,
Squash them,
Stop them dead.
Punish them,
Hurt them,
Flatten their heads.

"I can understand," Zardi said in a hushed voice. "I-I think it must be the stone Sula gave me—it's chosen its gift. It's translating what they're saying, and they're angry, really angry!"

The creatures continued to chant, their voices sounding more and more enraged. Zardi and Rhidan tried again to peer up through the canopy but the winged creatures could still not be seen. Zardi stopped, fear spreading through her as she realized that they were flying right toward the *Falcon*'s camp.

She turned to Rhidan. "RUN!"

19

The Roc

They broke into a sprint. Reaching the line of trees, they stopped to survey their camp.

In the middle of the beach, a huge fire was blazing. Beside it rested a barrel-sized gray speckled egg. Mo and Ali were laughing and rubbing their stomachs, while Tariq and Syed were getting ready to lever the egg into the fire. Nadeem was hobbling toward them with more firewood in his arms, and Mirzani, who was propped up on a makeshift chair, looked on with interest.

Kill them . . .

Punish them . . .

Flatten their heads.

The squawks were at a fevered pitch now, the flap of wings like the snap of a ship's sail. Zardi and Rhidan looked up to see five massive birds, each as big as a fishing boat, break the cover of the trees. Sinbad's men screamed as their eyes turned skyward.

The birds hovered in the air just above the sailors. Their feathers were the colors of oil on water—purple, green, and yellow—and their beaks were slashes of crimson. They fell into a V-shaped formation, their wings stirring up a whirlwind of sand. In their sharp, golden talons they each held a white boulder.

Rhidan grabbed Zardi's arm and pulled her deeper into the shelter of the trees.

"What are you doing?" she hissed. "We need to do something."

"I know, but we stay here until we work out a plan," Rhidan explained. "Those birds are here to do damage."

The bird at the front of the formation let out a screech and Zardi understood it as one single command: "*Attack.*"

Then the leader of the birds swooped toward the sailors and opened its clutches, letting the boulder fall.

Zardi cried out a warning as the huge rock fell through the sky. It missed Nadeem by a hair's breadth.

The birds' leader returned to the point of the V and gave another battle cry.

The second of the birds swooped toward Tariq and Syed, who were both scrambling away from the fire. The giant bird released the boulder, and the two men just managed to dive out of the way.

"Get to the forest," Rhidan yelled to the sailors. "They can't see you in here." Tariq and Syed dashed toward the trees.

Mo and Ali scurried to Mirzani's side, struggling to lift him out of the chair. "We've got to help them," Zardi said. "They'll never get here in time."

Rhidan nodded. They left the cover of the trees and raced toward the twins. Zardi frowned as Nadeem hobbled over to help the injured sailor too. Why hadn't he taken cover in the forest like the others?

The birds continued to shriek, but as Zardi reached

Mirzani's side she sensed a quieter, more mournful presence. A single bird who repeated just one phrase:

"Save my baby. Save my baby. Save my baby."

"The egg," Zardi said, suddenly understanding the giant birds' rage. "We've got to give it back. It's one of their babies."

"That egg is our lunch. Tariq and Syed brought it back," Nadeem protested.

"We'll do what she says," Mirzani said firmly. The effort of talking left him pale.

Zardi looked up and saw that the birds were reconfiguring, ready to attack.

"I can't believe you, Mirzani!" Nadeem's jaw worked furiously and he glared at Rhidan and Zardi. "Why should we listen to what she says? Dabis is dead because of her, because of both of them."

Zardi felt guilt lash at her. Nadeem was right. She and Rhidan had only brought tragedy to the *Falcon*.

She looked up again. The third bird in the formation had just peeled off and was flying toward them with yet another boulder. She couldn't let these birds hurt the sailors. She had to stop them.

Zardi stepped forward, touching the blue stone. It had helped her understand the birds. Would it help the birds understand her? Throwing her head back, she spoke as loudly as she could.

"Forgive us. We're sorry that we took your egg. Please let us give it back." The blue jewel was warm against her chest, and even though she formed the words in her head in her own language, a squawking sound came from her throat.

Falling back into a V formation. The massive winged creatures looked down at Zardi, their heads cocked to one side, listening. The leader gave a short, sharp screech that Zardi didn't quite catch and glided downward on outstretched wings. The bird landed a few arm spans away, and Zardi saw that it looked slightly different from its companions, with a beak the color of indigo night and a bright golden crest of feathers.

"We are sorry we stole your kin," Zardi said to the birds' leader, trying to sound calm. "My friends were looking for food. They should never have taken the egg."

"You do not belong here," the bird said, towering above her.

"We won't be here for long," Zardi explained. "We're trying to get home."

The bird stared at her, unblinking. "That would

be wise. Our enemy, the Queen of the Serpents, has ordered her army of snakes to kill almost everything on this island. She'll kill you if given the chance."

"The Queen of the Serpents?" Zardi repeated. Desolation Island was just like one of Nonna's pastries: far more layers than first met the eye with a surprise lying at its heart.

The great bird dipped her head. "How is it, featherless one, that you speak our language?"

"This stone, I think." Zardi showed her jewel to the bird. "It makes it possible for me to understand you."

The bird made a deep chirruping sound, beckoning the other four birds, and they fell in line behind her. "I am Lina, leader of the Roc," the bird said. "We are a peaceful race but will not abide the theft or murder of our kin. Violence will be met with violence. Do you understand?"

"I understand."

"Then let this be a token of our treaty, and we will not seek retribution." The bird plucked a feather from her golden crest and let it float downward.

"Thank you." Zardi caught the feather. It was a deep molten gold, and for a moment Zardi was reminded of the gold in her sister's eyes and her chest felt tight. She placed the feather in her tunic pocket and lifted her head. "My name is Zardi, and I vow that no one else in my camp will ever do anything to harm the Roc or their young."

"So be it for now and always. Please excuse me, I must recover my child." Lina stalked over to the speckled egg by the fire. Rhidan and Sinbad's men stood very still as the bird took the egg into her talons.

Lina soared into the air. The Rocs followed her ascent, their massive wings stirring up a storm of sand.

"Until next time, featherless one, keep safe," Lina called.

Zardi waved her hand in farewell. She liked this proud bird and realized it had been Lina's desperate thoughts she'd heard beneath the war cries. As soon as the birds were out of sight, Tariq charged out of the trees with Syed close behind him. He stopped in front of her, two spots of color riding high on the blade of his cheekbones. "I don't know what you said or how you said it, but thank you."

"You saved our lives," Rhidan said, looking at her proudly.

Mo scratched at his turban. "This island is full of danger. Even things that seem innocent are not."

"Maybe we should stick to fruit," Ali murmured. "It'll be a whole lot safer."

Zardi met Nadeem's eyes. He was glaring at her. Instead of making things better she'd made him hate her all the more.

"I'm sorry about Dabis," she said softly, remembering his angry words from earlier.

"Not as sorry as me," he replied and limped away.

PART THREE
Prisons

20

The Emerald's Secret

Zardi stood at the seashore and gazed out at the water, waiting for that rush of joy she felt when she first viewed the sea in Sabra. Nothing. All she could think of was Zubeyda and how the crew of the *Falcon* had been trapped on the island for nineteen days.

After almost three weeks on Desolation Island, the silvery-blue shore was dotted with shelters, as well as two roofed platforms for the food stores.

At the farthest end of the beach, the *Falcon* stood perched on stilts. Zardi rubbed her face wearily. It would still be weeks before they had enough coconut rope. She looked at the cracks that crisscrossed her palms—proof of the multitude of coconuts she'd already smashed open to pluck out their fibrous hearts.

She let her arms fall to her sides. She should be working, she knew that, but—

There's no point. You're not getting off this island. You're its prisoner.

That voice again, that dark secret voice from inside. She'd heard it every day, for the last nineteen days, ever since she had landed on the island. It often whispered but sometimes screamed when she refused to listen to it.

Zubeyda has been a praisemaker for twenty-eight days.
She only has sixty-two days to live.
You can't save her.
Baba will be killed.
You can't save him.
But you saved yourself.

"Shut up, shut up," Zardi said aloud. But the voice would not be quieted.

You never found the Windrose. You failed them all.

She kicked at the wet sand. She needed to do something, needed to run from the voice that robbed her of hope. She scanned the beach searching for Rhidan.

Nowhere to be seen. No surprise there, then. Irritation scraped at her again and she grabbed onto the feeling eagerly.

Over the last couple of days Rhidan had become increasingly secretive, often going off on his own for long walks. However hard she tried, she couldn't get him to tell her what he was up to. She walked toward the white pyramid at the end of the beach. From the top she'd have a good view of the whole south side of the island. As she got closer to the boulders, she saw Mo and Ali taking turns cartwheeling down the shore.

Mo grinned at her, his turban slightly askew. "I've just done fifteen in a row. Think you can beat it?"

"Of course," she replied. "But it'll have to be another time. Have you seen Rhidan?"

Ali wiped a hand across his sweaty brow and shook his head. "Maybe he's off trying to conjure up some of that purple magic."

Zardi shot them a warning look. "There's no more magic. He's told you that."

Ali grinned cheekily. "No harm in hoping." His gaze traveled over her shoulder and his face suddenly fell.

She turned to see Musty standing there.

The shipmaster glared at Mo and Ali. "I thought you two were going to help me gather more coconuts today."

The twins blushed.

"We were going to help," Mo began.

Ali shot a look of horror at his brother. "He means we *are* going to help."

"So why are you wasting time here?" Musty crossed his arms. "Don't you want to get home?"

"Of course we do," Mo said. "B-but you said you wanted to try harvesting in a new part of the island because there are no more coconuts around here." He uttered the last words almost accusingly and a faint tremor went through him.

Ali put a hand on his brother's shoulder. "He thinks he heard the roaring again last night."

The shipmaster went still, and every sinew in Zardi's body tightened. The roaring came every night; her skin prickled with sweat as she remembered the sound.

"I heard it as well," Zardi said. "It came from the east side of the island again."

A nerve jumped in Mo's cheek. "There's something out there, and I'm not going anywhere near it."

"It's probably that brass horse galloping about," Musty said brusquely.

Zardi frowned. She remembered the horse's metallic whinny, the sound of its brass hooves striking the ground. Neither of these noises was anything like the roaring she heard at night. She met Mo's and Ali's eyes. They looked as unconvinced as she felt.

"Besides," Musty went on reassuringly, "we're not going near the east side of the island." He took a roughly hand-drawn map from his pocket and tapped one corner of it. "We're going west."

The twins looked somewhat mollified. "All right, we'll go with you," they both said at the same time.

"Me too," Zardi said. "And Rhidan. I'll go find him."

"All right." Musty paused for a moment. "But will Rhidan want to join us? He seems to prefer his own company of late."

"Don't worry, Musty, he'll come with us, I'm sure."

"Come where?" asked Nadeem, striding up to them with Tariq and Zain at his side.

"We're going coconut harvesting on the west side of the island," Ali explained.

"Count me in," Nadeem said.

Zardi ground her teeth together. Why did he have to come? All he ever did was scowl and make her feel guilty. What a shame that his ankle was all healed up now.

"We're in as well," Zain and Tariq said.

Musty looked pleased. "Let's meet by the octopus tree. You'll need something sharp and a sack. Bring gloves if you have them. Be quick."

Zardi bid farewell to the shipmaster and scrabbled to the top of the white pyramid.

She spotted Rhidan straightaway. He was looking down at his feet, his figure casting a lonely shadow on the sandy ground.

Zardi expertly slipped her fingers and toes into the grooves of the outcrop's rock face before dropping to the ground.

She strode up to him. "Rhidan!" Her friend was concentrating so hard on his feet that he didn't seem to hear her. "Rhidan," she repeated. "Snap out of it. What is wrong with you?"

His head jerked up and he looked at her in bewilderment. "Nothing, I'm fine."

"Don't lie to me." She took a breath and tried to soften

her tone. "For the last two days, you've spent every second on your own. And when you are with people you look at your feet like you can't bear to be with them." She crossed her arms. "I'm not moving until you tell me what's going on."

Rhidan gave a low growl. "Why are you so impatient?" he asked, sounding exasperated. "I'm looking for something." He rummaged in his pocket and took out a green emerald. It easily filled the palm of his hand. "The other one of these, in fact."

Zardi felt her face pucker with confusion. It was one of the brass rider's eyes.

"Why?" she asked. "Is it for your memory box?"

"Ha, very funny, Zardi. You know I don't have a memory box. I stopped keeping one after you buried it in the garden and forgot where you put it."

"Oh yeah." She felt a stab of happiness at the memory of home. "Your amulet was in there. We had to uproot the whole orchard to find it again." She laughed. "I thought Nonna was going to have me on washing duties for life."

Rhidan ran his hand through his hair, and she noticed how much lighter it had become. The sun and salt air had turned it from silver to almost white. He looked torn. "I wasn't going to tell you," he said. "Not until I'd found the other emerald."

"Tell me what?"

Rhidan put a finger to his lips and led her out of sight beneath the overhang of the outcrop. He then rubbed the emerald between his hands. "The first time I did this, I was trying to get the sand off it." The jewel started to give off a deep green light.

The light bent and twisted. It grew arms and then legs, and Zardi gasped as a figure flickered into life beside her. It was a man who looked as if he were made out of green-tinted glass. He wore spectacles and had a neat, curling mustache and was no taller than her knee. A breath lodged in her throat. *Could it be? Is he a djinni?*

"You rubbed?" the man said in a dour voice, hovering up to eye level.

"Yes, I did." Rhidan pointed at Zardi. "Tell her everything you told me the first time I made you appear."

The emerald man sighed and turned to Zardi. "Right. Before you ask, no, I'm not a djinni. I am a herald; I am activated when you rub the emerald. I will take he who possesses this emerald to the chamber of imprisonment."

"And tell her about the brass rider," Rhidan insisted.

The herald jabbed his spectacles up his nose. "The brass rider, who you have obviously defeated because you have the eye, was a guard made for this island." He pursed his lips disapprovingly. "He was designed to stop meddlers and strangers like you from finding the chamber."

"So you built the brass rider?" Zardi asked excitedly.

The herald scowled at her. "Did I say that I'd created the brass rider? No, I did not! I am merely a guide. Created to take him who holds this emerald to the volcano where the djinni is imprisoned. No more and no less."

"Djinni?" Zardi could practically hear the crackling of her own excitement. "Did you just say djinni?"

The herald nodded once.

Her eyes met Rhidan's. "A djinni will be able to tell us where the Windrose guardian is!"

He grinned at her. "I know, but our green friend here can only show us the way to the prison. The other emerald eye is the key needed to open the door and—"

"And that's what you've been looking for," Zardi finished.

"Absolutely everywhere."

Zardi turned to the herald. "Is there no other way into the djinni's prison?"

"Another way in?" The herald shoved his glasses up his nose again. "Do you think my master, who went to the trouble of hiding a djinni and the ring that tethers her in a volcano, on an island that's almost impossible to land on, and created a man out of brass to guard the prison, would provide another way in?" He crossed his arms. "You're not supposed to find this djinni. She's dangerous." He spoke slowly as if they were very stupid. "May I leave now?"

Rhidan nodded.

The herald flickered and finally faded and the emerald became dull once more.

Zardi was suddenly struck by the absolute strangeness of it all. "I can't believe you didn't tell me about this before."

"I didn't want to get your hopes up," Rhidan explained. "I thought I'd find the other emerald first."

A horrible thought occurred to Zardi. "You don't think it got washed away, do you?"

Rhidan shook his head. "The brass rider was nowhere near the sea when you took his second eye out, but I don't know where else to look."

She rubbed her chin. "Maybe it isn't so surprising that you can't find it. We live on an island filled with pirates. They like shiny things. If there was an emerald to be found, maybe it's been found already."

"And maybe we need to start asking a few questions," Rhidan added.

Zardi nodded. "I told Musty we'd go to the west side of the island with him to gather more coconuts. A few of the others are going as well. We can start investigating straightaway."

21

The Valley of Diamonds

Musty led their party westward through the forest, the sun his only compass. Along the trek they were joined by Sinbad, and as the trees thinned out they found themselves atop a ridge. From this height Zardi had an excellent view of the island. Unknown landscapes spread out before her, valleys, lakes, rivers, and hills bathed in a soft, reddish light. To her left she could see spray being thrown up and hear a thundering noise. Peering over the edge, she saw a waterfall flowing down into a valley covered with yellow moss.

They climbed down the vale, the waterfall cascading beside them, throwing out plumes of mist. "It's beautiful here," Zardi said, bending down and drinking from the river that led from the bottom of the waterfall. Like the sea, the water here had a purple cast to it. Its clarity and brightness reminded her of Rhidan's eyes.

"It is beautiful indeed," Musty replied. "But we won't find coconut palms here; we need to head out for the coastline."

"Let's split up," Sinbad suggested. "We'll cover more ground that way." The captain pointed to those that were standing closest to him. "Zain, Tariq, Ali, and Mo, you're with me."

Zardi groaned inwardly; this meant Nadeem was with her, Rhidan, and Musty. She almost wondered whether Sinbad had done it on purpose. *He probably thinks he can force us to get along,* she thought to herself. *He's wrong.*

Musty looked at his map. "You take the northwest part of the island and we'll explore the west. We'll meet here by this river when the sun is at its highest."

Walking westward, Zardi could see that this part of the island was a patchwork of apple-green peaks and troughs. Her group walked in silence, and once again Zardi became aware of the absence of any wildlife. There was no bird cry in the sky or sign of creatures on the ground. Zardi remembered what Lina, the leader of the Roc, had said about the Queen of the Serpents and how she wanted to kill everything on the island. Wherever this serpent queen was, Zardi hoped she'd stay away from the *Falcon*'s camp.

"Let's ask them about the emerald," Rhidan whispered in her ear. "But we'll have to be subtle."

"All right, I'll take Musty, you take Nadeem," she murmured back. Rhidan looked sourly at her and she shrugged. There was no way that she'd be able to get anything out of Nadeem.

Zardi caught up with Musty, while Rhidan fell into step with Nadeem. "Hey, Musty, can I ask you a question?" she asked.

The shipmaster's face was flushed. "Go on, then. It might take my mind off this awful walk. This hill is as steep as the pyramids of Kemet."

Zardi smiled to herself. The hill was only slightly sloping. "I was wondering, how did you become a pirate?"

Musty sighed. "For sure, this life is not what I imagined for myself, but it was tragedy that threw me into Sinbad's path." His voice was soft, and sadness seemed to hang around him like mist.

"I'm sorry, Musty. You don't have to talk about it."

"It's fine." The shipmaster took in a deep breath. "Many years ago I had a wife and a daughter; they were taken from me by a fever." Musty's eyes were dull. "I started to drink, and soon the captains of ships refused to take me on. I thought I'd never sail again until I met Sinbad. He didn't judge me but merely said he respected my experience. I gladly became his shipmaster and said good-bye to the numbness of drink." Musty stood straighter. "Sinbad gave me back my life and a family of brothers. For those two gifts I can live with the fact that we spend some of our time pretending to be things that we're not." The shipmaster smiled at her. "The *Falcon* is my home."

Zardi nodded. Despite everything that had happened, the *Falcon* had become a home to her and Rhidan as well.

But it was not their real home. Home was a place where Zubeyda sang while picking mint from the garden, where Nonna would offer embraces when words wouldn't do, and where Baba would teach her and Rhidan the calligrapher's art and the importance of a steady hand to make a smooth stroke with a reed.

She probed on. "So, you're not a pirate for jewels and riches then?"

Musty honked with laughter. "What would I do with jewels and riches? I have no one to buy things for—"

"Enough!" snarled a voice from behind her. She whirled round. Nadeem was glaring at Rhidan.

"Fine," Rhidan said. "There's no need to get upset."

"Don't play dumb." Nadeem's lips were a thin line. "Why are you asking me all these questions?"

"I was just trying to make conversation. Excuse me for even bothering."

"You're excused," Nadeem spat back. "Don't do it again."

"Shhh!" Musty stopped abruptly. "I can hear the sea. We must be close to the shore!" He ran to the crest of the hill with Zardi, Rhidan, and Nadeem right behind him. They halted as the valley dropped away into sheer cliffs that overlooked a churning violet sea. There were no soft sandy shores here. No palm trees.

"We've come all this way for nothing," the shipmaster groaned. "Not a coconut to be seen."

"Maybe Sinbad and the others will have better luck," Zardi said hopefully.

The shipmaster rubbed at his forehead, leaving a red patch. "I hope so. We've got to make more rope if we are going to finish repairing the ship."

They trudged back toward the meeting point in silence, the mood bleak. As they got closer to the lake, Zardi quickly told Rhidan Musty's story.

"I don't think he has the other emerald," she finished.

"Are you sure?"

"Certain," Zardi responded. "What about Nadeem? Why'd he get so riled up?"

"It was weird. We were getting along quite well at first. He wanted to know a bit more about my magic, why I had it, why I'd lost it. I told him that I didn't really understand what was happening with me and that's why I wanted to find my real parents." Rhidan crinkled his brow. "Nadeem said he never wanted to see his family again, that if Sinbad hadn't saved him they would have sold him to the first person who came along."

Zardi thought of the anger that always seemed to bake beneath Nadeem's skin. "That explains a lot," she said.

Rhidan nodded. "Then I said how nice it must be to

have a permanent home on the *Falcon,* especially with all the treasure he gets to see from other ships. That's when he got all mad."

"Do you think he has the emerald?"

"Hard to tell," Rhidan said. "Nadeem's always defensive."

"Well, there are still plenty of people to ask. We need to find that emerald eye."

They arrived back at the river just before midday and waited for Sinbad's party to appear. Zardi was lying on the grass, gazing up at a cloud that looked a bit like a Roc, when she heard a holler of greeting. Zain was running toward them, his long braid streaming behind him, his face as red as a chili pepper.

"What's wrong?" Nadeem asked as soon as Zain was in earshot.

Zardi jumped to her feet. "Where are the others?"

"Diamonds," Zain managed to get out. "We found diamonds."

Zardi, Rhidan, and Nadeem stared at Zain in amazement. Musty was the one to break the silence. "What do you mean, diamonds? Have you found any coconuts?"

Zain waved his hand dismissively. "Musty, we found

a valley full of diamonds. We weren't going to search for any silly coconuts after that."

"You can't be serious." Nadeem's voice came out as a squeak.

"Come on, I'll show you," Zain said. "Sinbad sent me to get you all." He laughed maniacally. "Don't forget your bags. Your pockets won't be deep enough."

He tore off, heading northwest. The others followed him. "If only Zain would move this fast when working on the *Falcon*," the shipmaster muttered.

"Diamonds would make most people run," Rhidan replied wryly.

Musty pursed his lips. "But will diamonds get us home?"

They finally reached the edge of a hill dotted with golden bell-shaped flowers that swayed gently in the light wind.

Zain pointed down to the valley. Thousands of diamonds, some big, some small, some sharp, some smooth, lay on the floor of the gorge, sparkling in the afternoon sunlight. Many of the jewels were shot through with pinks and yellows and poked out between their crystal-clear cousins. Zardi squinted against the light and saw that the valley slopes were pitted with holes that led to darkness. The openings in the rocky surface reminded her of the brass rider's gaping eye sockets. She felt a chill slice through her even though the sun shone brightly above.

"They can't be diamonds!" Rhidan exclaimed, his eyes fixed on the translucent stones rising upward.

"Trust me, young one." Sinbad's voice boomed from somewhere down in the valley. "I've seen enough diamonds in my time to know."

Zardi peered over the edge of the crest to see Sinbad, Tariq, Mo, and Ali waving at her. They were already halfway up the valley's slope, their backs bowed by the weight of sacks stuffed full with jewels. She couldn't help smiling: Mo had adorned his turban with tiny diamonds.

"Welcome to our fortunes." A grin split Sinbad's face as he and his companions reached them on the crest and put down their heavy bags.

"Diamonds aren't going to fix the ship," Musty growled.

"Oh, Musty, stop being such a grump! We'll send another excursion party to find your precious coconuts. For now, you all need to come and help us gather as many diamonds as you can carry."

"Wait till we show the others at camp," Mo said eagerly.

"We'll be heroes!" Ali added.

Zain winked at Nadeem. "No need for you to be so precious about that emerald you found now, is there?" He laughed, sounding drunk on happiness. "There are plenty of jewels for us all to share."

For a stunned moment, Zardi and Rhidan stared at Nadeem.

Great! The boy who hated them down to the very soles of his sandals held the key to the djinni's prison!

22

Slither

Zardi looked up. The yellow ball of the sun was slowly beginning to melt into the pink of dusk. She rubbed the back of her neck. The day had almost finished and she was thoroughly fed up with harvesting diamonds. Her back ached from being stooped over for hours and her head throbbed from the dazzling light that the jewels gave off. Even more annoyingly, neither she nor Rhidan had been able to speak to Nadeem about the emerald eye as he was never far from Zain's or Tariq's side.

Zardi felt a nudge in her ribs and turned her head to see Rhidan holding up a diamond the size of a fist. "You know what? After you've seen a hundred of these things they kind of lose their appeal."

"Well, they haven't lost their value," Sinbad said, coming up behind them. "Come on, one last push. The sun is going down fast."

As Zardi bent down to scoop up yet another diamond, a strange hissing noise, like oil sizzling in a pan, filled the gorge. She stopped still. Out of the gaps that pockmarked the walls of the canyon, a dozen black and gold snakes the length and width of three men lying head to toe slithered into sight. Their jaws opened to show the ruby velvet of their mouths and the absolute white of sharp, long fangs as they glided closer to them.

Screams erupted all around Zardi. She remembered what Lina had said about the Queen of the Serpents. This had to be the queen's army.

"Run," Sinbad commanded. He grabbed a flat, sharp diamond from the heap in front of him. He held it out like a dagger, his eyes fierce. "No one is dying today."

Zardi and the others formed a closed cluster in the middle of the valley.

"We're not leaving you, Captain," Musty said.

Mo, Ali, and Nadeem grabbed some large diamonds and hurled them at the fast-approaching snakes, but the creatures didn't slow down. They began to hiss again, and Zardi's blue stone blazed against her skin as her mind tried to grasp at what the snakes were saying. But it was not words that ripened in her head, rather images—of fangs sinking into human skin, of coiled muscle crushing bone. Zardi gritted her teeth and tried to close her mind against the force of the snakes' desire to rip them apart. A high-pitched squawk came from the sky, and Zardi understood it immediately as the words *"We'll protect you."* She looked up. A flock of Rocs filled the air. They dove into the valley, talons flashing, their beaks open in harsh cries.

With a hiss the snakes fell back, watching their enemies with unreadable eyes. "The Rocs have come to help us," Zardi yelled, pointing to the birds as they landed, kicking up a flurry of diamonds. Sinbad nodded, eyes wide as he took in the sheer size of the Rocs.

Zardi had told the captain all about the Rocs and the incident with the egg, but from the looks of it, hearing about the giant birds hadn't prepared him for actually seeing them.

"On my back," a small, fluffy-looking Roc squawked. Zardi leaped up onto the bird's warm body and Rhidan clambered up behind her. With a beat of his wide wings they were carried into the air, leaving the teeming snake pit far below. As they climbed higher, Zardi saw that all of the Rocs were in the air, with Sinbad and the rest of his men in their clutches. "Thank you," Zardi called out. "You saved us."

The bird turned his head, his indigo beak catching slivers of light from the last rays of the setting sun. "You saved me once," the bird warbled. "Now we're even."

"I saved you?" she asked, mystified.

"I was an egg at the time, so you probably won't recognize me, but my mother told me of you. I'm Roco, by the way."

"Nice to meet you, Roco."

"Nice to meet you, too," Roco chirruped as they swooped through the darkening sky.

Rhidan nudged her shoulder. "Not everyone understands *bird*, Zardi, what did he say?"

She quickly told him who Roco was.

Her friend gave a low whistle. "Everything is so big

on this island. Those snakes were enormous, and Roco was just an egg a couple of weeks ago." He looked out at the fleet of Rocs with their grateful, yet still dangling, passengers. "Ask him something for me, will you? How did the Rocs know we were in trouble?"

Zardi asked, and found that her blue stone was warm but did not burn as it had when she'd first been trying to understand the snakes.

"I was out flying with my cousins when I saw the snakes attack." The young Roc made a fierce cawing sound in his throat. "They kill anything that moves. I wasn't going to let them kill you as well."

"Tell him thank you," Rhidan said, once Zardi had translated.

"You must stay away from that valley and the whole west side of the island," the young Roc warned, his squawk echoing in the darkening sky. "Especially at night. It's the home of the serpents and their queen. Everything that lies under the island earth is her domain as well."

"Who is she?" Zardi asked.

"We don't know where she came from," Roco replied. "But she sends her snakes to kill us and strip us of our feathers. She's not interested in peace, only destruction."

The baby bird gave a little sneeze, and Zardi realized that Roco didn't have proper feathers like the older Rocs, just downy fluff. He must be getting cold, now that the sun had dipped out of sight.

"Roco, we're in your debt," Zardi whispered as they wheeled through the sky.

"There's no debt. You saved my life and now I've saved yours," Roco cooed.

Below Zardi could see a cluster of enormous trees. She thought for a moment that they were completely bare, but as she got closer she saw that the branches sprouted leaves that looked like giant spiderwebs. They writhed in the wind like ghosts. She leaned forward and asked Roco about the white billowing canopies.

"Those trees are where we make our home," Roco replied. "We bind our nests with those silken leaves. They are lovely and sticky."

Too soon their flight came to an end, and the Rocs lowered Zardi and the other sailors onto the sandy shore of their camp next to the roaring fire. The other members of the crew ran up to them, surprise and fear shading their faces. They couldn't help but gawp at the Rocs with fascination. Roco loved the attention, walking back and forth, preening and ruffling his feathers.

He would have stayed on the beach all night if his cousins had let him. Instead, he was urged upward.

"Till next time," he warbled.

"Until next time," Zardi repeated, waving up at him until he was out of sight. Her fingers went to her tunic's pocket, tracing the softness of the feather that Roco's mother had given her on their first meeting. The Rocs were such incredible creatures, brave and clever, and thanks to Sula's stone she could understand them.

Ouch! She drew her hand from her pocket swiftly. The sharp end of the feather had pricked her finger. Zardi sucked at the wound and laughed to herself. *All right, the Roc may be my allies but they are still dangerous.*

Zardi suddenly heard a roaring sound behind her and whirled round, ready to fight again. Her eyes widened as she took in the scene in front of her. Sinbad and the twins had emptied their diamonds onto the ground and the crew of the *Falcon* crowded around the heap. The roar had been their collective cry of approval and amazement.

Rhidan met her gaze and held up his own sack, emptying his jewels onto the rapidly growing mound. He was followed by Nadeem, Musty, Tariq, and Zain. The crew was wild with excitement now, picking up diamonds and passing them round eagerly. Sinbad had to shout himself hoarse to get their attention.

Once he did, he told his men about the Valley of Diamonds and the snakes that they found there. "The snakes were bigger than you could ever imagine, but we faced them bravely, weapons in hand." The captain placed his hands on his hips. "There was no way they were going to stop us from getting our diamonds!" The crew whooped with approval.

Sinbad picked up a jewel that was as big as a fist and thrust it up into the air. "Men, our fortunes have been made!"

The crew began swinging each other in wide circles, their shadows jerky and long in the light of the fire that they danced around. Some of the men hugged, and others wept.

The captain held up his hands and continued with his speech. "Riches are important," he said softly, "but they aren't as precious as life." He looked at his crew sternly. "I forbid you, any of you, to go back to that valley. Death waits there. It was only thanks to the Rocs and their friendship with Zee that we're even standing here before you. She saved our lives."

Zardi ducked her head in embarrassment as the

crew began chanting her name. She looked up and saw Rhidan grinning at her proudly. She was about to smile back but stopped when she spotted Nadeem looking at her with eyes as flat and dead as those of the snakes in the valley.

She sighed softly. Nadeem had the emerald key that would release the djinni that could take them to the Windrose guardian, but as sure as the sun would rise the next day, she knew getting it from him would not be an easy or pleasant task.

23

What Lies Beneath

"Come on," Rhidan whispered. "We've got to follow him."

Zardi's gaze trailed Nadeem as he stalked away from the fire where the rest of the crew sat talking. As Syed began to brag about what he would buy with his share of the diamond haul once they got back to Arribitha, she and Rhidan slipped away.

The moon was full, a huge white disc in the sky.

Its rays touched on Nadeem as he walked toward the bone-white pyramid that split the beach in two.

"Nadeem," Zardi called. The boy's shoulders stiffened for a moment before he swiftly scrambled up and over the rocks.

Zardi and Rhidan pursued him, but instead of climbing over the outcrop they splashed through the water lapping the shore. They met Nadeem on the other side, blocking his way down the deserted beach.

"What do you want?" Nadeem's face was half in shadow.

Zardi hesitated. "We need to borrow your emerald."

Nadeem laughed. "I don't think so. Why do you need it anyway? You've got diamonds now."

"Do you remember what I told you this morning? That I'm looking for my parents," Rhidan said softly. "Well, that's just part of the story." He quickly told Nadeem about their quest to find the Windrose and its guardian before explaining that the emerald was the key to the djinni's prison.

"This djinni could get us to the Windrose," Zardi finished. A thought suddenly occurred to her. "And if we release her she might even send the *Falcon* home."

Rhidan looked at Nadeem hopefully. "So will you lend it to us?"

"No." The boy's voice dripped with a selfish joy. "I don't think I will."

"You'll get it back," Rhidan insisted. "I promise."

Nadeem shrugged. "I don't care about getting it back, I just don't want to give it to you."

"Why?" Zardi burst out. "This djinni could help us, all of us!"

"And you two get to be the heroes again?" The words exploded from Nadeem's mouth. "No way. It's like everyone has forgotten that it's your fault we're here in the first place. It's always how great Zardi is. Did you see what Rhidan did to that brass giant? Oh, and can you believe she talks to giant birds? Now you've saved us from those snakes." He shook his head bitterly. "Why should you be so special?" The words spewed out of him in a tarry mass.

Zardi's rage flared. But something held it back. It was as if she could feel Nadeem's jealousy. "We'll never replace you, Nadeem. The *Falcon* is your family, not ours. . . ."

"Don't you dare pity me!" Nadeem spat. "Pity yourselves." He grabbed the emerald from his pocket and flung it out into the inky sea. By the powdery light of the moon, Zardi watched the precious gem skim across the water and finally stop and sink.

With a scream of rage, Rhidan lunged for Nadeem. They quickly became a whirling mass of fists and kicking legs.

Yanking off her sandals, Zardi pounded toward the water. The sand was cold and slushy beneath her feet, but this in no way prepared her for the actual coldness of the sea as she plunged in. It cut through her, making her head ache, but with strong strokes she swam to where she saw the jewel sink and dived downward.

A dull silence engulfed her. The undersea world was blue-black like a bruise, the moon and stars cutting no shaft of light here. Using her fingers as eyes, Zardi searched the seabed. Fine grains of sand, knobby coral, long, sharp bits of shell grazed her fingers, and then she found it—a hexagonal object with smooth cut edges. Grasping the brass rider's emerald eye, she kicked upward.

In the cool moonlight she treaded water and stared at the emerald in her hand. Zardi grinned as she struck back toward shore.

"You're alive!" Rhidan ran up to meet her, his clothes

sopping wet. "Nadeem left and I swam after you, but I couldn't find you. . . ." He trailed off. "I thought you might be in trouble."

"I was fine," Zardi insisted.

"Still, you shouldn't have run off into the sea like that in the dark." Rhidan's face was serious. "You could have gotten hurt."

"You could have gotten hurt fighting Nadeem but that didn't stop you!" She smiled and opened up her palm. "Look!" The emerald glinted in the moonlight.

Rhidan stared at the gem, openmouthed. "I can't believe it. Zardi, you're amazing."

He quickly rummaged in his pocket and brought out the other emerald. "Tomorrow, we'll slip away from the others and then get the herald to direct us to the volcano."

"Why wait until tomorrow, when we can go tonight?" Zardi grinned. "We'll wait for everyone to go to sleep and then sneak away. We'll be back by dawn." She gripped the emerald key tightly. "Hopefully, with a djinni who has the power to get us to the Windrose. If we free her she's bound to want to help us."

Rhidan closed his hand over the emerald. "We go tonight."

Back at camp, sailors were yawning and stretching their limbs in the firelight, far too sleepy to notice that Zardi's and Rhidan's clothes were wet. Nadeem was nowhere to be seen, and before long, the crew of the *Falcon* headed to their beds. Zardi and Rhidan did the same.

She lay like a statue, listening to the even breathing of the sailors who surrounded her. Far away, from the east side of the island, a roar thundered across the bay. None of the sailors even flinched.

Maybe they're all pretending to sleep just like me, she thought. *Maybe they don't want to think about what else is on this island.* Zardi shuffled down under her rough covers and stared up at the thatched roof of her shelter. The roaring finally stopped, leaving just the sound of snoring. All she had to do now was wait for Rhidan, wait a little while longer . . .

"Wake up," a voice hissed in her ear.

She looked up groggily to see Rhidan crouching over her, a flaming torch in his hand.

"Come on, sleepyhead, let's go."

In one fluid motion she sprang to her feet and fastened her archer's belt around her waist. They tiptoed past the sleeping sailors and plunged deep into the forest. Once in the heart of the trees, Rhidan handed Zardi the torch, fished the emerald out of his pocket, and rubbed it.

The herald appeared, his green glow even brighter at night. "What time do you call this?" he asked grouchily.

"Time to visit the djinni," Zardi said, holding up the other emerald for him to see.

"Are you sure you want to do this?" The herald yawned and rubbed his eyes. "This djinni was locked away for a reason."

"What reason?" Zardi tried not to show she was bothered by the herald's question.

"Well, I don't know exactly," the herald muttered. "But I'm sure it's bad."

"We know how to handle ourselves," Rhidan said confidently.

"Fine, but don't say that I didn't warn you." The green guide hovered shoulder height to Rhidan and Zardi and then burst ahead, leading them through the humid forest.

As they emerged from the trees, they came to a mountain range. They scrambled over the lowest part and were hit by the freezing air coming off a series of sand dunes that rose up before them.

"Where are we?" Zardi asked, lifting her torch a bit higher.

"The east side of the island," their guide said huffily as he led them up the first sand dune. "But we still have plenty of ground to cover before we reach the volcano."

"You're taking us eastward?" Zardi asked uneasily.

The herald's eyes became sly. "That's right. You've heard him, haven't you? Roaring in the night."

"Who is *him*?" Rhidan demanded.

"Why, the Cyclops of course," their guide said, arching an eyebrow. "His name is Okre. He was here first. Desolation Island is his island more than anybody else's. I'm surprised he hasn't been over to your camp for a visit yet."

Zardi swallowed.

"Oh well," the herald continued. "I'm sure he'll come visiting soon. He always comes in the end."

"He can come if he wants," Zardi said fiercely. "Once we release the djinni she'll get us off this island, every single one of us."

"I'd like to see that." The herald chuckled. "She helps no one but herself. You'll find that out if you don't run into Okre first."

"Take us on a route that avoids him," Rhidan said firmly.

The herald smirked. "He lives in the volcano as well."

"You never mentioned that before," Rhidan accused.

"You never asked. Want to turn back?"

"No, we don't," Zardi snapped. "Just get us to the volcano."

"Your funeral." Their annoying guide floated off down the dunes.

Zardi and Rhidan slid and slipped in the soft sand as they followed him, the cold air rushing across their faces.

The night air grew colder still, but finally they slid down the last dune and found themselves on a flat expanse of rocky ground. Their torch had almost gone out, but as they stood still it flared into life once more. Rhidan took it from Zardi and held it up.

The volcano towered in the distance. They followed a path filled with coarse rocks to reach its base.

"Here we are," the herald said, pointing to a crack in the rock face. "You'll find her in there."

"What about the Cyclops?" Rhidan looked around nervously.

"Oh, he'll be in there as well," their guide replied. "Keep your voices down. Okre's probably asleep at the moment and you *really* don't want to wake him." He tipped his head at them. "I bid you farewell."

"Farewell!" Rhidan exclaimed. "You're supposed to be our guide, and you haven't *guided* us all the way to the prison yet."

"This is as far as I go," the herald said. "I have no idea where she is in the volcano anyway." He sniffed and shoved his glasses up his nose. "What you're failing to understand is that the person who made this prison really didn't want anyone to release her. Perhaps you should take the hint."

"We're not turning back," Zardi said resolutely.

"Good luck. You'll need it." And with that the little green man faded from sight.

For a moment Zardi felt bereft. It wasn't like the herald had ever been especially friendly or even nice, but he had been a companion on this journey.

"Ready?" Rhidan asked. His hair looked more silver than the watching moon above their heads.

"Ready!" she replied. Together they plunged into the bowels of the volcano.

24

Cyclops This Way

The heat hit them first, and then the sulfurous smell of rotten eggs. The pungent gas burned their throats and nostrils, and Zardi's eyes streamed with tears. She suddenly remembered chopping onions with Nonna back in the kitchen in Taraket. Thinking of home made her feel braver.

Zardi wiped away the sweat from her stinging eyes as she tried to see through the boiling vapor that burst out of the vents in the ground. In the distance she spotted something that filled her with excitement and fear.

A tunnel.

She pointed it out to Rhidan and they walked toward the cavernous passageway. Billows of heat pumped from it, lifting their hair. By the flickering light of their torch Zardi saw bones and excrement littering the tunnel's floor.

"You might as well have a sign at the entrance saying 'Cyclops This Way,'" Rhidan said in disgust.

"A sleeping one, hopefully," Zardi reminded him. "Come on. There's only one way forward." Taking a deep breath, she strode into the mouth of the long tunnel.

As they walked farther down the path, a deafening rumble filled the passageway.

"Is that what I think it is?" Zardi asked, her voice all but drowned out by the noise.

"Snoring," Rhidan said after listening for a moment. "Okre is still asleep then. He sounds just like Nonna, only a hundred times louder."

Zardi laughed despite herself. For a moment it didn't seem to matter that a sleeping Cyclops was at the end of the tunnel. "Nonna could snore for Arribitha. Do you remember how she would doze off in front of the fire and then insist that she was just deep in thought?" Zardi's throat began to feel tight. "And Zubeyda wasn't much better, always saying she needed an extra hour in bed or she'd get pimples." Zardi laughed again but this time it felt much more like she was crying.

Rhidan put a hand on her shoulder. "I miss them too," he said. "Every night, I go to bed thinking about Nonna, your father, and Zub, what they must be feeling. How scared they must be."

"Me too," Zardi replied brokenly. "I hurt with it, knowing that I haven't put things right yet."

"Let it hurt, Zardi," Rhidan said. "Take the pain and make it something else. Let it make you stronger and smarter."

The snoring was earsplittingly loud now, but finally Zardi could see the end of the passageway and the huge stone cavity it spilled into. As they crept into the high-ceilinged chamber an overpowering festering smell filled her nostrils. Squinting in the low light she saw the slumbering form of a giant.

Okre's face was in the shadows, but the flickering flame of the torch revealed the shaggy jet-black hairs that covered his tree trunk legs, wide torso, and barrel chest. The beast's feet were big enough to crush a man beneath them and they ended with long twisted nails that could stab and slash.

Zardi scanned the walls, looking for any sign of a doorway that might lead to the djinni's prison. Then she saw it, an iron door at the far side of the cavern, next to Okre's hull-like left shoulder.

The entrance had a faint green glow pulsing all around it, similar to the light that had surrounded the herald. She turned to Rhidan and they shared silent words with a glance. They had found the entrance to the djinni's prison.

"How are we going to get over there?" Rhidan mouthed beneath the loud snoring.

Zardi shook her head. The Cyclops was practically wedged into the cavity, his bulk covering the entire floor space. There was no way they'd be able to creep round the edges. A bitter taste bloomed on her tongue as she realized that they only had one choice.

She turned to her friend. "We go over him."

Rhidan's mouth dropped open. "You're actually crazy, you do know that?"

"It's all right. He's so big he won't notice us."

Zardi crept toward the sleeping beast. She lightly placed her trembling hands around a bunch of thick bristles on the Cyclops's massive leg and pulled herself up onto his shin.

The beast did not stir.

Finding her balance, she carefully took one step and then another.

Still the Cyclops did not move.

She turned her head and looked at Rhidan. The torch in his hand quivered, but on meeting her gaze, he slotted it into a crevice in the wall and climbed onto the Cyclops's leg.

They journeyed over Okre's body, past his bulging kneecaps, across the brawny muscles of one of his thighs, and onto the hard ridge of his stomach.

Eagerness nipped at her. The door ringed in green was still a fair distance away but they were making good progress.

They stepped onto Okre's chest, and Zardi bit down on an exclamation of surprise as a powerful tremble suddenly ran up her legs, forcing them to buckle beneath her. Both she and Rhidan fell onto their hands and knees—hard.

The Cyclops snorted in his sleep and scratched irritably at his chest, just missing her head with his sharp, twisted claws. Beneath her palms Zardi felt a strong, steady vibration. It was the creature's powerful heartbeat. Each dull thunk was a mini earthquake. She and Rhidan tried to crawl forward, but the thudding heartbeat was too strong, and they began to slide off the beast's chest.

Zardi looked up and around, searching for another way to get to the djinni's prison. A thin sliver of ledge jutted out of the chamber's wall just above the Cyclops's chest. It was frighteningly narrow but they might be able to walk along it to the iron door.

"It's too narrow," Rhidan mouthed when she pointed it out to him.

"Have you got a better idea?" She pulled herself up onto the ledge and Rhidan followed.

The ledge was much narrower than the sultan's arch in Taraket. They had to walk on the tips of their toes, with their backs pressed to the wall, to remain on the jutting piece of rock. Rhidan leading, step by step they drew closer to the djinni's prison.

The cavern shuddered as the Cyclops coughed and shifted his body. The beast turned his head, and Zardi and Rhidan took in a full profile of Okre's grotesque face. His one eye was set in the center of his brow, and his hairy head was as large and uneven as a rain-battered boulder. His fleshy nose was bulbous and badly pitted, and inflamed pustules covered his skin. As the Cyclops snored, his lips curled around two tusks. They were yellow in the firelight and looked sharp enough to slice through rock. His breath was the worst thing, though, a combination of rotten fish and sulfur, and in his new position he was breathing right on them.

Rhidan looked as if he was about to pass out from the smell.

"Don't you dare faint," Zardi ordered.

In her head the words had sounded quiet, but clearly not quiet enough. The Cyclops opened his eye—its red iris was like a candle's flame. Drawing back his lips, Okre roared.

"RUN!" Rhidan shouted. With surprising nimbleness he edged along the narrow ridge. Zardi followed him, the wall scraping at her back.

Okre's head brushed the top of the cavern's ceiling as he stood, dislodging small fragments of rock. With his massive clawed hand he swiped at them, but Zardi and Rhidan were just out of reach.

The iron door was almost below them, its emerald aura burning brighter. Zardi's eyes raked the front of the door, searching for the lock.

There you are.

A simple indentation in the shape of a hexagon was in the wall next to the door. Rhidan had seen it too, and he sprinted along the narrow stone width toward it, his feet a blur.

Zardi screamed as a meaty fist smashed through the ledge in front of her. The Cyclops's clenched hand just missed Rhidan. He wobbled for a second before throwing his body back against the wall, arching his feet so that he was perched on the tips of his toes. Across the chasm that had opened up between them Zardi could see his chest rising and falling with the effort of keeping his balance.

She ducked as Okre swiped again. Out of the corner of her eye she could see that Rhidan was just above the door now. All he needed to do was climb down and place the emerald key in the wall.

But I have it.

Swiftly, she took the emerald from her pocket. "RHIDAN, CATCH!" she yelled, tossing the jewel at him.

He held up a hand and caught it easily. He then knelt down and grabbed hold of the ledge before dropping down to the ground. He fitted the key into the lock and the iron door swung open. He hesitated for a moment before diving through it.

The Cyclops paid him no attention. He only had eyes for Zardi. *Lucky me,* she thought. Okre watched her carefully, with a calculated calm that scared her far more than his fists.

The door had now swung back fully, and inside, Zardi could see a room lit by a white glow. She heard the sound of clattering.

"Zardi, hurry," Rhidan called. "I can't hold this door open for much longer."

Zardi eyeballed the Cyclops. A black, swollen tongue shot out of his mouth, and he licked his saber-sharp tusks and growled in anticipation, enjoying the moment. For an instant she considered loosing an arrow, but knew the second she unclipped her bow he would be upon her. *I need a distraction.*

Her hand crept to the pear-shaped blue stone around her neck with its smooth edges and sharp tip. Before she could have second thoughts, she ripped the jewel from its gossamer casing and leaped forward. While in midair, she slashed the sharp stone across the Cyclops's cheek, leaving a crimson ribbon. She fell to the ground, winding herself as the air left her lungs in an excruciating rush.

The Cyclops roared in pain and clutched at his cheek, blood seeping between his thick, hairy fingers. Zardi took her chance and tumbled her aching body across the floor and through the door. It closed behind her with a resounding thud. But she could still hear the Cyclops's angry roar.

She lay on the floor, and would have felt delight if her chest hadn't hurt so much. Rhidan knelt beside her, peering at her anxiously. Torches that flowered with white fire sat in iron sconces in the wall.

The sound of something rattling cut through Zardi's pain-filled haze. She looked up to see a crystal ring on a large stone pedestal vibrating angrily. Blurred red light radiated from it. Rhidan gulped. "Do you think—"

"The djinni is in there?" Zardi finished.

Rhidan nodded.

"We better go find out." Zardi staggered to her feet, slipping the bloodied blue stone back into its gossamer setting around her neck.

"Wait," Rhidan barked as Zardi approached the stone pedestal. "Maybe we need to think about this a bit more. The herald said she was dangerous."

"So is the sultan. That's why we're here." Zardi

snatched up the ring and let it rest in her palm. "We just need to rub and the djinni will appear. That's what Nonna always said."

"Rub and your wishes will come true," Rhidan murmured, his eyes filled with memories. He came to stand next to Zardi. "We'll do this together."

They both put their thumbs to the ring's crystal band and rubbed.

25

The Djinni's Price

A deep red light ignited in the center of the ring. Zardi and Rhidan stepped back as the light blasted upward, becoming a ball of red magic that twisted, turned, and expanded.

The air rippled with heat, forcing Zardi's eyes shut despite themselves. A cool hand took hers, and she knew it was Rhidan's. She could feel the crystal ring between their joined palms.

"Zardi, whatever happens, we don't let go of the ring," Rhidan yelled.

The heat fell away and there was a trill of laughter. "Silly, children. Just because you hold the ring does not mean that you can control me. Clearly, there is much you need to learn."

Zardi cracked an eye open. A woman of fierce beauty was perched on the stone pedestal looking at her. The woman wore long robes of red silk and her skin was the color of rain-soaked earth. A flowing mane of braids trailed over her shoulders, and her eyes were dark brown, slanted, catlike. Inappropriate laughter bubbled up in Zardi's throat. They had found the djinni. . . .

"You got past Okre." The woman's voice had a lilt. "Impressive work. Zardi, isn't it? At least I believe that is how your friend referred to you."

Zardi nodded. "That's my name, and his is Rhidan."

"What a pleasure to meet you both." The woman was looking at Rhidan intently, as if something about him puzzled her. "My name is Khalila and I'm a djinni, but I've got a feeling you know that already or you wouldn't be here."

"We've come to ask for your help." Zardi paused. She could hear the Cyclops outside, roaring and pounding at the chamber's door and was glad of the distance between them. So many of her hopes, and Rhidan's, lay with this djinni, she didn't know how or where to start.

"Why don't you start at the beginning?" Khalila said, looking at her long fingernails. "Mortals tend to find it easier that way."

And so Zardi did. She spoke of the sultan's reign of terror, her father's imprisonment, and how her sister had been made a praisemaker. "She only has sixty-two days left till the Hunt," Zardi finished, the words feeling like cold pebbles in her mouth. "If I don't find a way to stop the sultan, she'll be . . ." Zardi clenched her hands into fists and forced herself to say the next words. "She'll be killed."

"But we're not going to let that happen," Rhidan said firmly. "That's why we have to find the Windrose." He swiftly went on to tell Khalila about Sinbad, Sula, and the sorcerers of the Black Isle.

"So you want me to tell you where the Windrose guardian can be found?" Khalila asked as they fell silent.

Zardi and Rhidan nodded.

"And help the *Falcon* get back to Arribitha."

They nodded again.

"Anything else while you are here?"

Zardi couldn't believe how nice the djinni was being. Why had the herald been so afraid of her? Why had Khalila been imprisoned here? She pushed the questions aside and pounced on the djinni's last words.

"Will you save my sister and father from Sultan Shahryār?" Zardi asked.

Khalila's deep brown eyes suddenly became shiny. "And who has kept *me* safe? A thousand years ago, Eria, the great wizard, shackled all djinnis who would not obey him to earthly objects." The djinni waved her hand, and a thin cord of red light appeared. It ran from Khalila to the ring in Rhidan's hand. "It is impossible for me to be parted from this ring. It is my tether."

Zardi stared at the flickering red line, remembering what Sula had told them back in Sabra. "I know. Eria cursed you and all the djinnis who did not join his ranks. You are bound to the ring and have to accept the wishes of a mortal master."

Khalila clicked her fingers and the red cord faded from sight. "For centuries, I was handed down from generation to generation as each of my masters grew old and died. I accepted my lot, but destiny decided that my sorrow was not to end there." An aura of flickering flames surrounded her, and the djinni's beautiful face twisted with anger. "I was married once too, you know, to a mortal man. He was my husband but also the master of my magic. I granted every one of his wishes, but how was my love rewarded? I was kidnapped. That ring you hold was taken from my husband and was locked up in this place. And he never came to find me."

Zardi and Rhidan exchanged a tense glance as the djinni's flames began to flicker even more violently.

"No one has come looking for me either." Rhidan stepped toward Khalila and held out his amulet, showing her the inscription etched there. "My father doesn't even want to know me. But here I am. Our quest isn't just about stopping the sultan. I need to get to the Black Isle to learn the truth about my family. I need to understand. You see that, don't you?"

Khalila was looking hard at the words on the amulet. The flames around her died down and became less red and more a sunny yellow. "Yes, I do. Thank you, I see things more clearly now."

Rhidan looked pleased with himself.

"Who kidnapped you?" Zardi asked softly.

"One of my husband's enemies," Khalila replied. Her tone did not invite further questions. "Listen, mortals, the only way I can leave this place is if a human wishes it."

"We could wish it. We could get you out of here." Rhidan eyes were bright. "If you promise to help us first."

Khalila appeared to think about the offer for a moment and then inclined her head. "What this woman Sula told you in Sabra is true. You can only find the Black Isle with the Windrose. I will take you to the Windrose guardian and maybe even use my magic to take you to the Black Isle with the help of the Windrose's guidance, but that is it. I will not help this girl, Zubeyda, nor will I help the crew of the *Falcon*. Why should I extend charity to strangers?" The djinni swung her sheet of fine braids over one shoulder. "You must understand that Eria's curse was devised so that I could only serve one human master at a time. That master is my husband and he is still alive. But there is a way I can grant you wishes. I will use my own life essence." She slipped down from her stone pedestal. "Understand me. I will become a shadow, neither alive nor dead, if I use too much of my essence. You are free to make wishes, but I will choose which ones I will grant." She held out her hand for the crystal ring and

Rhidan dropped it into her palm. "And when the time comes, when I have helped you in your quest to get to the Black Isle, you must promise to wish me back to my husband. Do we have a deal?" She slipped the ring on her finger and held out a hand.

Zardi fought the urge to spring forward and shake the djinni until she agreed to help Zubeyda. Once upon a time, in a kitchen in Taraket, Nonna had accused Zardi of being an impatient seed—but she refused to be that today. As long as they got to the Black Isle it didn't matter that Khalila wouldn't save Zubeyda. Rhidan's father, Iridial, would help her. Rhidan would make him.

"We have a deal," she said, and Rhidan shook the djinni's hand.

"Come, it's time we leave this island," Khalila commanded. "I feel like I've been here forever. Rhidan, make your wish."

"I wish you to take us to the Windrose and its guardian," Rhidan said, his voice steady.

"So be it," Khalila replied.

26

The Riddle

The djinni clasped her hands together. They glowed like fiery embers as she murmured an incantation.

Zardi felt herself being ripped out of the world, in an uprising of color.

Suddenly she stood on stark black ground, interrupted only by a broken white line that ran down its center. In the distance she could just about make out a sparkling fortress against a blue sky.

"What is this place?" Rhidan asked.

There was a cracking sound and a painted metal sign hoisted to a wooden pole pushed out from the black ground beside them.

It read:

WELCOME TO POSTREMO

Khalila laughed. "We're playing the game already, I see. *Postremo* means 'future' in djinni language." The breeze ardently trailed its fingers through her many long braids. Seeming to forget them for a moment, she drank in the air and gave a sigh of pleasure. She then strode forward, with Zardi and Rhidan running to keep up with her long, lithe strides.

Khalila tipped her head at the glinting fortress ahead. "In there you will find what you seek. He knows that we've arrived, of course," she mused. "Knowing Oli, I'm sure he can't wait to meet us."

"Oli?" Zardi repeated. "Is Oli the Windrose guardian?"

Khalila nodded.

"You know him?" Rhidan's face lit up. "Can't you just ask whether we can borrow the Windrose?"

The djinni laughed. "Oh dear, I don't think so. For the last few hundred years I've heard that Oli has been testing those that would seek to claim the Windrose with a riddle. He will not deviate from that."

"What kind of riddle?" Zardi asked.

"I believe that it's got something to do with his true name," Khalila replied.

"But I thought you said he was called Oli." Rhidan frowned.

"His true name is a secret."

"Why?" Zardi asked. "What does it matter if anyone knows his true name?"

"Questions, questions! I'd forgotten how annoying mortals can be, especially young ones," Khalila snapped, and an aura of small flames ignited around her body. "Those with the right knowledge can use a djinni's true name against them. That is how Eria managed to shackle so many of us."

"So your real name is not Khalila," Rhidan said hesitantly.

"I started to call myself Khalila when Eria cast his spell that bound me to this ring. I no longer remember my real name." Sadness hung around the djinni like heavy perfume.

Zardi noticed that Rhidan was tugging on his amulet anxiously, and his lips twitched as if he was trying to stop himself from saying something. He lost the battle.

"If Eria was a wizard, does that mean he was related to me?" Rhidan finally asked.

Zardi winced. Telling an angry djinni that your ancestor was possibly some kind of djinni jailer didn't sound particularly wise to her.

"Because—I mean—well—" Rhidan wiped his brow. "If he was, I'm really sorry."

Khalila laughed. "What an odd little person you are, Rhidan. You are not related to Eria. He was a wizard. You are a sorcerer. Eria's magic is different from yours; he was not born with the ability to absorb magic from nature like you."

Rhidan flushed.

Khalila smiled a strange smile. "Besides, I don't think a child should be held responsible for the actions of his forefathers. Retribution should be visited on the person who did the wrong and no one else. Don't you think, Rhidan?"

He nodded but looked uncomfortable, and Zardi felt the hairs on her arms stand on end although she didn't really understand why.

Khalila stopped and traced the scar on Rhidan's cheek. "I'm glad we see things in the same way."

The djinni smiled even more widely, and Zardi

noticed for the first time how neat and sharp her pearly teeth were.

There was some kind of hidden meaning to Khalila's words, but Zardi was not interested in trying to work it out. She straightened her spine. The only puzzle she was interested in solving was Oli's. "What happens if we get the riddle wrong?" she asked.

Khalila turned to her, the smile sliding from her face. "You would be at his mercy, and I'm afraid that I would not be able to help. His domain, his rules." The djinni clucked her tongue sympathetically. "It's not all doom and gloom. If I get stuck here at least I'll have some company. He can be insufferably smug but I suppose I will have to learn to cope with it."

"We appreciate your confidence in us." Zardi stomped off toward the fortress.

"You're annoyed by my words," Khalila called after her.

"No, just don't give up on us yet," Zardi said, not looking back. She glanced at Rhidan as he caught up and saw that he was looking at her proudly.

Khalila glided to their side. "I wish you both all the luck in the world. You may not believe this but I want to take you to the Black Isle."

Zardi was surprised to see truth in Khalila's eyes.

"Don't worry, we'll get there," she told the djinni. "We just need to solve the riddle first."

They continued to walk toward the dazzling fortress in the distance. As they got closer, Zardi realized with amazement that the building was made entirely of glass and was so tall it scraped the sky.

Their footsteps were whisper soft on the strange surface beneath their feet. Zardi glanced down at the ground and could see flecks of stone held fast in a black casing that could have once been liquid.

"Did Oli make all this?" Rhidan asked, kicking at the black surface.

The djinni nodded. "Many, many years ago, when the wizard Eria tried but ultimately failed to put the world under his yoke, he gave Oli this place as a reward for his unfailing loyalty." Khalila's face looked disapproving. "This is my first time here, but it is clear that Oli has been very busy designing this place."

As they got closer to the glass fortress, images of themselves were thrown up by the reflective surface of the building. Hundreds of Zardis looked back at her. Some were tall, others were short. In some she looked like an old woman, like Nonna, and in others she looked just like her sister. Zardi felt her eyes fill with tears as she stared at the face that was hers but somehow also Zubeyda's. This girl, whoever she was, looked terrified.

Khalila clicked her fingers in front of Zardi's face. "He is playing games with you. You must not let him inside your head."

Zardi tore her eyes from her reflections. Khalila was right. Looking round, she saw that Rhidan was also staring at the mirrored glass, completely transfixed.

Zardi shook him. "Stop looking. Oli is toying with us."

Rhidan blinked hard and took a step back. "Yes, of course. I knew that person wasn't me. Couldn't be me."

"Who did you see?" Zardi asked.

Rhidan scratched at his arm, his nails leaving trails of red. "It doesn't matter—a trick of the light."

There was a humming noise, and a pane of glass rolled to one side as if invisible hands had drawn back a curtain.

They strode through the entrance and into a marble room lined with books. Bright light flooded down from small circles in the ceiling, and a man, as beautiful as an ancient god, stood waiting for them. He reminded Zardi of one of the statues in her garden at home: regal, body perfectly carved, cold.

"Ah, Khalila, good to see you after all this time,"

the man said, tucking a heavy-looking book under one arm. "You don't look a day over a millennium."

Khalila inclined her head, clearly taking his words as a compliment. "Hello, Oli." She looked him up and down. "I must say, this current appearance is very pleasing."

"It's the Adonis look." Oli flexed one of his defined biceps. "I've been employing this look for the last two centuries, on and off."

"Yes, you've always liked your myths and legends." Khalila smiled. "The Oli I knew before liked appearing as Pan the satyr."

The djinni shook his head. "Horns and a potbelly. What was I thinking?"

Khalila wrinkled her nose. "We all make mistakes."

Oli's face became serious. "Truer words you've never said." He looked at Zardi and Rhidan. "You have made a mistake coming here today. You will not win the Windrose." He cocked his head to one side. "However, as you have come with Khalila, I will do you the kindness of letting you scurry away now."

Rhidan looked at Oli squarely. "I'm afraid that's not an option."

"So be it." The djinni's handsome face twisted into an arrogant smile. "If you want the Windrose, you'll have to win it off me. The name of the game is a riddle. And the riddle is to guess my name."

"When do we start?" Zardi asked.

"Such eagerness." Something akin to admiration tinged Oli's voice. "You know, I have been reading about you and Rhidan with much enjoyment." He took the book he was holding out from beneath his arm. The simple leather cover was imprinted with just four words: *The Book of Wonders*. "Such a shame that your story will end here."

"That's our story?" Zardi asked, her voice a squeak of surprise.

"As it is lived, it is written," the djinni replied. "My library is filled with people's lives."

"Zardi, ignore him," Rhidan growled. "He's playing games with us *again*."

"Believe what you like." Oli placed the heavy book on the shelf.

"The riddle, please." Rhidan's voice was calm.

The djinni clasped his hands together, and, as they glowed amber, the outline of a door suddenly appeared on the wall behind him. "The Windrose is behind this door. Guess my name and you can order me to open it. Fail to guess my name and you will die here. No amount of begging or pleading will change this." Oli's face was stern. "Do you understand me?"

Zardi looked at Rhidan. She felt as though someone had spooned out her insides, leaving behind just the husk.

"Maybe we don't have to do this," Rhidan said.

"Yes, we do," she replied, trying to keep her voice steady. "We need to do it for Zubeyda and Baba. Time's running out."

Rhidan tugged on his amulet and turned to Oli. "We're ready."

"Then let us begin," the djinni intoned.

Heavy words, lightly thrown,
Shall reveal what is unknown.
Smooth as oil, rough as grain,
I will heal internal pain.
Sweet and savory I can be;
You must sow the seeds to see.
Answer now, no time to wait,
I'll burst open, never late.

Oli fell silent. He clapped his hands together and a spark burst into life at the bottom right corner of the door.

Zardi watched as the spark slowly began to edge up the door's outline, leaving a golden trail in its wake.

"You have until the golden spark reaches its end point to solve the riddle," Oli said. "After that the door will be sealed and your lives will be mine."

"They are so young." Khalila looked at them pityingly. "It's a shame that there is no other way."

"They have made their choice. Age has nothing to do with it."

Zardi could feel Rhidan trembling beside her. She grabbed his hand and pulled him away from the two djinnis. "Come on, you're brilliant at riddles. Let's solve it."

"All right." Rhidan's voice wobbled but his eyes were determined. "What we need is logic and patience." He started to pace. "We'll look at each clue in isolation." He began to look more confident. "Then we search for a pattern, the thing that links them all."

"'Heavy words, lightly thrown, shall reveal what is unknown,'" Zardi recited.

Rhidan rubbed his chin. "That's easy enough. Oli is just setting up the premise of the riddle. Telling us that his words can reveal the answer."

"What about the next line?" she asked. "What is as

smooth as oil and as rough as grain at the same time?"

"Slow down there," Rhidan said evenly. "He's not necessarily saying that this thing has to be rough and smooth at the same time. Maybe it is like the sea, calm sometimes and rough at others."

"Yes, of course," Zardi murmured, thinking of all the times she'd looked out at the water while sitting on Desolation Island's shore. She frowned. "But you can't compare the sea to grain. It's a different roughness. The roughness of grain is like sand or something."

Rhidan's eyes widened. "Glass!" he exclaimed. "Glass is made out of sand. It starts off being rough and ends up being smooth." He surveyed his surroundings. "Look at this place, what do you see?"

"Glass!" she repeated, looking at the see-through walls of the fortress. Her heart beat a bit faster. They had the second part of the riddle, and a proper clue to Oli's name. Zardi's gaze fixed on the door: The golden line was about a third of the way around the frame.

"Healer of internal pain," Rhidan muttered to himself. "That's got to have something to do with medicine, right?"

Zardi nodded. Unbidden, an image of Sula came into Zardi's mind. Sula the medicine woman. Sula massaging salve into Rhidan's hand. A thought, shadowy yet stubborn, danced at the edges of her mind.

"So we have two clues, glass and medicine." Rhidan was pacing furiously now. "But what about the next two lines, 'Sweet and savory I can be; you must sow the seeds to see.'" He recited the lines once, then twice, his brow a map of furrows. "Yes, that fits," he murmured after a moment. "I think he's talking about a cooking ingredient." Rhidan tapped his head. "But that doesn't help us at all. Most things grown from seeds end up in the kitchen." He punched a fist into his palm. "It could be anything. Pomegranates, oranges, sesame seeds, barberries, tomatoes—"

"Wait a second, say that again," Zardi urged as that whisper of a thought suddenly started to become much more solid.

"What, tomatoes?"

"No, no, the one before."

"Barberries?"

"No, the one before that!"

"Sesame seeds?"

Zardi didn't respond. It was like a mosaic image all slotting into place and the whole picture showed a humble, honey-colored seed.

"Sesame," she whispered, although it took all her self-control not to shout the word from the top of her lungs. "Don't you see? It fits with each part of the riddle. Sesame can be used in sweet and savory dishes, and if you plant sesame seeds they produce flowers, which generate more seeds." She gripped his hand. "Nonna told me once that I was impatient like a sesame seed. She said that the pods burst open when they are ripe, like they can't wait to be eaten."

Rhidan's eyes lit up. "'I'll burst open, never late.' It fits perfectly with the last part. But what about the rest of the riddle? What on earth has sesame got to do with glass or medicine?"

"I'm not sure where glass comes into it, but do you remember when you burned your fingers? Sula used a salve and said that it had sesame oil in it to take away the sting. She said sesame oil cures all kinds of pain."

Rhidan was nodding. "But what about glass? It's the only thing not to fit." He looked over at the door that led to the Windrose.

Zardi followed his gaze. The golden seal was almost all the way round. "Listen, Rhidan, forget about glass, will you? For just one second!" Desperation made her words sharp, even to her own ears.

A wounded look passed across his face.

She rubbed at her forehead. "Sorry, it's just that sesame fits with the rest of the riddle. It has to be rig—" She was stopped abruptly by Rhidan, who clicked his fingers loudly.

"What if that first line isn't talking about glass at all?" he said. "What was it again? 'Smooth as oil, rough as grain.'" Rhidan's face was flushed. "Sesame seeds feel like grain, right?"

"Right," Zardi said.

"Well, if you press sesame seeds for long enough you get oil. Grain and oil."

Zardi whirled toward Oli. The djinni was on the floor doing push-ups, while Khalila stood a little distance away, looking bored.

"Have you got an answer for me?" Oli jumped to his feet and dusted off his hands. "You really should get a move on. That door is going to be sealed any second now." He looked ridiculously smug as the golden spark raced toward the finish.

Rhidan glared at the djinni. "Yes, we have an answer."

"Sesame. Sesame is your name." Zardi pointed at the door. "Open, Sesame. Open the door."

The Windrose

The djinni's smug smile slid from his face, and the golden seal around the door spluttered for a second and rolled back to its starting point.

"What . . . h-h-how did you guess?" The djinni's shoulders sagged as the door swung open to reveal a marble staircase.

"Teamwork." Zardi grinned at Rhidan.

"Extraordinary!" Khalila's smile made her beautiful

face exquisite. "I see now that neither of you should be underestimated." She turned to the djinni. "I believe you have a Windrose to show us, Sesame."

"Do not call me by that name." He looked furious.

"The Windrose, Sesame," she repeated. "Show it to us."

"Afraid not, Khalila. I will show the Windrose to *her.*" Oli pointed to Zardi. "She is the one who used my true name and issued the command. She is the one I will take to the Windrose."

"Wait a second!" Rhidan cried. "We worked the riddle out together. We should both get to go."

"You're welcome to try," Oli said with a smirk, some of his old arrogance returning. "But you'll be burned to a cinder first."

"And why's that?" Rhidan demanded.

"Only the person who made the command can cross the threshold." Oli headed toward the open door.

"It's all right." Zardi put a hand on Rhidan's arm as he opened his mouth to protest further. "Let me go with him and get the Windrose. Then, when I come back, I can give it to you."

"Wrong again." Oli tapped a slippered foot impatiently. "The Windrose calls on all four elements to find those things that want to remain hidden and that includes fire. Only the keeper of the Windrose will be able to withstand its heat. Anyone else who touches it will be burned. Badly."

Zardi met Rhidan's gaze and blanched at the expression on his face. He looked as if someone had just ripped his heart from his chest. *He should be the keeper of the Windrose,* Zardi thought. *He's the one that made it appear on Sula's table.* "Oli, please," she pleaded. "There must be a way I can give the Windrose to Rhidan."

The djinni looked amused. "Sure, there's a way. You could always die. Ownership would then pass on to the next person to touch the Windrose."

Rhidan's eyes were filled with disappointment, but he managed to raise a smile. "Well, that would be a bit extreme. It's all right, Zardi. Go and get it."

"All right," she replied quietly, still feeling guilty. She joined Oli by the open door and together they crossed the threshold. She looked behind her to see Khalila put a hand on Rhidan's shoulder. Then the door slammed shut, taking all light with it.

The way ahead was dark, except for a spot of flickering blue at the top of the tall staircase. She didn't ask Oli which way to go. There was only one way, toward the light. She felt out the steps with the tips of her feet, climbing each one slowly. The djinni followed.

Neither of them spoke as they ascended the steep stairs, but Zardi could feel excitement and something else radiating from the djinni in waves. Her heart thundered in her ears.

She continued to climb the stairs but the blue light seemed to be forever out of reach, and Zardi found herself thinking about Sula again. The medicine woman had told her she had a destiny to fulfill, that her path might take her from Rhidan's side. Zardi wondered if this climb upward was the separate path of which Sula had spoken.

Suddenly, she was at the top of the staircase, and the azure glow that had seemed so far away was all around her. Ahead, beneath a roof made entirely out of glass, stood a fountain. Blue liquid flame pumped from its head, pooling into the fountain's basin. Oli guided her right up to the font. Despite its intense heat she made herself look down into the depths of the pooled flame. A golden disc, with a tree emblazoned at its center, spun in the bowl of fire. The rubies studded around the inner ring burned like embers and the words etched onto the gold bled into each other as the disc whirled.

The Windrose.

"Here it is." Oli pushed her closer. "Won't you take it?"

"But how?" Zardi asked, her mouth dry. "It will burn . . . M-my hand will burn."

Oli's voice was scathing. "All things have a price. You have come to take something from this fountain. An object that can lead you to anything in the world, all the riches, all the knowledge that you've ever wanted. Did you think that it would come for free?"

"I've paid you," she snarled back. "I answered your riddle."

"That you did, and in turn I paid my price, I brought you to this place." He looked down at her. "Take hold of the Windrose or walk away but know that you only get one chance."

Zardi began to tremble like a palm leaf in the wind. Of all the challenges she had faced since leaving home, this was the one she wanted to run from. She looked at her rough, callous hand. It was shaking. *I could leave the Windrose,* she thought. *I could leave now.*

Zardi pushed away the traitorous voice. She could not fail. The Windrose was the key to everything.

She leaned forward but reared back as the heat struck her face. She could feel a thickness in her throat. A hard ball of dread filled her stomach, but before her courage could desert her, she plunged her hand into the fiery basin.

Time stood still. Pain unknown, until now unimaginable, shot through her hand as the flames covered it. A blanket of unconsciousness tried to smother her, but she kicked it off and forced herself to look at her burning hand, which even now reached for the Windrose. Through the flickering, blue-tinted flames she could see her skin blister and shrink. The skin over her knuckles began to peel back, showing red, and then the white of bone. Still she reached, but her hand was too far away from the golden disc. She needed to expose more of herself to the flame. She pushed her forearm into the fiery basin, and the flames grasped it greedily. The blue stone around her neck swung forward. The gossamer thread that held the jewel began to melt and there was a cracking sound as the flames touched the gem. The stone shattered, the hot pieces falling onto the exposed skin of her chest and neck.

With all of her being Zardi wanted to pull away from the fire, as despair joined pain in her mind—her hand was being destroyed and she'd lost her stone, the stone she had promised Sula she would look after.

Why go on? her thoughts whispered. *Pull back, give up.*

A howl of pure agony left Zardi's lips, but with her last shard of will she fought against the voice in her head and pushed her whole arm forward. She lifted the Windrose from its fiery bath and with a sob she fell back from the flames and onto the floor.

28

To the Future

All her pain ended as suddenly as a summer storm. Zardi looked down at her hand: It was undamaged, and in it she held the golden Windrose. "I don't understand." She gaped at her hand stupidly and then up at the djinni.

"It was a test." Oli looked utterly fed up. "And you passed it rather impressively."

"So, my hand was never really burning?" Zardi asked

in amazement, placing the Windrose gently in her lap.

"It *was* burning," Oli said. "That was the price. You had to be prepared to sacrifice it to be able to take possession of the Windrose. If you had withdrawn your hand without the Windrose, the burns would have remained. No magic could have undone them. But now that your hand has been through the fire, you will be stronger."

Zardi let Oli's words settle on her and sink in. The djinni would never know how close she'd come to quitting before she had the Windrose. She flexed her hand, still not quite believing that she wasn't hurt.

The golden disc tingled with pleasant warmth as she grasped it. She wearily got to her feet and stepped away from the fountain. Through the glass roof, she could see a thousand stars in the night sky. It had grown dark outside. How long had they been in Postremo? Zardi suddenly felt homesick for Desolation Island and the crew of the *Falcon*. "If we're all done here, I'd like to leave," she whispered.

Oli led her down the winding stairs. All the way, she grasped the Windrose tightly, its circular edge sharp against her skin. It was really hers!

Zardi reached the stone door and stepped into the book-lined room.

"You're back." Rhidan ran up to her, with Khalila following. "Are you all right?" His eyes raked over her.

"I'm fine, really." On the long walk down the stairs she'd been of two minds as to whether she would tell Rhidan about the fire fountain and what had happened to her. She decided she would tell him, but not right now.

Rhidan's brow furrowed with worry. "What happened to your neck?" He briefly touched the base of her throat.

Zardi's fingers crept up to her neck and she could feel a tiny ridge of smooth, cold stone embedded in her skin. She prodded at it but it didn't hurt. For a moment she couldn't think of what it could be, but then the answer rushed over her. It was a fragment of the jewel that Sula had given her. Zardi felt a grin break over her face. The stone wasn't destroyed; she still had a tiny bit left.

"It's my stone," Zardi said. "And I'll explain later, I promise." She held up the Windrose for him to see. "Look what I've got."

Rhidan's eyes widened, and he reached out to touch the Windrose.

"I wouldn't do that if I were you," Oli said. "You don't want to get burned, do you? Only the keeper of the

Windrose can touch it."

Rhidan's hand stopped in midair. For a moment, disappointment worried his brow, but then pride blossomed on his face. "Zardi is the keeper of the Windrose. I wouldn't have it any other way."

Zardi smiled at her friend, relieved that he wasn't annoyed at her for being the one to say Sesame's name and be taken across the threshold.

"So, keeper of the Windrose, which way is it to the Black Isle?" Khalila arched an eyebrow.

"I don't know, I . . ." Zardi faltered. "I don't even know how to use it." She looked over at Oli hopefully.

The djinni looked mutinous. "You come here, guess my name, take the Windrose, and now you want me to give you instructions?" He folded his arms. "I am not telling you a thing."

Khalila held up her hands. "Luckily, I know." She pointed at the Windrose. "Those words etched around the circumference are the ancient names of the four winds. It means the Windrose can harness the power of air." She pointed to the etched tree, the roots that turned into waves, and the glowing rubies along the rim. "As well as earth, water, or fire. You need to focus your mind on the Windrose and then on the place you want to go. I'd call on air for its help. It is the easiest element to control."

"But we're inside," Zardi protested.

"It doesn't matter," Oli said reluctantly. "The elements can find you anywhere and lead you to what you desire."

"Ask the Windrose to guide you. I will fix on the wind it chooses to give us and will use my magic to transport us to the Black Isle," Khalila promised.

"Wait," Zardi replied. "We need to go back to camp first. We can't just leave without telling Sinbad and the others. Khalila, I command you to take us back to Desolation Island."

"You misremember, you are not my true master. I will grant your wishes only if I choose to," the djinni retorted. "I never want to see that place again."

Rhidan spun round to face the djinni. "Listen, I know our deal is that if you transport us to the Black Isle, we'll wish you back to your husband. But right now, we've got to go back to the island."

Khalila considered his words for a moment. "I've got another idea. One that doesn't involve us going back to that place."

"Go on," Zardi said.

"You could wish Sinbad and his men home and I'd grant it, even if it means using my life essence."

"We wouldn't get to say good-bye." Rhidan turned to Zardi.

"True." Zardi smiled sadly. "But Sinbad's journey was never supposed to be ours. I just want them to get home."

Rhidan turned to the djinni. "Khalila, I wish you to send Sinbad and his men back to Arribitha."

"And don't forget the diamonds," Zardi added swiftly.

"So be it." Khalila clasped her hands and murmured an incantation, but unlike last time her hands did not glow with fire. "Something's wrong." She frowned. "I tried to send the crew of the *Falcon* back home but they're still on the island."

"Why wouldn't your magic work?" Rhidan asked.

For the first time, Zardi saw something very much like fear pass across Khalila's face.

"I'm not sure," the djinni said hesitantly.

"Maybe you're a bit rusty, my dear," Oli offered. "And transporting a whole crew, while in a different dimension, isn't an easy task even when you're at the top of your game."

Khalila looked glum, and Zardi felt a surprising pang of sympathy.

"I guess that must be it," the djinni said.

"You need to start slow, baby steps and all that," Oli went on. "I am more than happy to send you back to the island, so you can try there."

Zardi's eyes narrowed. "What's the price? There is always a price to pay for magic, right?"

"You learn fast. I don't have a price so much as a desire." Oli looked almost embarrassed. "You see, I'm bound to remain in this place until my master, Eria, returns."

"A guard dog with nothing to guard now the Windrose is gone," Khalila commented snidely.

Oli ignored her. "And boredom is the worst torturer."

"I don't understand," Zardi said. "What can I do?"

"Let me see your future." Eagerness bloomed in Oli's voice. "Once I've seen your future, I can record it in the *Book of Wonders*. I won't have to wait so long to find out what happens next. Will you let me see?"

"I guess. If it means you'll really send us all back to the island," Zardi said.

"It's a promise." Oli clasped his hands together and murmured something under his breath. His hands glowed, and he touched Zardi's forehead. Black exploded across the whites of his eyes.

Zardi shared a bemused glance with Rhidan as a smile split the djinni's handsome face. Whatever Oli was watching in her future, he was enjoying it. At long last, the smile faded and the black seeped from his eyes.

Oli clapped in delight. "I'd better write this all down before I forget." He hurried over and pulled the heavy leather book off the shelf.

"What did you see?" Khalila's face was pinched.

"I'm sure you'd like to know." Oli stared at the other djinni with a knowing look on his face, and Khalila lowered her gaze.

Zardi frowned. Something was going on between the djinnis that she didn't understand, and she certainly didn't like it. She folded her arms. "Actually, I'd like to know. It's *my* future."

Oli licked his fingers and flicked through the *Book of Wonders,* looking for a blank page. "Well, I don't want to spoil all the fun, but know that the Black Isle will not give you the answers you seek. You won't even reach there in time for it to make a difference. Zubeyda's Hunt will go ahead and there is nothing you can do to stop that."

"You're wrong," Zardi ground out.

"Of course he is. He's just toying with you," Rhidan said reassuringly. "We have the Windrose and once we find the Black Isle, I'll convince my father to help us and—"

"Ah yes, your father, the mysterious Iridial." Oli laughed. "Oh, Rhidan, I long to read your future, but I don't want to ruin the ending for myself, and the end lies with you, I think." He tucked the *Book of Wonders* under his arm. "Time for you to go—there's much still to come!" Oli clasped his hands together. Words flowed under his breath.

"Wai—" Zardi began. But it was too late. She, Rhidan, and Khalila were ripped through space once again.

29

Spelltrap

"Ouch," Rhidan complained as Oli's magic dropped them back on the beach. "Isn't there a less painful way to travel?"

"Sure there is," Khalila said. "But Oli clearly wasn't feeling that generous."

Zardi scanned the shore, searching for Sinbad and his crew, but all she could see was the carcass of the *Falcon* up ahead. She shivered as a cool breeze danced off the sea and rushed over her, making the hairs on her arms stand on end. The low sun in the sky told her that it was nearly dusk.

Fear gnawed at her. “This is wrong.” Zardi broke into a run, heading for the *Falcon*. Rhidan’s footsteps pounded behind her. Where was everyone? Where was the fire that should have been built by now, its smoky plume spiraling into the sky?

The herald’s warning about Okre sounded loudly in her head. *He’ll come visiting soon. He always comes in the end.*

“I hope you don’t expect me to run after you,” Khalila griped. “I’m not getting sand in my slippers.”

Only yesterday the *Falcon*’s hull had been riddled with gaping holes. Now they were filled up with some kind of sap that had grown hard and shiny. Zardi reached out and touched its smoothness.

“How’d they do this so quickly?” Rhidan asked, catching up with her.

“Get away from there!” A gaunt man with wild white hair ran toward them, shouting and brandishing a long stick with a sharp rock strapped to its end.

Zardi squinted in the failing light. The man looked incredibly familiar.

“Musty?” Rhidan asked uncertainly.

The white-haired man stopped short, recognition lighting up his face. "You're alive!" he exclaimed. "How can this be? Where have you been for the last month?"

"What are you talking about?" Zardi asked. "We've only been gone a few hours."

"What nonsense are you speaking?" Musty shook his head as if trying to dislodge their voices. "No time for games. There is work to be done. I must finish the ship." He strode away, dragging his long stick behind him.

"But where is everyone else?" Zardi chased the frighteningly thin old man. *How had Musty become so skinny, so quickly*?

They caught up with Musty next to a pile of coconuts. He was busy splitting them in half with his makeshift axe.

"Musty, please, where's Sinbad, the rest of the crew?" Zardi persisted.

"Gone, gone, gone," Musty chanted. "A beast, some called him a Cyclops, came and kept on coming, night after night. Picking us off, gulping us down. Those of us that made it after the first night thought that the beast must have taken you and Rhidan."

Zardi felt sick as she thought of Okre attacking her friends. She'd never see some of them again.

"But we haven't even been gone a day." Rhidan's voice was thick with confusion and upset.

Angry color flooded Musty's face and he stopped chopping. "Are you taking me for a fool, boy? I know how long it's been. A moon has waxed and waned since I saw you last."

"I think I'd better explain." Khalila appeared by their side. "Time moves differently on different planes," she said. "In Oli's dimension four hours passed, here four weeks."

"And you didn't think to tell us?" Zardi glared at Khalila and quickly calculated how long Zubeyda had been praisemaker. *Fifty-six days,* she realized. *Only thirty-four days left until the Hunt.*

The djinni tossed her braids over her shoulder. "I didn't think it mattered. I wasn't expecting to come back to this place."

Musty stared at her with deep suspicion. "Who are you?"

"A djinni," Rhidan said quickly. "And a friend."

Zardi bit her tongue. Khalila was many things, but she wasn't a friend. A friend would have told her earlier that time moved differently in Postremo. That Zubeyda only had little more than a month left to live.

The djinni held out her hand to Musty. "I'm Khalila. I'm sorry to hear about your shipmates."

Musty shook her hand. "Did I hear right? You're a djinni?"

"You don't look surprised," Khalila commented.

"I met a djinni once before, and he wasn't half bad," Musty said. "So, you're hardly going to send me running into the trees screaming." The shipmaster's eyes took on a glazed look. "Besides, I've done all my screaming and all my running away."

"You can't blame yourself for running from the Cyclops," Rhidan said, placing a hand on the shipmaster's shoulder. "We've seen him. He's a nightmare come to life."

"Who said I was talking about the Cyclops?" Musty shook off Rhidan's hand. "I'm talking about that thing. That she-devil, the Queen of the Serpents."

Zardi's eyes met Rhidan's. Her horrified bafflement reflected in his violet eyes. She remembered Roco talking about the Queen of the Serpents.

"She made mincemeat of that Cyclops," Musty whispered. "A more bloody, more grisly sight I've never seen."

"I think you'd better start from the beginning," Zardi said, finally finding her voice.

Musty began his story, leaning heavily on the handle of his axe as if each word left him weaker.

"We tried to fight him." Musty's voice cracked with grief. "But we were no match for his strength or greed. Our numbers dwindled, and wherever we hid the Cyclops always found us. Then Nadeem offered us a way out."

"A way out?" Zardi repeated.

"He told us that we had an ally." Musty snorted. "He had met someone called the Queen of the Serpents. The night after we lost Syed and the cook, the queen told Nadeem that she'd give us refuge. Sinbad made the only decision he could. He moved us into her kingdom, deep in the bowels of the earth." Musty's eyes clouded at the memory. "The queen and her army of snakes then hunted down the Cyclops, tearing him limb from limb."

"The Cyclops is dead!" Rhidan exclaimed. "So everyone is safe now."

Musty let out a chilling laugh. "Safe?" he sneered. "You mean safely locked up. After the battle, the queen took us all prisoner. Nadeem became her advisor, helped to keep us locked up like animals in cages so that we could work on her blasted flying contraption."

"But you aren't in prison," Khalila murmured.

Musty cast his eyes downward. "She was going to feed me to her favorite snake, Satyan. She told me I was old and worn out. But Sinbad begged for my life and she set me free."

"But why'd she listen to him?" Rhidan asked.

Musty was silent. His sunken, brown cheeks became ruddy.

He's embarrassed, Zardi realized with some confusion. "What is it, Musty?"

"Well, you see, the queen is rather fond of the captain," the shipmaster finally managed to say.

"You mean she *fancies* Sinbad," Rhidan replied.

"It's more than that. She's in love with him," Musty revealed. "To save me, he promised to be her consort and spend his days praising her beauty with poetry. She agreed, and I became an exile." Musty lifted his axe and brought it down on a coconut. "Enough. I must finish the ship if I'm going to get my crew home."

Zardi led Khalila and Rhidan to one side. "We need a plan."

"Let me guess," Khalila said drolly. "Please can you get my friends out of the Queen of the Serpents' den and send them home?"

"That's pretty much it," Zardi replied. "We can't leave this island until they're safe. And don't forget Musty."

"Fine, but only because I want to get off this island once and for all." The djinni frowned. "And I need the practice. Do you know how embarrassing it is to be told by another djinni that your skills are rusty?"

Oli's words about the Black Isle and how its sorcerers were not the answer to saving Zubeyda catapulted into Zardi's head. "Well, if you need the practice, save my sister and father as well."

Khalila cracked her knuckles. "Sure, why not. That will show Oli."

Zardi tried to keep her face composed. She couldn't believe how easily the djinni had agreed. Could her family's fate be so easily resolved? She imagined Zubeyda and Baba walking through the door of their home in Taraket. The look on Nonna's face. Zardi quickly made the wish that would free her friends and family before Khalila could change her mind.

"Keep your eyes on Musty," the djinni said. "He'll be back in Arribitha in a moment as will the crew of the *Falcon*." Khalila clasped her hands together, and Zardi looked over at the shipmaster, expecting him to disappear in a flash of light. But he didn't. He just continued splitting coconuts.

"Khalila, I don't think it's—" She stopped as she turned to face the djinni. The color had drained from her face.

"I have no magic," Khalila said hoarsely. "It's not there."

"Of course it isn't," a voice like dry leaves said.

Zardi spun round. A woman, part snake, part human, towered over them. Her golden, wide-set eyes were ignited with glee, and more than twenty snakes, all ivory except one, which was red and gold, waited at her back.

"No, no, no." Musty's howled protest was filled with dread and Zardi saw him drop to his knees as a ring of snakes surrounded him.

The Queen of the Serpents, Zardi thought, looking back at the woman-creature in horror. Time slowed as she took in her appearance. The queen's head was wide and flat like a snake's, and her jaw tapered to a sharp point. The skin of her face and arms was fish-belly white and covered with a whisper-thin membrane of iridescent scales that sparkled in the amber light of the setting sun. Her hair was a knotted mass of rattail silver strands that reached her powerful-looking violet-colored tail, and her upper torso was dressed in a silver breastplate. Around her waist she wore a belt of silver hoops, and hanging from it was a strange-looking glass orb filled with red light.

"I stole your magic, djinni," the queen hissed. "Who knew that my creator's spelltrap would work so well?"

"Spelltrap?" Khalila questioned. "What a ridiculous idea. I have been alive for over two thousand years. There's no such thing."

"Oh, really?" The queen took the orb full of red light from her belt and dangled it from her finger. "This tells me differently. This is your magic. Every drop of it." She giggled, and the light twinkling sound was monstrous coming from her mouth. "I captured it when you tried to transport the crew from the island."

Khalila whirled toward Zardi and Rhidan, her dark brown eyes now black with rage. "I don't believe her. Wish something, anything."

"Save us from her," Rhidan said swiftly. "I wish it."

Khalila closed her eyes and brought her hands together, but, again, no red glow illuminated her palms. She tried twice and then three times but still there was no light. The djinni's breath rattled in her throat. "I don't understand—how has this happened?"

"Vanity aside, I really have been frightfully clever," the queen said. "I set up my creator's spelltrap in the jail where I'm keeping Sinbad's men. The first time you tried to take my prisoners, the spelltrap caught your magic and held it." The queen grinned, showing white, even teeth. She looked round at them, her eyes resting on Zardi. "From what Nadeem told me of your character, I was sure you would come for your friends. So I let that worn-out shipmaster go free and sent one of my guards to watch him. As soon as you arrived I was informed."

Khalila was a blur as she leaped from the ground and grasped at the spelltrap. The queen's snakes were faster, though, and four of them surrounded their liege, protecting her. The red and gold snake shot out toward Khalila with its velvety pink mouth open, showing sharp fangs. Zardi grabbed Khalila and dragged her from the attacking snake before releasing her bow from her belt and nocking an arrow. She stood firm.

The queen let out a hiss that Zardi understood as a command: *STOP.*

Zardi thought about the fragment of blue stone embedded into her skin. *My stone, it still works.*

The red and gold snake halted in its tracks, frozen, and then with jerky movements came to rest beside the queen, its sides heaving heavily.

The queen glared at Khalila. "Try to touch me again and I will not stop him from ripping out your throat." She stroked the red and gold snake's head. "Satyan would be more than eager."

Khalila did not reply. The fight had gone out of her. She watched with dull eyes as the queen reattached the spelltrap to her belt.

"Come, it's time that we leave this place," the queen commanded. "You've had me waiting long enough."

"I don't understand. What do you want with us?" Zardi asked, her bow still raised.

"My plan for you will be revealed in my own good time." The queen pointed at the arrow. "I really wouldn't bother with that. Before you even fire one, my snakes will be upon you and the results won't be pretty."

Zardi surveyed the serpents in front of her. There were so many.

The queen laughed. "Yes, I made sure that I brought my personal guards with me. Nadeem told me that you are a good shot, and many other things besides. He really has been incredibly helpful. For instance, I know all about your quest to find the Windrose and the Black Isle."

Rhidan flinched, and Zardi recalled how they'd both stood on the beach pleading with Nadeem to give them the emerald eye, how they'd told him everything about their quest, the Windrose, even about wanting to free a djinni.

Zardi glared at their captor. The queen met her gaze. *She doesn't blink,* Zardi realized. *Just like a snake.*

"Of course, Nadeem had no idea just how important his revelations were." The queen smiled to herself. "You see, we have something in common. You want to go to the Black Isle. Well, guess what? So do I. You are going to help me get there. And by the time I'm finished with those sorcerers there will be nothing left but corpses. . . ."

PART FOUR
Reckonings

30

The Flying Machine

"If I see another feather, I am going to poke my eye out with it," Rhidan growled, throwing a giant, downy plume away. "Thirty-three days," he murmured. "I've been in this stinking prison for thirty-three days."

"Why does she want to fly to this Black Isle anyway?" Mirzani peered down at the plans for the flying machine and fixed another feather into one of the glider's giant wings.

"We still don't know." Zardi tightened a cord that connected the wings to the wooden triangular frame at the nose of the machine. She stood back, her eyes sweeping over the two giant wings made entirely out of Roc feathers and the leather harness that hung beneath it. Despite herself she was proud. The crew had done a great job of following the plans that the queen had given them.

"At least we're almost done." Mirzani's narrow face broke into a smile. "We'll be out of here soon."

Zardi could hear the excitement in the sailor's voice at the thought of being free, and she suddenly found herself remembering the day that she, Rhidan, Musty, and Khalila had been brought to the queen's lair. They'd been led deep underground through a set of tunnels as twisted as the roots of the tree etched on the Windrose. The way had been dotted with flickering torches lit with something other than flame, and giant snakes had guarded every bend. Eventually, they had been dumped in this prison. The crew had been quick to welcome them, but they had demanded explanations as well. Zardi and Rhidan had told them everything, introduced them to Khalila, and even explained about the quest for the Windrose.

Zardi rubbed her hands over her face tiredly. That had been over a month ago. Time was measured by the bowls of foul-tasting slop that were shoved through the hatch at the bottom of the prison door morning, noon, and night. Each day, Zardi expected the queen to come and ask whether she had the Windrose in her possession. But she never did, and every evening Zardi went to sleep knowing that in Taraket Zubeyda was ever closer to death.

Just one day until the Hunt, her thoughts screamed. *Just one day until Zubeyda is killed.* Zardi closed her eyes to stop tears from falling, but in the darkness she saw her sister's terrified face, saw her mouth open in a scream for help.

"I'm coming, Zub," she whispered. "I'm going to get out of here and find a way to save you."

"We can finish it today. Just one last push, boys," Ali called, walking from the adjacent room where the prisoners took turns sleeping on rough sheets over hay. He looked over at Zardi and at Khalila, who was sewing two pieces of leather together. "Um, I mean boys, girl, and djinni."

"But what happens then, eh?" Mo asked as he coiled up a length of rope.

"The queen will let us out, of course," Ali said.

"Brother, has your brain gone to mush in this place?" Mo scratched irritably at his bearded face. "She's never going to let us go free. She'll feed us to her snakes."

"You're wrong," Mirzani said fiercely. "Sinbad won't let us be eaten. He'll save us."

"When was the last time you saw Sinbad or that traitor, Nadeem?" Zain pitched in from across the room, his long hair was unbraided and a tangled mess. "It's just us down here."

They fell silent at the sound of a key being turned in the lock. The door hadn't been opened since Zardi and the others had been thrown into the cell.

Nadeem, adorned with a plum-colored cloak, swept into the room, followed by Satyan.

"Look at this," Zain sneered. "You speak of the sneak and he appears with his beastly snake. What'd you want, Nadeem?"

"I've come for these three." Nadeem pointed at Zardi, Rhidan, and Khalila. "The queen wants to see you."

Zardi's stomach clenched uneasily as she, Rhidan, and Khalila rose to their feet.

"Nadeem, we need to talk," Ali said firmly. He paused, his face wrinkling into puzzlement. "Why are you wearing that cloak?"

"I'm the queen's advisor. It's only fitting I dress like this," Nadeem replied primly.

"You look and sound ridiculous," Tariq replied, coming into the room, stretching and yawning.

"I do not," Nadeem said, his voice rising. "What I do is vital. I help the queen plan and make decisions."

"So, what's your queen's plan for us?" Tariq asked. His swamp-colored eyes narrowed.

Nadeem looked confused. "You know what the plan is. Once the machine is finished, you'll go free."

"And you believe that?" Zain came to stand at Tariq's side. "We're her prisoners. She can't be trusted and neither can you."

Nadeem hunched his shoulders. The words from his former friend were cutting deep. "You're not prisoners; you're keeping up your end of a bargain," he snapped. "The queen got rid of the Cyclops and now we're helping her build her machine. That's fair, isn't it?"

"Fair? We're locked up like animals," Zain spat.

Nadeem shook his head. "You'd all be dead if it wasn't for her. How about some gratitude?"

Satyan, who stood beside him, added a long, low hiss.

Nadeem scowled at Zardi, Rhidan, and Khalila.

"Come on, let's go." His gaze traveled over the sailors in the room. "The queen wants her glider finished by tonight. The sooner you finish, the sooner you'll get out." He swept out of the room, his cloak billowing behind him. Zardi, Khalila, and Rhidan followed, with Satyan at their back.

Nadeem locked the thick wooden door, ignoring the two green snakes that stood outside the prison, guarding it. He strode down the corridor. Zardi and her companions followed, prodded by Satyan.

Huge snakes hung from the ceiling and brushed the prisoners' faces with scaly skins and flickering tongues.

Zardi saw Rhidan take his amulet off. "What are you doing?" she asked.

Rhidan put the amulet in his pocket. "It feels wrong to wear it with all these snakes around. I can't explain it."

But the snakes didn't seem to bother Nadeem at all. He walked along the tunnel pompously talking about his role as the queen's advisor.

Zardi was almost relieved when they reached the throne room and she saw the queen sitting there on a raised platform made out of jade. At least Nadeem would shut up now. About twenty ivory snakes lined the edges of the room. As Nadeem led them closer to the queen, Zardi had to suppress a shudder as she realized that the platform was not made of jade but was actually alive with the wriggling mass of hundreds of tiny green snakes. They curled around the silver throne like scaly adornments.

"Thank you, Nadeem," the queen said as they stopped in front of her. Satyan slithered up the throne to stand at her side. "You may leave now."

Nadeem hesitated. "My queen, I'm your advisor. How am I to advise if I don't know what's going on?"

"Do not be so preposterous," the queen retorted. "Of course, you've been helpful, but your usefulness has almost run its course. You're lucky I haven't put you in the prison with the rest of your friends. Continue to annoy me and I'll do just that."

"But—"

"No buts. GET OUT."

Fighting to hold back tears, Nadeem turned on his heel and stalked out of the throne room.

The queen fixed her unblinking gaze on the three of them.

"Tomorrow is a momentous day. My flying machine will be finished and I'll begin my journey to the Black

Isle." She looked at Rhidan and Zardi and rose to her full height. "I'll be needing the Windrose."

"We haven't got it," Zardi said swiftly.

"Turn out your pockets," the queen said calmly. "I know one of you has it."

"We haven't got anything," Rhidan said firmly. "Why do you want to kill the sorcerers on the Black Isle anyway?"

The queen grimaced. "This really is getting tiresome." She clicked her fingers at Satyan, and the snake struck out, wrapping his length around Khalila's chest.

"Release me," Khalila commanded imperiously.

"Tell me, djinni," the queen demanded. "Which of you has the Windrose?"

"You may have my magic," Khalila rasped, "but I am the master of my own tongue."

"Hmm, perhaps Satyan can squeeze the answer out of you. Without your magic, you'll have bones that can break." The queen clicked at Satyan again, and the snake tightened its length about the djinni.

The sound of cracking ribs reverberated around the underground cavern walls, and Khalila let out a pained cry.

"Stop it, please!" Zardi said, flinching at the expression of agony that crossed the djinni's face.

"Then turn out your pockets," the queen repeated softly. "Both of you."

Zardi slipped her hand into her trouser pocket, the warmth of the Windrose brushing her fingertips. She placed it next to the amulet, which Rhidan had also put on the floor. The Windrose's ring of rubies glinted in the light of the chamber, making the amulet with its silver snakes and purple stone look positively dull in comparison.

"Let Khalila go," Rhidan demanded. "We've done as you've asked."

But the queen did not appear to hear at first. Her face was strangely masklike and she couldn't seem to take her eyes away from the objects in front of her.

"Let her go," he said again more forcefully.

The queen jolted out of her trance and hissed a command at Satyan. Zardi once again understood her word: *STOP.*

The red and gold snake leisurely uncoiled his length and released Khalila. She fell to the ground with a groan. The snake's fierce hiss filled Zardi's head with images of what it wanted to do to them. Zardi wondered why she could understand the queen's hissed commands as words but not Satyan's? Maybe serpents were just too different from other creatures, and their thoughts were impulses not words.

Zardi knelt by Khalila's side. "Are you all right?"

"Sure. Just give me a moment to catch my breath," the djinni said defiantly.

Zardi wanted to believe Khalila, but the way she was holding her side told a different story. She helped the djinni to her feet.

"Where did you get this?" The queen's voice was trembling, and Zardi looked up to see her slither forward and pick up the amulet.

"From my pocket," Rhidan replied.

"I suppose you think you're funny, you annoying little worm." The queen's voice was now steady. "I'll ask you again. Where did you get this?"

"My father gave it to me," Rhidan replied.

"Your father?" The queen started to laugh.

"Yes, my father!" Rhidan snapped. "I don't see what's so funny."

The queen traced the interlocked snakes of the amulet gently, turning it over in her hands. She stopped as she read the inscription on the back of the amulet. "So he didn't want you either."

Either? Zardi shared a confused look with Khalila.

Rhidan's face flooded with angry color. "It's got nothing to do with you."

"Oh, but it has." The queen looked at him. "You see, Iridial is my creator. And it looks as though he wanted you just as much as he wanted me."

31

The Sorcerer's Creation

Rhidan's knees sagged. He looked as if he might faint or scream but did neither. "You're lying." Rhidan raggedly wiped his sleeve across his face. "Give me back my amulet."

"Your amulet?" She came close, her fetid breath choking them. "I was there when he forged it. This talisman was my creator's key to all of his spells." She read the inscription again and sniffed the amulet. "There's no magic in this. Did he not even keep that promise?"

Zardi remembered how Rhidan had used the magic from the amulet on the brass rider, but she wasn't about to tell the queen that. "What was a sorcerer from the Black Isle doing here?" she asked instead. A disturbing thought occurred to her as she glanced over at Khalila and thought of the djinni's prison in the volcano and its emerald key. Had Iridial built the brass rider; had he imprisoned Khalila? "Did Iridial create the brass giant?" she asked.

The queen glared at her. "Brass giant?"

"Yes, the huge metal thing that was guarding this island," Zardi said.

The queen shook her head impatiently. "That thing was not built in my creator's workshop. I have no idea where it came from, but if I did, why should I tell you?"

"Well, tell me why my father was on this island," Rhidan said. "If he really created you, tell me."

The queen looked at him with something akin to fondness in her eyes. "I'm going to do you a favor, son of Iridial. I'm going to give you the answers you crave because I appreciate what it is like not to know. This will be my only kindness."

Rhidan nodded.

"My creator settled here to do his experiments," the queen began.

"Experiments?" Rhidan asked. "What experiments?"

"Iridial is a great inventor and an even greater sorcerer. He traveled all over the world collecting spells and adding them to his collection of enchantments. He studied the three main forms of magic—Fitra, Alama, and Kanate; learned, channeled, and innate—and was consumed with the idea of creating an elixir that would increase a sorcerer's ability to harness magic from nature."

"Impossible," Khalila interrupted.

"Once upon a time, maybe," the queen conceded. "But my creator discovered that a snake's venom, when combined with other magical components, could produce a powerful elixir that allowed a sorcerer to channel an infinite stream of magic from nature. He bred many types of snakes, but the only venom that worked was extremely poisonous. Even a drop too much could kill. He needed to find a way to make the venom safer. That's why I was created."

"I don't understand." Rhidan's hunger for more knowledge was apparent in every line of his body.

"Iridial hypothesized that if he fused his blood with the blood of a snake, he could create a new type of snake whose venom would not be poisonous to sorcerers."

"And you're the result?" Zardi asked in amazement.

"I am far more than a result," the queen hissed. "I am perfection."

The queen's long forked tongue snaked out, and she licked her thin lips. "He was horrified at first, of course. He didn't want to create a creature like me, a being that could talk and think for itself. He just wanted a snake from which he could extract venom. But he made peace with this and we were happy for a while. I even helped him with his experiments."

"Where is he?" Rhidan demanded. "What happened to him?"

"Once Iridial finally perfected the elixir, he decided to return to the Black Isle and share his knowledge with his people. He asked me to look after his workshop and guard his research and serpents. He said he would come back for me. But he never did. My only companions were my dear snakes." Her smile was sharp. "I've learned much from Iridial's books and notes. The moment Nadeem told me of the Windrose I knew my destiny. Now I will find Iridial and kill him and the others that would dare to breed snakes for their own selfish wants. I may not have magic, but I can do well enough with the inventions he left behind, like the spelltrap." She hurled the amulet at Rhidan, who caught it in midair. "This thing is the past." She looked down at the Windrose. "This is the future."

"It is not yours to take," Zardi warned, but the queen ignored her and grabbed the Windrose.

Her scream was piercing as the magical object seared her hand. She dropped it and staggered back.

Satyan was at her side in an instant. He slithered back and forth in front of his queen, as if to protect her from the enemy he couldn't see or hope to understand.

Zardi scooped the Windrose off the ground. "Like I said, it is not yours to take. I am the keeper of the Windrose and I am the only one who can withstand its heat or make it work."

The queen cradled her hand, her eyes streaming with angry tears.

"Perhaps I should get Satyan to kill you right now," she gasped out. "You wouldn't be the keeper of the Windrose then."

Zardi held her face in a portrait of disinterest. The queen had no idea how close she was to the truth. If she died, the next person to touch the Windrose would become the keeper.

"The Windrose would be useless if Zardi died," Rhidan said. "Only she can use it."

"Fine, she comes with me."

"Never," Zardi spat. "I won't help you kill innocent people."

"Then you sentence yourself to death with your crewmates."

"Please!" The word sounded misshapen coming out of Rhidan's mouth. "Please spare them."

She shook her head. "I made a promise to my snakes: sailors' flesh. They have been very patient." She grinned. "I think it's time you all get back to work. NADEEM!"

There was the sound of hurried footsteps.

"Yes, my queen?" Nadeem bowed, his face stony.

"Take these three to the prison."

"Yes, my queen."

"Then fetch Sinbad so that he can join me for dinner. Give him a little of the draft if he becomes unruly."

They've been drugging him, Zardi realized with horror. *That's why Sinbad has not come for us.*

"Yes, my queen." Nadeem stood there for a second, looking unsure.

"Well, what are you waiting for?" the queen hissed. "Be gone, I have much to prepare." She looked at Zardi. "We leave tomorrow morning. Be ready to direct me to the Black Isle or I will kill you and then ensure that your friends suffer even more painful deaths than necessary."

Zardi glared at the queen. She needed time to think. Her eyes dropped to the spelltrap that hung from the queen's belt. Khalila's magic. It was their last hope.

Almost as if Satyan could read her mind, the snake moved closer to his queen's side, protectively.

Now is not the moment to strike, Zardi thought. *But I will. I'll find the queen's chamber and steal the spelltrap while she sleeps.* The plan beyond that was still shadowy, but she knew one thing. *I'll need help.* Her eyes fixed on Nadeem.

Silently, they followed him from the throne room and into the long corridor that led to the prison. Satyan followed once again at the back of the line.

Nadeem no longer bragged or crowed about his status as the queen's advisor. As they walked, he looked shrunken somehow.

But will he help me? Zardi wondered. *He has to! Time is running out and I'm all out of options.*

"I need you to distract Satyan," she told Rhidan and Khalila in a whisper.

"Follow my lead." Rhidan dropped to the ground and began scrabbling around in the dirt. "Where is it?" he wailed. "Where's my amulet?" Satyan was at his side instantly, hissing furiously.

Nadeem looked back. "What's going on down there?"

Zardi ran to his side. "Rhidan's lost his amulet."

"Tell him to stop being so pathetic," Nadeem snapped. "He's not the first person to lose something. Better just to forget it."

"It doesn't have to be that way." Zardi grabbed onto his words like a drowning person. "Sometimes we can save what we thought was lost. Just like you can save the crew."

Nadeem pinched the bridge of his nose. "How many times do I have to say it? They're not in danger."

"Not in danger? Once the queen's machine is finished, she's going to feed the crew to her snakes. She said so."

"She doesn't mean it. She's just trying to scare you."

"Nadeem, she's going to kill them. Believe me, please. You're the only one that can help us get out of here."

Nadeem pushed his hands through his thick black

hair, looking over at Satyan, who was circling Rhidan menacingly. Rhidan was raking his fingers through the dirt like a person possessed.

Khalila suddenly pointed to a far corner and cried out. "Over there! I just saw something catch the light."

"You know, I never wanted any of this to happen." Nadeem's voice was papery thin. "I was just trying to keep everyone safe. It's such a mess and I don't know how to put it right."

"You can put it right," Zardi told him. "We both can. You just need to leave the door to the prison unlocked and I'll do the rest."

Nadeem's eyes flickered with fear. "I'll get caught." He looked over nervously at Satyan, who had followed Rhidan over to the corner and was making impatient hissing noises.

"Just put us back in our cell and then pretend to lock the door behind you. How are the snakes going to know the difference?" Zardi replied calmly. "But first, tell me where the queen sleeps."

"Why?" Nadeem asked.

Zardi hesitated. Could she really trust Nadeem? *Trust is the friend of trust.* Zubeyda's words came to her suddenly. "I'm going to take the spelltrap from the queen while she's asleep," she revealed. "If Khalila has her magic back she can fix all of this."

Nadeem swiftly checked that Satyan was still occupied with Rhidan before speaking. "Tonight, wait until you hear the guards on the door fall asleep, then turn right at the top of the tunnel where your cell is," he said in a whisper. "Follow it until it branches into two. Take the left branch. You're looking for the second door along. That's the queen's chamber."

"Thanks, Nadeem."

"Promise me one thing," he said after a long moment.

"What?"

"Don't leave me behind, all right?"

"I won't."

Nadeem turned toward Rhidan and Satyan. "Enough!" he hollered. "Rhidan, get off your knees and get moving."

Zardi gave her friend the tiniest of nods to show that the need for a distraction was over. He scrambled to his feet and dusted himself off, stopping as he reached his pockets.

"Can you believe it?" Rhidan said, pulling out the amulet. "It was here the whole time!"

Satyan gave a hiss of annoyance and Nadeem took

Rhidan roughly by his arm. "Come on. It's time to take you back to your cell."

They fell into line again with Nadeem leading the group. As they walked into the tunnel that housed the prison, Zardi peered all the way down the snake-filled passageway. At the end of it—give or take a few twists and turns—was the queen's chamber. Tonight she would be visiting.

"Here we are." Nadeem held open the cell door and they filed inside. "Good-bye," he said from the doorway.

"Good riddance, more like," Rhidan muttered under his breath. Khalila sat down with a sigh, clutching her side.

"Good-bye, Nadeem," Zardi replied.

The door closed.

The key jiggled in the lock.

And Zardi breathed a sigh of relief as it failed to make a full turn. Nadeem had kept his promise.

"So, how was the meeting with the queen?" Ali asked.

Zardi turned and saw all of the crew standing there next to the flying machine, their faces hungry for information.

"Let's just say it was full of surprises," Rhidan said tersely.

"Did you see Sinbad?" Tariq asked eagerly.

Zardi shook her head but told them that, from what she could make out, Sinbad had not abandoned them but had been drugged in some way.

"So what did the queen want?" Zain asked.

"Me," Zardi replied. "She wants me to use the Windrose to direct her to the Black Isle."

"What about the rest of us?" Mirzani asked.

"She's going to let you all go tomorrow," Zardi lied smoothly. She felt awful about not telling her friends the truth, but panic made people stupid. If they knew about the queen's plan, and that the door was unlocked, they'd probably flee down the tunnel only to be met by the snakes.

Rhidan frowned at her, his eyes demanding answers, but Zardi wouldn't give them to him, not while the others listened. Keeping the secret meant keeping them alive.

32

The Sleeping Sailor

"How's Khalila?" Zardi asked, her back resting against the stone wall.

"In a lot of pain, but she's sleeping now." Rhidan crouched down beside Zardi. "Are you going to tell me why you lied to everyone and said that the queen will be letting us go tomorrow?" He peered at her hard. "And what were you speaking to Nadeem about?"

"I'm going to get Khalila's magic back," Zardi said and quickly explained her plan.

Rhidan's cheeks flushed with excitement. "What are we waiting for? Let's go."

"I'm not risking your life," she said firmly. "One of us can do it."

"It is not your choice to make. I've just found out that my father is some kind of crazed inventor who created a snake woman," her friend replied. "On top of that, Khalila told me that it was probably my amulet that drew us to this island in the first place. Apparently, magical objects have a way of being drawn back to the place where they were forged." He grimaced. "This is my mess. I'm coming with you."

Zardi studied her friend. His jaw was set determinedly. There was to be no arguing with him. Secretly, she was relieved that she wouldn't be alone.

As the sailors finally went to their room to sleep, Zardi and Rhidan crept over to the door and waited until the sound of the guards' even breathing could be heard. "It's time," Rhidan whispered.

Zardi gently pulled the door open. The width of the two sleeping snakes blocked the doorway. Taking a deep breath, she and Rhidan stepped over the bodies.

Leaving the prison behind, they bolted down the tunnel and didn't stop until they turned the corner. They gulped down mouthfuls of dank air. The way ahead split into two paths. Zardi pointed to the left branch. "The queen's chamber is this way."

They edged forward. Rhidan froze and pointed to a heavily breathing snake that hung from the ceiling. Its eyes were wide open and it was staring straight at them. A spasm of fear went through Zardi.

Calm down, she told herself. *Snakes don't have eyelids.* "It's asleep," she whispered.

The tunnel sloped downward, and when it leveled off, they spotted a wooden door set into the wall. A warm golden light eked out from beneath it. Some way beyond was a second door that stood in complete darkness. *The queen's chamber.* Zardi stopped still as an echo reached her. "Can you hear that?"

Rhidan cocked his head and then all color bled from his face. "Snakes!"

Zardi's stomach twisted. It wasn't just snakes. She could hear the queen's hissing voice reeling off orders. The voice was still far away, but it was getting closer. Her knees felt hollow. Her plan to steal the spelltrap while the queen was sleeping was unraveling like a ball of twine falling through the air. . . .

"The queen is coming," she mouthed to Rhidan. She pointed to the door just ahead of them. "In there, now!"

They pushed the door open and slipped into the dimly lit room. The coiled tension in Zardi's muscles relaxed as she looked around. The chamber was empty except for a wooden chest in one corner, and a grand-looking bed with a large stone chair beside it.

The lamps that hung from the ceiling spluttered gently, and they heard the slight rise and fall of breath that came with sleep.

Zardi and Rhidan stepped closer to the bed. It was surrounded by gauzy drapes, woven from golden thread that revealed the silhouette of someone sleeping. Gently parting the veil, they both looked down at the slumbering figure. *Sinbad.*

His face appeared peaceful at first, and Zardi felt a flash of annoyance that he could be so serene while his crew slept in a stone prison, locked up like animals. But as she peered closer, she noticed lines around his eyes and mouth that had not been there before. His face looked waxen and drawn. Zardi reached out to touch the captain's shoulder but Rhidan stopped her.

"She's outside the door," he hissed. "We've got to hide."

Zardi's eyes quickly took in the room. "You hide behind the chest and I'll take the chair."

Rhidan gripped her hand. "Be safe." He dived behind the chest.

Zardi ducked behind the stone chair just as the door to the chamber opened. Peeping from her hiding place, she saw the queen sweep in, accompanied by four ivory snakes. The serpents remained by the door but the queen headed straight to the bed and firmly pulled aside the drapes.

"Wake up, my darling," the queen entreated, stroking Sinbad's cheek. "We need to talk." But the captain continued to sleep.

With a polite cough Nadeem stepped into the room.

"What do you want?" the queen asked curtly.

"My queen, you really should get some rest. You haven't slept at all."

"Can't you see I'm busy?"

"Yes, my queen, but he won't awaken. You'd need to brand him with a red-hot iron."

The queen hissed angrily. "How much sleeping draft did you give him?"

"The whole flask," Nadeem answered nervously. "He was demanding to see the crew again. He wouldn't calm down."

"You're useless!" the queen screamed. "Leave us."

Nadeem left, his head bowed.

The queen turned to the ivory snakes and ordered them to do a patrol of the tunnels. The snakes slithered out of the room, the door closing with a thud behind them.

Zardi crouched lower in her hiding place as the queen sank into the chair next to the bed, the spelltrap swinging from her belt.

"The flying machine is finished," the queen said to the sleeping captain. "And I will fly at first light." She gave a little sigh. "I'm loath to leave you, but I've been waiting for this moment a very long time. I found the plans for the machine right here in this chamber, Iridial's old workshop." She took Sinbad's hand into her own. "Destiny brought you to this island, my love, so that your crew could build my glider. Once I get my revenge on the Black Isle, I will come back to you." She squeezed his hand. "Your men will be dead by then, and you will be angry, but in time you will forget and we will be happy."

Zardi listened as the queen continued to talk to Sinbad, outlining their future together. Eventually, though, her words began to blur and tumble into each other and the queen dozed off.

A shock of silver hair popped up from behind the chest. "She's asleep," Rhidan whispered. "Get the spell-trap. I'll listen at the door."

The queen was snoring as Zardi reached out from behind the chair, straining for the spelltrap. Trying to keep her hand steady, Zardi placed her thumb and forefinger on the clip that linked the spelltrap to the queen's belt and gently began to press it open.

The queen muttered something in her sleep and shifted in her seat, pulling the clip from Zardi's fingers.

Zardi pursed her lips, trapping a swear word she'd learned on the *Falcon*.

A movement glimpsed out of the corner of her eye made her look up. Rhidan had his ear to the door and was waving urgently at her. "Something's coming," he mouthed.

Zardi looked down at the spelltrap. She was so close! Her hand reached for the clip again.

"Get down!" Rhidan's voice was low but sharp. He dropped to the ground and rolled under the bed. Zardi slipped back behind the chair just as the chamber door crashed open.

Satyan slithered in, accompanied by Nadeem and six large ivory snakes.

The red and gold snake raised his head, as if sniffing the air for something. *Can snakes smell?* Zardi wondered desperately.

Satyan glided forward and hissed loudly in the queen's ear. She awoke with a start.

"I can't believe I fell asleep," the queen hissed to Satyan, her voice blurry and thick. The snake hissed something, and Zardi's mind was filled with images of herself, Rhidan, and the crew of the *Falcon,* their faces pinched with fear. The queen rose from her chair.

"Are you sure that everyone and everything is where it should be?" the queen asked. "I cannot afford any mistakes. We're too close."

Satyan hissed again.

"Nadeem," Zardi heard the queen say, "Satyan tells me that you checked the prison and that everyone has been accounted for."

"That's right, my queen." Nadeem's voice betrayed no hint of his deception.

"And how did my flying machine look?"

"Perfect, my queen. When I went to collect it from the prison only the shipmaster was awake. He was putting the final touches to it."

Zardi frowned. The machine had been finished earlier that evening. *What had Musty been doing to it?*

"And have you taken it to the launch point?" the queen continued.

"It's in position, ready for tomorrow."

The Queen of the Serpents clapped her hands like an excited child. "Then we're one step closer to executing my plan." She paused. "Our work is not finished, though. I must blend the plague that I will take to the Black Isle."

She went to Nadeem and stroked him under the chin. "You've been most helpful and will be rewarded. Tomorrow, once I'm gone, some rather unpleasant things are going to happen to your crewmates. I have given orders that you are to be spared, but if you try to interfere you will be killed. Understand?"

Nadeem nodded.

"Good, and make sure you look after Sinbad." The queen looked fondly at the captain before slithering out of the door, the snakes and Nadeem following behind her.

Zardi watched, sickened, as the spelltrap, their last hope, left her sight.

33

The Falcon's Cry

Zardi's whole body shook. "What are we going to do? The spelltrap's gone!"

"I don't know." Rhidan's face was pale. He looked over at Sinbad on the bed. "Maybe he'll have some ideas." He shook the captain's shoulder roughly, but Sinbad did not stir.

Zardi rubbed her face, hard. She needed to feel something. She needed to start thinking. "That's not going to work," she said wearily. "Don't you remember? Nadeem said you'd need a hot iron to wake him."

Rhidan's expression was thoughtful. "We have the Windrose."

Zardi took it out and looked at it uncertainly.

"Give him the lightest of touches," Rhidan said firmly.

Zardi took a breath and touched the Windrose to Sinbad's bare arm. The captain let out a surprised gasp of pain.

"Sorry, Captain." Rhidan put a finger to his lips. "We had to wake you."

Sinbad sat up, rubbing at the red welt that had sprung up on his arm. He had lost a lot of weight, and Zardi tried not to stare at the bones that she could see under his skin. Sinbad, who'd always seemed so strong and capable, now looked like a fragile bird.

"I can't believe you're really alive." Sinbad's voice was croaky. "Nadeem told me that you'd come back, but I didn't trust his words. How could I? He betrayed us all."

"He said he didn't mean for any of this to happen." Zardi slipped the Windrose into her pocket. "He's the one who helped us get out of our cell."

"And then you came to free me?" Sinbad said.

"Um, actually we came to try to steal the queen's spelltrap," Rhidan explained. "There's a lot you don't know."

"Then tell me," Sinbad insisted and Zardi could hear a trace of the old authority in his voice.

As briefly as possible, Zardi and Rhidan told Sinbad all that had happened since they'd seen him last.

"We thought that if we could get the spelltrap and give Khalila back her magic, she would be able to get us all out of this place," Rhidan finished.

"But the queen does not intend to sleep again tonight," Sinbad murmured.

"That's right," Zardi said. "We need a new plan and we were hoping you could help."

Sinbad snorted. "Look at me." He held out his bony arms. "I'm as weak as a babe in swaddling. Every time I stand my legs feel like dough."

"How did this happen?" Rhidan asked.

Sinbad shook his head. "I had the run of the place at first. Like a favorite pet. I found an abandoned tunnel that led me to an unguarded exit next to a volcano. I began to look for a way to get my crew out, but she must have gotten suspicious because she started drugging my food. I'd pass out for hours at a time, sometimes days." The captain rubbed at the burn on his arm. "For a long time, I stopped eating or drinking so that she and Nadeem couldn't drug me, but then I got weak and had to eat again." He hung his head. "I've let everyone down."

"No, you haven't," Zardi insisted. "But your men do need you. Tomorrow the queen is leaving and her snakes will slaughter your crew. We need to get them out of here."

"The abandoned exit!" Some of the old fire returned to Sinbad's eyes.

"We could go now and sneak everyone out while the snakes are asleep," Rhidan said excitedly. "The ship is practically finished. If we can get them off this island they'll be fine."

"We can't forget Nadeem. He helped us," Zardi said firmly.

"We won't." Sinbad threw his long legs over the side of the bed and stood up. He swayed dizzily, and Zardi and Rhidan reached out to steady him. They exchanged a worried glance.

Sinbad threw off their arms impatiently. "I'll be fine. Let's go."

They cracked open the door and saw that all was

clear. As quickly as Sinbad's legs would allow, they headed down the tunnel toward the prison.

Suddenly, something large, red, and gold dropped from the ceiling in front of them.

Satyan.

He gave a high-pitched hiss, so piercing it forced Zardi, Rhidan, and Sinbad to their knees. Out of every crevice and hole in the walls, a tide of snakes filled the darkness.

Zardi, Rhidan, and Sinbad staggered to their feet. Standing back-to-back they were ready to fight, but the serpents did not attack. They were waiting for someone.

The queen did not leave them waiting for long. The army of snakes parted as she glided toward Sinbad, her face twisted with fury.

Satyan hissed something at her, and she nodded before he slithered away.

The queen's gaze moved over to the captain. "And where did you think you were going?"

"My sweet, I have no idea," Sinbad replied, with real dread and confusion in his voice. "They came to me while I was asleep and dragged me out of my bed. I could not stop them. I was far too weak."

The queen frowned, weighing his words.

Sweat trickled down between Zardi's shoulder blades. Sinbad couldn't afford to lose the queen's favor. It was the only card they still had. But would the queen believe him?

Sinbad held out his arm where the angry red welt was still visible. "Look what they did to me," he practically sobbed out. "They told me they would do the same to my face unless I went with them." He pouted sadly. "They hate me for leaving them in that prison. They all do. I can never go back to being their captain." He looked at her with big eyes. "They wanted to ransom me to you for the freedom of the crew."

His last words cracked through the queen's reserve and she slithered forward and caressed Sinbad's cheek. "I couldn't bear it if they had done anything to you."

Sinbad turned his face and kissed her scaly fingers. "I'm just so grateful that you saved me from them." For a second Zardi was reminded of that dashing sailor in Taraket, the actor who convinced a crowd of people that he had fought a mighty beast and had real treasure on his ship.

The queen beamed with pleasure at Sinbad's words and brought him to her side. "I will protect you from them. They'll be taken back to their prison. You'll never have to see them again."

"Let me go!" a panicked voice cried. Zardi turned to see Nadeem coming down the passageway, being led by Satyan. A large ivory snake was wrapped around his arms and chest.

"Ah, the little traitor has finally joined us."

"I'm no traitor, my queen," Nadeem rasped.

"So, how is it that these two are free?"

"I'm not sure, my queen." Nadeem groaned as the ivory snake squeezed his body.

Sinbad took the queen's hand and stroked her palm. "My sweet, Nadeem has been a loyal helper to me. I cannot believe that he would betray you and let these two go free. Believe me, there is no love lost between them."

"Well, how did they get out?" the queen demanded.

Sinbad interlocked their fingers. "Perhaps he accidentally left the door unlocked. These things happen."

The queen narrowed her eyes. "Then that makes him a fool if not a traitor. Regardless, he's going to prison with the rest of them."

"My queen, please—"

The queen shook her head.

Nadeem turned to Sinbad. "Captain, don't let them put me in the cell," he pleaded. "She's going to kill the crew."

Sinbad looked at Nadeem coldly. "The ship is dead to me, and so are all those that served on it." His gaze swung over all of them. "The *Falcon*'s cry is now silent."

Zardi felt chilled despite herself. She knew Sinbad was acting, but his words held a note of intensity. She suddenly remembered him explaining why he'd chosen a falcon as the namesake of his ship. He'd said that the falcon was fiercely loyal and could never be silenced. That it would fight for its master until its last breath. Despite everything, Zardi had to stop a grin from tugging at her lips. Sinbad was giving them a message. He would be coming for them.

"Captain, please," Nadeem wailed.

"Silence him." At the queen's command, Nadeem's mouth was covered by the snake that encircled his chest.

Sinbad sighed. "I want to go to my chamber."

"We'll go in a moment," the queen trilled. "I will put these little annoyances into their cell first."

The queen let forth a series of orders. The meaning was clear: *Remove them*. The snakes charged at Zardi,

Rhidan, and Nadeem, taking their legs out from under them. They fell backward onto a carpet of scaly skin. Moving as one, the serpents carried them along the tunnel and into their cell, tossing them onto the hard prison floor. The door then slammed shut, the key turning fully in the lock.

"I can't believe he abandoned us." Nadeem clutched his arms around his legs.

Zardi ignored him and put her ear to the door. The faint breathing of the two snakes guarding the prison was audible but all else was silent. She turned to Nadeem. "He hasn't abandoned us. All that talk about the falcon was a code. He's coming back."

There was a cough behind them, and Zardi turned to see Khalila and Musty coming out of the shadows. Behind them stood the whole crew of the *Falcon*.

"You didn't get the spelltrap," the djinni stated flatly.

Rhidan's mouth dropped open. "How did you know we even went to get it?"

Khalila smiled grimly. "I may not have my magic, but I've been alive for a long time. I know human nature." She folded her arms. "Time has also taught me another lesson. Always have a plan B."

Plan B

"Khalila told us what the queen has in store for us, and we're not just going to sit around waiting to be eaten," Zain said. "Tomorrow morning we're going to bust out of this place." He picked up one of the heavy tools that they had used to build the flying machine and slapped it against his hands. There were whoops and growls of agreement from the others.

"They'll rip you to shreds," Zardi said, imagining

this tired and weak crew going up against the tightly honed skills of the queen's killer snakes.

"Wait, it's not such a crazy idea," Rhidan said. "Not if you couple it with Sinbad's abandoned tunnel."

"Sinbad?" Musty asked. "What of him? Is he all right?"

Rhidan quickly told them about their meeting with the captain and his promise to come back for them.

Nadeem held out a golden key. "We can get out of here easy enough, but even if we fight our way through to the tunnel and get outside, the snakes will hunt us down before we get to the *Falcon*. You have no idea how fast they are."

"No, you're the one who knows everything about the snakes." Tariq glowered at Nadeem. "They're your friends."

"Nadeem is in this prison and is under threat just like the rest of us." Khalila's voice cut across Tariq's. "Besides, he's right, the snakes are fast, but that's where the second part of plan B comes in."

"There's another part?" Zardi stared in wonder at the djinni.

Khalila nodded. "But its success lies solely on your shoulders, Zardi."

"Go on," she replied.

"You need to leave with the queen tomorrow on the flying machine. And as soon as you can, you must dispose of her—but not before you get the spelltrap."

"What do you mean, 'dispose'?"

"I've put a lever to the left of the glider's holding bar," Musty explained. "The lever will collapse the wings of the machine and unhook the harness. This gives you the chance to lose the queen. You'll have the element of surprise on your side. If you pull the lever again the wings will extend themselves, but you'll have to hook the harness back on yourself."

"Whatever happens tomorrow, you need to be on the left-hand side of that machine," Khalila added. "Choose your moment, defeat the queen, and grab the spelltrap." Khalila stared at her hard. "Then come back to us."

"But if you've left the prison, how will I find you?" Zardi asked.

"Use the Windrose," the djinni replied. "Call on the element of air. Then just imagine us and fix us in your head. The wind will come and guide you."

Zardi let the words sink in. Already she was thinking of the place where she would try to dispose of the queen, but as she gazed into the hopeful faces of the crew, she couldn't help but feel scared. There were so many things that could go wrong. "What do you think?" she murmured to Rhidan.

"I think this is our only choice," Rhidan said softly. "You must defeat the queen, whatever it takes."

"I'll do it." Zardi looked around at the faces she knew so well. Her throat tightened. Some would fall tomorrow, of that there could be no doubt. But they had chosen to fight, and those snakes had no idea what was about to hit them.

No one slept much that night. Instead they busied themselves creating weapons. Some used the materials they had left from building the flying machine. Others sharpened rocks and sticks to a fine point. Rhidan even fashioned more arrows for Zardi's bow.

When the key turned in the lock, the crew of the *Falcon* scurried to hide their weapons.

The door opened and the queen slithered in. As always, Satyan was at her side and a ring of ivory snakes surrounded her. The queen was resplendent in silver armor. Her silver belt was heavy with various objects including a black bottle that hung beside the spelltrap. Zardi wondered if this was the plague of which she'd heard the queen speak.

"It is time to go." The queen's unblinking gaze fixed on Zardi.

Zardi lowered her head as if in defeat.

"My queen." Nadeem threw himself to the ground in front of her. "Please, I don't want to die. I'll do anything." He looked around desperately. "They're going to try to escape. They have a plan. See, I am still loyal to you."

"Why, you—" Rhidan leapt toward Nadeem, but the queen's laugh stopped him.

"I am not interested in this worm's information, Rhidan." She looked out at the crew. "Please feel free to try to escape. My snakes much prefer to hunt before a feast. But I wager that you won't get far."

She turned to leave the room but stopped as if she'd forgotten something. She turned back and stared at Rhidan. "Farewell, Iridial's son. I'll say hello to your father for you. Just before I kill him." She smiled and then exited the cell. The prison was now silent except for the sound of Nadeem sobbing.

Zardi's eyes met Rhidan's. "You can do this," he said.

"So can you," she whispered back. Hugging him, she quickly followed the queen while her legs still allowed her.

As the queen locked the door, a crazy thought tickled

the back of Zardi's mind. The snakes wouldn't be able to operate that lock and get into the cell. Had the queen been playing games with them all this time?

"What are you smiling about?" the queen hissed.

"I misjudged you," Zardi said. "Your snakes can't unlock the door. You have no intention of feeding my friends to them."

The queen's whole body trembled. For a moment Zardi thought it was with sorrow, but then she saw mirth scuttle across her enemy's face.

"What a ridiculous idea," the queen snorted. "The snakes have no use for keys. When the time comes they will simply smash through the prison door with their heads."

Hate blistered Zardi's insides. She'd thought this creature capable of kindness. She wouldn't make that mistake again.

Their walk through the network of tunnels was brisk, and Zardi had to run to keep up. Coiled snakes lay watching them as they raced past. Finally, they came to a narrow, steep passageway and each step took them closer to the bright outside.

Light scalded Zardi's sensitive eyes as they emerged from the hole, forcing them shut. She opened them again, this time slowly. They were on top of a steep, grassy hill, and the flying machine stood waiting. "Where are we?" Zardi asked.

"The southeastern tip of the island," the queen replied. "This is the tallest peak, barring the volcano. We'll need the height to get air under the wings. We'll sink like a stone otherwise."

"You seem to know a lot about this," Zardi said.

The queen looked down at the island laid out below them. "I've had ample time to read Iridial's notes and learn how to fly this machine."

Satyan hissed something and the queen laughed. "He is eager to get to the cell. He's worried that the others will start without him."

Zardi balled up her hands. "Let's go."

The queen whispered something to Satyan and kissed the serpent's head before he disappeared into the tunnel. Beckoning Zardi to follow her, the queen slithered over to the glider and positioned herself on the left-hand side of the machine.

Khalila's words echoed loudly in Zardi's head. *Make sure you get the left-hand side of the glider.* "Actually, I need to be on that side."

The queen looked at her scornfully. "Why?"

She shrugged. "I like to be on the left when it comes to travel. My grandmother always told me it is good luck."

The queen's face twisted with suspicion. "What game are you playing?"

"No game. We don't even know if this glider-thing is going to work; we might need all the luck we can get." She blew a lock of hair out of her eye. "If I'm worrying about being on the wrong side, the Windrose won't work. It's your choice."

The queen slid over. "Fine."

Zardi ducked under the wings of the flying machine and took her position behind the holding bar. She quickly slipped the leather harness that hung from the top of the frame over her head and around her midriff.

The queen did the same. "Right. On my count, push off this hill as quickly as possible. Three, two, one."

The queen swiftly slithered forward and Zardi ran alongside her. They pushed off and the glider jolted off the precipice, dipping dangerously.

This is never going to work, Zardi thought with horror as she felt the wind whistle past her ears. *We're going to die.* But then, amazingly, the air was caught and swelled beneath the wings, sending the glider surging upward.

"We're airborne!" the queen screeched. She looked over at Zardi. "Now to the Black Isle. Which way?"

Holding on to the bar of the glider with one hand, Zardi took the Windrose from her pocket. She thought of a gust of wind and then fixed in her mind the image of the trees with the silky explosion of leaves she'd seen the night the Rocs saved her from the valley of diamonds. The leaves would tangle the queen up and leave her trapped. Out loud she said, "I want to go to the Black Isle." Excitement spurted through her as a gust suddenly sprang up, steering them westward. *It really works.* "We go with the wind," Zardi explained.

They traveled in silence, a gentle wind directing them across the island with faint pushes and tugs. Zardi's heart sped up. There, in the distance, were the specter-white web leaves, stretched out between the branches of a cluster of massive trees.

The queen tensed beside her. "This is Roc territory." She scanned the horizon. "We'll need to get through here as quickly as possible."

Zardi's hand crept toward Musty's lever. They were directly above the silken webs now. Gripping the holding bar tightly with her right hand, she pulled the lever hard with her left. Her whole body dropped as the harness gave way and the wings collapsed, almost folding in half.

The queen gave a high-pitched scream as she flopped downward. Her hand slipped off the bar, and she was left dangling by five fingertips. They plummeted toward the web-laden trees. Zardi swung toward the queen, fingers reaching out to seize the spelltrap from the silver belt. The queen hissed, arching her body back so that it was out of reach.

The webs were just a few arm spans away now, their billowy width ready to receive them. *The queen was supposed to get caught in the webs,* Zardi thought. *Not me.*

She yanked on the lever and the wings extended themselves again. Air hit the feathered arcs, pushing them upward.

At the same moment, the queen hauled herself up, both hands now back on the bar. "I don't know what you did to my machine," she snarled. "But you'll pay." She lashed out with her tail, hitting Zardi full in her stomach.

The machine spun wildly in the sky, tumbling away from the silk canopies.

The queen got ready to strike again, but Zardi was quicker. She swung her body forward and grabbed the queen's belt with her right hand. She pulled, but the metal links of the belt held firm. A violent spasm went through her right hand as sudden strength coursed through it. A metal link snapped and Zardi swiped the belt away and slung it around her neck.

What happened to my hand? Zardi asked herself even as her joy at getting the spelltrap chased the question out of her head.

The queen gave an awful scream of rage and opened her mouth wider than any human ever could to reveal two fangs. She surged toward Zardi's throat.

Zardi's fingers found the Windrose in her pocket. She brought it out, searing the queen's cheek.

The smoke-raw smell of burning flesh filled Zardi's nostrils, and the queen gave a howl of pain, instinctively putting her hands to her face. Without hold, the queen plummeted downward with a scream.

Relief washed over Zardi, but almost instantly a weight yanked at her legs. She looked down. The queen had Zardi's ankle. She grinned evilly, the burn on her face puckered and weeping, as she slowly pulled her way up.

35

The Graveyard

Zardi kicked out, her arms trembling from the effort of holding onto the glider's bar, but still the queen dragged her way up Zardi's body. The flying machine plunged toward the ground.

She's going to kill us both.

As she tore through the sky, Zardi caught a glimpse of the massive trees with their webbed canopy. The same tree where the Rocs made their nests.

The Rocs. They must be close by.

Desperately, she let out high-pitched squawks begging for help.

The trees juddered and a torrent of oily color surged up from the canopy. Soon the beat of the mighty wings was all around them. Zardi's head was filled with the Rocs' angry voices as they registered that their enemy was in their midst. The birds surrounded the flying machine, pecking furiously at the queen, slashing at any exposed flesh with their crimson beaks and golden talons. The machine continued to drop. Zardi's arms thrummed with pain, her fingers began to slip . . .

Then the weight was gone.

Zardi looked down. All she could see was the black "O" the queen made with her mouth as she fell toward the ground. Then she was obscured, hidden by the multitude of Rocs diving after her.

Zardi gave a shuddering sigh.

"Thank you," she screeched out in the Rocs' language, her voice loud and full with joy.

Zardi tugged the harness over her body again and angled herself so she caught the edge of the wind. With the Windrose still in her hand, she thought of a boy with silver hair and violet eyes. An answering gust of wind announced itself, guiding her northward, and she followed it. She placed the object in her pocket.

"Wait," a voice called from behind her.

She turned her head to see Roco approaching.

"You saved me again," Zardi said as the young bird reached her side. "You all did."

The young bird chirruped in a pleased-sounding way. "We're happy to help. That queen has killed far too many of our number." He chirruped again. "Where are you going now?"

"To my friends." Zardi quickly explained the danger the crew of the *Falcon* were in and the abandoned tunnel that Sinbad had found. "I need to get the spelltrap to Khalila."

"I'll help," Roco said.

"It's too dangerous."

"I'm coming," Roco screeched out stubbornly.

They followed the guiding wind, the rising sun caressing all corners of the island. From her position, Zardi could see an emerald valley with a crystal-clear lake that reflected the sky: clouds, a Roc, and a girl gliding through the air. It was almost impossible to believe that so much pain and hurt existed in this place. But Zardi believed it. She'd seen it, and understood far more than she wished why this place was called Desolation Island. On top of a tall hill, she suddenly spotted the brass rider's horse. It stood absolutely still and Zardi wondered if it had frozen in place, but then it tossed its head and Zardi heard its lonely whinny echoing across the valley.

Lakes, waterfalls, and green hills soon gave way to a mountain range and then sand dunes. Down below, Zardi could see the volcano that had once been Khalila's hated prison and she thought instantly of her sister held prisoner in a watchtower in Taraket. *Today is the day of the Hunt.* Zardi let the thought creep into her head. She had refused to think about the Hunt until now, until there was at least a chance of saving her sister. She touched the spelltrap that hung around her neck. *You are the last hope. Khalila is the only one who can save Zubeyda now—but she'll need her magic back first.*

The guiding wind suddenly vanished as the glider stopped directly over Khalila's old prison, and the absence of it was as piercing as a falcon's cry in her head.

Figures, small as ants, were running through a canyon leading away from the volcano. Dark wriggling lines pursued them.

Snakes.

Zardi tipped the glider and hurtled downward with

Roco at her side.

Suddenly, the people below didn't look like ants anymore. They looked like her friends. Tariq and Musty, Zain, Mo and Ali, Mirzani and Nadeem, Sinbad and Rhidan.

Her eyes searched for Khalila, and she found the djinni at the center of the group of sailors running from the snakes that poured from the large hole in the canyon wall, Satyan leading the charge.

"I don't think the abandoned exit is abandoned anymore," Roco said as they hovered above the hunters and the prey.

"No, it isn't. We've got to stop those snakes."

Roco gave a chirrup of understanding. He soared downward, picked up one of the canyon's large boulders, and dropped it on top of two large ivory snakes. Not pausing, he plucked up another large boulder and crushed an azure snake and its orange companion.

But it was not enough. A hoard of snakes had overtaken the fleeing prisoners, cornering them so that their backs were against the rocky wall of the canyon.

Zardi could see that Rhidan was using her bow and arrow to deadly effect. Sinbad parried the fangs of one snake with his sword, the rusty blade a bloody blur in his hand, while Nadeem, Musty, Ali, and Mo stabbed forward with their sharpened sticks. There was a satisfying crack as Zain and Tariq lashed out with mallets, knocking back the heads of any snakes that came too close.

Zardi was parched, her tongue stuck to the roof of her mouth. Sinbad and his crew were fighting bravely, but wave after wave of snakes attacked them, and their defense couldn't hold much longer. Knowing that surprise was her only weapon, she angled her glider at the cluster of snakes swarming her friends.

Collapsing the wings, Zardi landed hard, scattering the serpents like grain. The ground punched the air from her but she managed to get to her feet.

A few steps away, by the canyon wall, she could see Rhidan, Khalila, Sinbad, and the others. Smiles of relief split their faces as their eyes fell on the spelltrap that hung from the belt around her neck.

The sound of hissing suddenly swelled up behind her. She turned. The scattered snakes were now quickly reorganizing themselves.

Zardi ran to give the queen's belt to Khalila. The djinni instantly unclipped the spelltrap and tried to find a way to open it. The Queen of the Serpent's belt fell to the ground, its vial of plague discarded.

"I can't see how I get the spelltrap to release my magic," the djinni screamed in frustration.

Sinbad turned to his men as Zardi joined them. "Khalila needs more time and we're going to give it to her. We'll hold this line until she releases her magic." He turned to the djinni. "You get behind us and open that thing."

Khalila frantically began to smash the spelltrap against a rock.

The crew of the *Falcon* formed a line and braced themselves, their odd assortment of weapons at the ready as the snakes surged forward, with Satyan at the fore.

"Welcome back," Rhidan said. "I knew you'd do it."

Despite the charging snakes, Zardi felt a warmth gather in her chest. He'd always had faith in her. "I just hope Khalila opens the spelltrap soon," she replied. Rhidan held out her bow and arrows but Zardi shook her head and took the Windrose from her pocket.

"This will be my weapon," she said, feeling its heat beneath her fingertips as she slipped in between Rhidan and Nadeem.

The snakes threw themselves at the line but Zardi and her friends worked as one, burning, shooting, cutting, and thrusting. Beating back wave after wave.

From farther up the line, there was a scream of grief, and Zardi turned to see Ali's lifeless figure being ingested in one gulp by an ivory snake. Zardi pushed down her own cry of horror, knowing that if she screamed she might not stop. Sinbad had to hold Mo back as the twin tried to throw himself into the pit of snakes.

They continued to fight, but sorrow and weariness hung all around them, weighing down their arms and their hearts. The serpents seemed to sense their despair and pushed forward even harder. Zardi felt as if the crew's defense would buckle at any moment under the onslaught.

A shadow covered them, and Zardi looked up to see Roco above. He tore a boulder from the side of the canyon and dropped it on the attacking snakes. For a moment, the aerial attack dispersed the snakes once again.

"How are we doing with that spelltrap?" Sinbad hollered, his face streaked with blood and slippery innards.

"I've almost cracked it open," Khalila gasped out as she smashed the thick glass orb against the rock again.

The snakes pressed forward once more. Zardi hit out with the Windrose, the object burning its way through scaled flesh, but she could feel herself tiring. A gap widened in their defense, and Satyan did not pause.

He surged toward Khalila.

"No!" Zardi sprang forward to protect the djinni, but Nadeem was faster. He dived in front of Khalila, pushing his stick upward as the snake launched himself at the djinni. The shaft pierced the scaly skin of Satyan's belly and lodged there. But even as Zardi saw the snake's eyes cloud with death, Satyan pitched forward and sunk his fangs into Nadeem's neck.

With a whimper Nadeem let go of the stick, and the snake slumped to the ground, unmoving. The boy swayed on his feet. Zardi scrambled to his side, helping him to the ground. The puncture wounds in Nadeem's neck pumped out blood in a torrent. She put her fingers to the injury. His skin felt slippery, and the air around them smelled of iron. She pressed down hard, but blood still seeped through her fingers.

"I wanted to do the right thing just for once," he gasped out, his lips pale. "To be a hero, not a coward." He was blinking fast, his eyelids beating like a butterfly's wings. "Do you remember when you called me a coward on the shores of the Tigress? Even then, even before I knew you were a girl, that hurt me more than made sense."

"Nadeem, I'm sorry. You're not a coward. You're a

hero and heroes fight," Zardi sobbed out. "You can't give up."

Nadeem opened his mouth to say something, but his body bucked, once, twice, and then he was still beneath her hand. His eyes were wide and staring.

Gently, as if she were handling a piece of precious porcelain from Mandar, Zardi lay Nadeem flat on the ground and closed his eyes. Her heart ached for the misunderstood boy who would never grow up to be anything else but that.

On the fringes of her vision there was a flash of red light. Through the crystal of her tears, Zardi looked over to see Khalila holding the two jagged halves of the spelltrap in her hand. Red light was pumping out of it and streaming into the djinni, who gave a cry of ecstasy.

"Finish them," Rhidan yelled. "I wish it. I wish it right now."

The red light cut off, and Khalila clasped her hands together and muttered an incantation. Her hands glowed like embers once again. She held her palms out toward the serpents and a pulse hit every single one of them, propelling the snakes backward, flipping them through the air. They slammed against the base of the volcano, slid to the ground, and lay quite still.

36

The Hunt

"This is not the time for a tour of the island, Khalila. What are we doing here?" Zardi demanded as the two of them stopped beside a large lake. "You promised that you would help me save my sister. So help me before it's too late." Her heart felt as if someone were clenching it in a fist as she said the words. She wished that Rhidan was with her, but he was with the crew back at camp.

"There is still time, but not much," Khalila replied. "But first I need to explain something to you."

Zardi ground her teeth in frustration. The memories of Nadeem's blood under her fingertips and the sound of Mo's wails as his twin brother was killed were fresh in her mind, building up to form a throbbing pain behind her eyes. "Explain what?"

"You extended charity to me," the djinni said softly. "You risked your life to get the spelltrap and give me back my powers." Khalila looked uncomfortable. "Djinnis do not believe in owing favors. So I will give you what you want but then the debt is cleared, understood?"

Zardi's stomach lurched. "You're really going to save Zubeyda?"

The djinni nodded. "And we'll stop Shahryār. I think that is far overdue."

"But djinnis can't kill, Sula told me that."

"Don't let that concern you. Make your wish."

"I wish you to save Zubeyda." Zardi said the words quickly before the djinni could change her mind. "Stop the sultan." She shuddered with anticipation as she said the last words.

The djinni clasped her hands and they began to glow

with red fire. She murmured an incantation under her breath, and a red pulse flew from her palms and hit the surface of the lake, throwing up pillars of steam.

Through the vapor Zardi could see a cluster of trees, their branches heavy with oranges. A veiled girl in white stumbled through the trunks. The familiarity of the scene stole Zardi's breath. She'd seen this image on Sula's table—remembered how the fleeing figure had turned and it had been her own face looking out at her.

"I don't understand," Zardi said to the djinni.

"That is Zubeyda. The Hunt has begun," Khalila explained. "The sultan is not far behind. Don't worry, we're going to save her. Fear not, you won't be alone."

A wave of vapor rolled off the lake and surrounded Zardi, blinding her. When she could see again, she was among a cluster of trees in the sultan's palace grounds.

"Zardi?" The whispered word echoed faintly in her mind.

Zardi winced and put a hand to her temple as she felt Zubeyda's consciousness bump up uncomfortably against hers. Somehow she and Zubeyda were sharing the same space. Zardi could sense her sister's relief, but there was also terror and confusion.

Holding up her palms, Zardi saw the scars of hard work that crisscrossed their surface and knew for sure that this was her body. She looked down at herself. She was dressed in white and could feel the softness of the veil covering her hair. Within the pocket of her dress, the warmth of the Windrose touched her thigh. Amazingly, Khalila's magic had transported the Windrose to this place as well.

"What are you doing here?" Zubeyda's voice had become a bit stronger.

"I'm here to save you," Zardi replied, saying the words in her head rather than out loud.

"But how can we both be here at the same time?"

"Zub, I—"

The sound of snapping branches came from deep in the copse of trees, and Zardi turned. The thick foliage made it impossible to see anything, but she knew that the sultan was coming.

"Zardi, we've got to run," Zubeyda's whispery voice gabbled out. "The sultan told me that if I reach the walled garden without getting caught then I win the Hunt. He promised that he'd let me go, that he'd let Baba go."

"Where's the walled garden?" Zardi asked, her eyes

scanning the palace grounds. All she could see were trees and more trees.

"I don't know," Zubeyda cried. "None of the sultan's prey has ever found the garden. The sultan has always won. . . ."

"It's just another part of his sick game." A wave of hate slammed into Zardi. "But we're going to beat him." Her fingers closed around the Windrose in her pocket. "Guide me to the walled garden," she murmured.

Almost immediately, a light wind teasingly ruffled her scarf, brushed past her left cheek, and skipped away. She raced after it, plunging through the trees. Twigs and thorns tore at her bare feet. *Because shoes would have been far too much of an advantage,* Zardi thought, feeling the crash of a new wave of hatred.

Zardi ran on. She didn't know where Khalila was, and there was no time to care. She was going to win the Hunt. She was going to get her sister to that walled garden. She was going to put her family back together. She was going to save Baba and get Zubeyda back to her sweetheart—

A crashing sound came from her right. Zardi turned to see the sultan galloping toward her, his hunting jackals leading the way. Zubeyda's screams filled Zardi's head, warring with the sound of the wildly barking jackals that chased them. Barks that Zardi understood.

Hunt.

Hunt.

Hunt.

She hurtled forward, swearing when the long sleeve of her dress caught on the branch of a tree. Yanking it away, she felt a slash of pain as the sharp branch sliced at her arm. Blood tinged the white of her dress, and Zubeyda's sobs filled Zardi's head. The sound of the jackals kept getting closer.

"Zub, it's all right, don't cry," Zardi pleaded. "Be strong. All is well and I won't leave you." Her sister's sobs became a whimper, and Zardi searched out the guiding wind again and continued to run. Up ahead she could see a low curved wall that surrounded a beautifully landscaped orchard. *The walled garden, I just need—*

One of the sultan's jackals darted through her ankles, tripping her up. Zardi pitched forward, the Windrose flying from her hand into the undergrowth. She slammed into the dirt, the scarf coming away from her head, her cheek grazing the ground.

The jackals surrounded her, howling and gnashing their teeth. Meaty breath warmed her face. Zardi could feel Zubeyda collapsing in on herself like a paper puppet as fear overwhelmed them both. Her sister's presence became thin, less than a whisper.

Zardi slowly turned to face Shahryār. Khalila was still nowhere to be seen. The djinni had deserted her and there was no escape. But she would not give the sultan the satisfaction of looking scared.

The hunter drew his horse to a stop, his eyes widening as he looked at her. "You," he snarled. "Where is Zubeyda?"

"She's safe." Zardi's fingers scratched the dirt around her, looking for a weapon. Her hand eagerly closed around a large rock. She felt a pulse of strength go through her fingers and the rock cracked in her grasp.

Zardi looked down at her right hand in surprise: It didn't hurt, and somehow it felt stronger than it ever had before. *No, that's not true.* Her memory wheeled back to her battle in the sky and how she had snapped the queen's metal belt. Her thoughts then twisted even farther back, to the point when she'd thrust her right hand into the fountain of blue fire to gain the Windrose. Oli had said that enduring the flames had made her stronger. *He was talking about my hand. The fire has changed it.*

"I'll find her," the sultan promised, leaning forward in his saddle.

"I won't let you hurt her." Zardi stood and glared at Shahryār, flexing her right hand. There was a flare of warmth in her head. It was Zubeyda's presence, urging her on.

"And what is a little kitten like you going to do?" The sultan snorted. "This is Rhidan's doing, no doubt, swapping you and Zubeyda." He dismounted and strode toward her. "I'm pleased that the boy's sorcery has finally manifested itself. Before I kill you, you'd better tell me where he is."

"How did you know he was a sorcerer?" Zardi demanded, not taking her eyes off the approaching hunter.

The sultan pursed his lips. "I've always known, but if you are not going to answer my questions, why should I answer yours?" He put his hand to his scabbard and withdrew a curved sword. "Come, I've got much to do. Once I've killed you I will track down Zubeyda and then find Rhidan." He stalked forward, a thin smile cutting his face in two. "An unexpected bonus, getting to hunt more than once in a day."

The sultan's eyes blazed with anticipation and he lunged toward her, his sword held high.

Zardi leaped forward as well, her hand reaching for the sultan's throat.

He gave a choked gasp of surprise as she gripped his windpipe and lifted him off his feet.

She squeezed harder, enjoying the feeling of power as she felt the fragility of his neck. *I could crush him.* The sultan's face was turning blue, but he smiled contemptuously at her despite his rasping breaths. Zardi found her hand clutching even more tightly.

Rage fought with another feeling deep inside her. It was not Zubeyda but her own conscience. *If I kill him I'm no better than he is, no better than a monster.*

"You won't take my life," the sultan croaked out, reading her hesitation perfectly.

And Zardi began to shake because she knew he was right.

"No, but you will be stopped." Khalila's voice was suddenly in Zardi's head.

Zardi's right hand began to tingle, and a red pulse exploded from her fingertips, blinding her for a moment. She could hear the jackals whining with fear.

As her eyes got used to the light, she could see that scarlet energy was still streaming from her hand and flowing into the sultan's body.

He screamed as his skin began to harden and crack, turning to bark before her gaze.

"What magic is this?" the sultan cried. "Whose magic?" And for the first time Zardi saw fear darken Shahryār's eyes.

His turban unraveled and fell to the ground, and a riot of leaves and vines thrust out through his scalp. He gave an anguished cry as branches, heavy with buds and new leaves, pushed out of the sides of his torso and roots sprang from his feet.

Zardi pulled back from Shahryār and watched in amazement as the bark crept up his neck, spread across his jaw, and covered the mouth that used to so love to sneer. Bit by bit the skin of his face crusted over, until just his eyes were left. Finally, all traces of the sultan disappeared, leaving in his stead a young-looking tree.

One of the hunting jackals took a fancy to it, moseyed forward, and lifted his leg to urinate on the roots.

In her head, Zardi could hear Zubeyda laughing with delight, but Khalila's presence seemed quieter, almost mournful.

"Time to go, Zardi," the djinni said softly. "Our business is finished here. I will send your sister and father back to your house. They will be safe. No one will seek retribution, I have seen to that."

"Can't I see my father or Nonna?"

"I'm afraid not," Khalila said. "I am finding it difficult to stay here."

"Give me one moment, please. Let me say good-bye to Zubeyda."

There was a ripping sound, and Zardi saw her sister appear in front of her wearing the white gown of a praisemaker, the hem streaked with dirt and the sleeve with blood. Zardi looked down and found that she was back in her own tattered boy's clothing.

Zubeyda threw her arms around her. "I missed you so much."

The warmth of Zubeyda's embrace flooded through Zardi, filling her with memories of home and chasing away the terrors of the last ninety days. She began to shake. "The sultan's gone," she said into Zubeyda's lavender-scented hair. "He's really gone." Tears scalded her cheeks. The curse that had hung over Arribitha for fifteen years had been lifted.

Zubeyda gently wiped the tears from Zardi's face.

"And it is all thanks to you, my darling, clever, brave sister. You saved me. Now you just need to tell me how!"

"I will, but I can't right now. In a moment, you're going to be sent back home with Baba. You don't need to worry about anyone else coming after you." Zardi's gaze was suddenly caught by a glint of light in the undergrowth, and she knelt down to pick up the Windrose, slipping it into her pocket. She turned to face her sister. "Tell Nonna and Baba that I miss them, that I love them, and that I'll be home soon, but I made a promise to Rhidan and I need to keep it."

Zubeyda nodded. "Baba will have much to do now that Shahryār is gone. Who will be our ruler now?"

"Aladdin!" Zardi exclaimed. "There are rumors that he is still alive. Maybe Baba can find the prince and make him the new sultan."

Zubeyda smiled. "It would be good to have the prince back in Taraket, but even better to have you and Rhidan home."

"Soon." Zardi kissed her sister's warm cheek. "Say hello to Omar for me." And in the next instant she was back on Desolation Island on the bank of the lake with Khalila beside her.

The djinni looked exhausted. The transformation of

the sultan, and the magic used to transport Zardi to Taraket, must have cost the djinni deeply. She had put her life force at risk. Zardi remembered how Sula had said that djinnis could become the walking dead if they used up too much of their life essence.

"Thank you, Khalila," Zardi said. An image of the sultan, bark creeping up his face, roots springing from his feet, shot through her mind. "What you did was amazing."

The djinni held up her hand. "What I did was repay a debt. Now you will stick to the terms of our agreement. Once you and Rhidan have reached the Black Isle you will make the wish that will reunite me with my husband. No questions."

"No questions," Zardi repeated.

"Come," Khalila commanded. "It is time we rejoined the others on the beach."

37

The Farewell

"Are you sure this is right?" Musty frowned down at the nautical map he had in his hands.

"I may not have the strength to transport you back to Arribitha," Khalila snapped, "but are you really doubting my ability to conjure a map?"

Zardi grinned to herself as she saw Musty go rather red in the face. "Well, there's no need for that tone," he said. "Magic is one thing. Navigation is something else entirely."

Sinbad slapped a hand on Musty's shoulder. "I think the map will do nicely." He gave the djinni a courteous bow. "I thank you for everything that you have done. With your help we will easily get back to Arribitha."

The djinni sniffed dismissively and stalked off.

Sinbad laughed. "Musty, you're a braver man than I to make an enemy of a djinni. Remember what she did to the sultan?"

Musty looked worried. "I think I'd better go and apologize." He ran after Khalila.

Zardi looked over at the captain. "So, when will you set off?" she asked.

"There is no time like the present." Sinbad looked out at the horizon. "The ship is fully repaired and we've taken on enough fruit." He laughed. "And let us not forget that we have on board more diamonds than there are grains of sand in the deserts of Arribitha."

"Your fortune is made," she replied with a smile. "Will you go back to Sabra?"

Sinbad nodded. "Now that the sultan has been taken care of, we can go home and I can pick up the crew I left behind." He paused, as if choosing his next words carefully. “I plan to find Assam when we dock. And if he’ll accept, I’ll give him a share of my fortune.”

“That’s a wonderful idea.” Zardi stared down at her feet. “When you do find him please tell him I’m sorry for everything that happened.”

“Why don’t you tell him yourself?” Sinbad asked. “Reconsider, and come with us.”

Zardi gave him a look.

Sinbad sighed. “Yes, I know. You have to get to the Black Isle and reunite Rhidan with his long-lost family.”

“Something like that,” Zardi responded, thinking of all the mixed feelings Rhidan had about his father.

“It is a shame. I have gotten used to having the two of you around.”

Zardi looked at Sinbad and then past him to the sailors who were busy filling the ship’s wooden stores with star fruit. “You have become like family to me,” she whispered.

“To family, then,” Sinbad said, holding out his hand to her. “To those members who are here and those that are gone.”

Zardi grasped his palm and found comfort there. The loss of Dabis seemed long ago, but the absence of

Ali was still an open wound and the image of Nadeem being buried stayed behind her eyes.

A squawk from above made them look up. Roco swooped downward with Rhidan on his back.

"I'm sure he'll want to tell you how his trip went." Sinbad squeezed her hand. "I'll send someone to come and find you both once the *Falcon* is ready to leave."

Zardi watched as Sinbad walked away. Sadness welled up inside her as she realized that soon she would really be saying good-bye to the captain and his crew.

Rhidan jumped off the Roc's back. A bag slung over his shoulder slapped against his hip as he did so.

"How did it go?" Zardi reached out and stroked Roco's soft, downy head.

"Roco was right. The tunnels are empty. The snakes were all destroyed."

"So what'd you get from your father's workshop?"

"Just a few bits that I thought Iridial might like to see again." Rhidan patted his bag. "We have to travel light, right?"

"Very light," she replied. Khalila had made it clear that she'd used far too much of her life essence recently. She could not whisk them away to the Black Isle. They would be traveling a different way. Zardi looked up to where the flying machine rested on the highest part of the pyramid outcrop. It was all patched up and ready to go. She just hoped the pyramid was tall enough.

"Sinbad is leaving the island today, and so should we," Zardi said.

"I'll get us some water." Rhidan patted the Roc's feathers. "Tell Roco thanks, will you?"

"Sure," she replied. "I'll come and find you later."

Rhidan strode off, leaving Zardi and Roco alone.

"He wanted me to thank you for helping him today," Zardi warbled.

"I like helping," Roco replied.

She gave the baby bird a fierce hug. "You've been brilliant. Helping us to fight the snakes, flying all of our injured back to the beach after the battle. You didn't need to do any of it."

Roco rubbed his soft cheek against hers. "You're my friend. For always."

"Always, Roco." Her eyes fell on the flying machine again. "I've got something to tell you," she said, pulling back.

He cocked his head to one side, curious.

"We're going today. We're leaving the island."

"Will you come back?" he asked.

Zardi shook her head.

"Never?" Roco squawked.

"No, never."

The bird gave an impatient ruffle of his feathers. "You're wrong, Zardi," the Roc said. "We'll meet again. Maybe not here, but somewhere."

He chirped the words out with such authority that she found herself replying, "I hope so."

Roco started to beat his wings. "Until next time, then," he sang out and soared into the air.

"Good-bye," Zardi sang back, waving until he was just a dot in the sky. She looked around, searching for Rhidan, and found him sitting on the sand next to Khalila. "Roco's gone," she said, sitting next to them.

"It looks like today is the day for good-byes then," Rhidan said. "I've just said a few."

"Good-byes are tricky things," Khalila murmured. "Hard but necessary. You realize that, once you've been alive as long as me."

"I realize it now," Zardi said. "But not having a chance for good-byes is even more awful." She felt a stab of sadness that she never got to say farewell to Nonna or her father.

"I never got to say good-bye to my husband before I

was kidnapped and imprisoned on this island," Khalila continued. "I think about that a lot."

"Well, we made a deal," Rhidan said. "Once we get to the Black Isle we'll wish you back to him."

"Yes, you will. And I am hoping that by then I will have answered a few things for myself." She thrust her shoulders back. "But that is the future. What of the present?"

"Once the *Falcon* leaves we'll take the flying machine and set off," Zardi promised.

The djinni yawned and stretched. "It will be a long journey for you both, but I will be glad of the rest. I still don't quite feel like myself."

Zardi frowned. She wondered if Khalila's recent extensive use of her powers had had anything to do with why the djinni had taken so long to work her magic against the sultan. It seemed ungrateful to ask the question though.

The djinni removed her ring and gave it to Rhidan. "Look after this for me. I'll be inside its realm, so keep it safe."

Rhidan put the ring on his finger.

They heard the sound of footsteps approach them. They turned to see Mirzani running toward them.

"Capt'n Sinbad told me to fetch you. We're about to cast off."

The three of them got to their feet and followed Mirzani to the shore where the ship had been pulled into the sea. Sloshing through the water, they watched as Mirzani made his way to the *Falcon* and climbed aboard.

Sinbad stood at the prow of the ship and looked down at them. His crew crowded around him. "The time has come, my friends. The end of our journey with you." There were shouts and waves from the crew. "I hope our paths will cross again one day."

Zardi smiled as she looked up at them all, the rigged-up multicolored sails of the *Falcon* a riot of color behind them. With Sinbad standing proud at the prow of the ship, she was reminded of the man she'd met three months ago in Taraket. The captain and the storyteller who kept an audience captive with his tales of monsters and magical charms . . . What stories he could tell now!

"Farewell!" Rhidan called.

Zardi's throat felt too tight to utter any words, so she waved as hard as she could instead.

The *Falcon* sailed forward through the waves, weaving through the white rocks that jutted out of the water, throwing up spray as it went. Before long the ship had disappeared over the horizon.

Khalila gave another stretch and yawned once more.

Rhidan took off the ring and placed it in his palm.

"You read my mind," Khalila said. "Rub if you need me for anything. Otherwise, I'll see you when we get to the Black Isle." She clasped her hands together and then twisted and turned in front of them before disappearing into the crystal ring. Rhidan slipped it back onto his finger.

"Just us again, then," Zardi said.

"I like that." Rhidan grabbed her hand. "Come on, let's get off this island!"

They ran full tilt along the beach, up toward the outcrop where the flying machine stood. Zardi could feel the warmth of the Windrose in her pocket, and she felt something unlock inside her at the thought of their next adventure, a destiny unwritten.

Somewhere out there, the Black Isle was waiting. . . .